VICKI B.

COMING OF THE STORM

QUEST FOR DARKLIN VALE

BOOK I

This is a work of fiction. All characters and events portrayed in this novel are either products of the author's imagination or are used fictitiously.

COMING OF THE STORM

Cover by Driven Digital Services
Editing and typesetting by Kingsman Editing Services

First Edition January 2026
ISBN: 978-0-9990605-5-1

vickibwilliamson.author@gmail.com

Dean, Alexander, Sophie, & Charlotte
Embrace your imagination and feel the magic.

Black Tower
Century
Backaroon Mountains
Juice Mine
The Greatlands
Creeks Baine
Haunted Forest
Abster
Darklin Vale
Mt. Kitamin
Roadstead
Elven Realm
Big Blue
Doom

The consciousness of Charmot awoke in a split second. One moment the world was normal—flowing with a steady cadence. Life and death happening in their own time. Then a being of such evil permeated the landscape that, for a moment, birds quieted; deer stopped in their tracks. A cloud seemed to pass overhead as the whole world froze.

He gave a mighty stretch, bulging the sense of time and space. The world had suffered his whims before. Fallen victim to his pure need to subvert and consume. They thought him gone, thought they had bested him. But he was back, and this time he wouldn't only take this world; he would take all of them. It had taken him a millennium, but he had the answer.

Even now he sensed her. Smelled her. She was the key. He would bring her to him, subvert her. She would think to use him. But he would use her.

CHAPTER ONE

With the buzz of the city around her, Officer Naomi Clark rounded the corner in a sprint. Just ahead of her, maybe a half block away, ran the perp. She squinted light-brown eyes. From this distance she saw a figure in jeans, a black hoodie, and white tennis shoes. If asked, she would say it was male, but she had yet to see his face.

When she lost sight of him in a pack of civilians, Naomi put on an extra burst of speed. Passing an alley, she glanced down without slowing. She was right, as the fleeing figure had not gone that way. On the intersecting street, she caught sight of the police car that even now, her partner, Officer Sam Hunter, drove to intercept their flight.

They had been cruising the city, watching and waiting, talking about Sam's oldest son and how he was excelling at sports. How the younger couldn't catch a ball to save his life but had the talent of Van Gogh with paints. Naomi enjoyed hearing stories about Sam's family—the normalness of it kept at bay the knowledge that her life lacked all that his offered.

Meeting just months after Naomi's birth, her mother and Nathaniel Clark hit it off. He had always wanted a family, and here was one ready-made. Though the family wished for more children, it wasn't to be. When her mother died before Naomi's tenth birthday, she put aside her own sorrow and took over caring of her policeman father. An only child, Naomi strove to be all he could ever want, yet somehow, she always came out lacking. Throwing herself into, not only her studies at school, but she also cooked and cleaned and made his life as worry free as possible. When asked what she wanted to be when she grew up, it was inevitable that she would choose the law.

When the hooded individual paused to glance back, she saw a mixed-race man, skin a tinge darker than her own. Glistening from a sheen of sweat, he panted for a moment, then bent over before bolting across the street and up the sidewalk in front of the buildings. His uneven, limping gate gave her confidence that his flight was coming to an end. When she saw the black-and-white accelerate to the next block, she dove deep and ran to catch her quarry.

The man in the hoodie chose one of the passing shops and wrenched the door open, then ran through. Barely slowing, Naomi followed only to stop short. The man had one arm wrapped around a woman's shoulders and a pistol pressed into her side.

"You stop right there," he yelled. Putting her hands up in a slow-down gesture, Naomi took a small step forward.

"I said stop!" The tremble in his voice had her worry spiking. Whether it was from fear or exhaustion, it just might push him to do something foolish.

"Okay." She nodded at him, halting in her tracks. "No need to bring this lady into all this. Let her go and we'll talk about it."

"I don't want to talk about anything." Sweating, gaze jumping furtively around the store, the man shoved the muzzle of the pistol harder into the woman's side, causing her to cry out. Naomi kept her eyes on the man. Even from a few feet away, she could smell the stench of his sweat and fear.

She saw a small motion behind him and registered her partner sliding up to the rear of the man and woman.

"Come on, man. We can discuss—"

"Shut up! Just you shut up!" Gesturing with his weapon,

the gun man motioned for Naomi to step to the side. As she moved, so did he, putting himself closer to the door. With his gun pointed away from the hostage, Naomi flicked her gaze to Sam just as he gave her a nod. Together, they rushed the man. Reaching him seconds quicker, Naomi grasped his gun hand with both of hers. She stuck her index finger in the trigger guard, effectively stopping the man from firing. Sam grabbed him from behind, freeing the woman. Together, the two officers grappled with the man and began to take him to the ground.

Just as Naomi thought the fight was won, the man threw a wild punch, hitting her in the temple and knocking her to the ground. She took his weapon with her as she fell, the pistol spinning a few feet away on the highly polished floor. Dazed, she shook her head, making her way to her hands and knees. With Sam's arm around his throat, the man pulled him forward and gave a vicious kick to Naomi's ribs. She fell to her side. For a moment, she was filled with pain, unable to catch her breath. Looking over her shoulder at the combatants, the room seemed to ripple, and Naomi thought she heard chanting. She closed her eyes and sucked in large breaths, filling her lungs before pushing the breath out again. This time when she opened her eyes, everything was as it should be. The only sounds a soft radio, the distant wail of sirens, and the harsh breaths of the men on the floor. Through the haze of agony, she watched the two men wrestle with each other. The perpetrator grabbed Sam by his arm, which was still at his throat, and, bending, flipped the officer over his shoulder. Before she or Sam could react, the man had Sam's weapon out of his holster. The perpetrator took a step back and swung the gun to point at her partner. Naomi drew her own.

Looking down the barrel of her service weapon, Naomi's brain squeezed, causing her to hesitate. The stolen pistol discharged, she jumped, then she looked from him to Sam. Sam lay still, a red stain spreading across his chest. Her gaze swung back to where the gunman once stood, only to see an empty doorway.

*****

Officer Clark stepped from the police station and the door closed behind her. A small breeze blew strands of her dark-brown hair across her face. Then, the day was calm.

To protect and serve, she thought.

That's all she had ever wanted to do. She always wanted to help people. To make their lives easier. Safer. Vivid in her memory was the image of her stepfather leaving home on his way to work. He had looked larger than life in his uniform. Crisply ironed, shoes shined, weapon on his hip. She had thought of him as a hero—and she had always wanted to be one, too.

Now everything had changed.

For two years, she had done her job. Kept the community safe. Been part of a team with Officer Hunter, and they, in turn, were part of something bigger. Until yesterday, she never had cause to draw her weapon. And she froze.

Naomi blinked, letting the image play in her mind.

Until yesterday.

She still didn't understand how it had happened. Why it had happened.

The man. Why didn't he give them a chance to handle the situation peacefully? She hadn't had any alternative. She had tried to get him to calm down, but he had taken Sam's gun. He had fired on her partner before she could return fire.

But that was not completely true.

She had hesitated. She hadn't meant to. She'd hesitated and the man was gone. Sam was on the floor. She had thought he was dead. Thank God for the abilities and speed of the EMTs.

The perp would be found—someone who assaulted an officer always was. But Officer Sam Hunter—her partner for five years—was injured, may never come back to work, and no arrest would change that.

Now, she was on administrative leave. She had to turn in her badge and gun. There had to be an investigation. She had to go to counseling. Would anyone else know she had hesitated? Did it matter when she knew? Once again, she wasn't enough. Just not good enough. Her stepfather had told her again and again she didn't measure up. She wouldn't ever be enough.

She still wanted to be a cop, maybe needed to, but this changed everything. She thought she had proved her worth, but old habits didn't just go away.

CHAPTER TWO

Naomi gasped and sat straight up, jerked from the dream. She threw back her covers, spun to put her bare feet on the floor, and dropped her head into her hands. Taking deep, steady breaths, she tried to calm herself.

This wasn't the first nightmare she had. She had been having them for as long as she could remember. It was just the dream itself she couldn't recall. Even now, a mere moment after waking, the crux of the dream was leaving her.

Darkness.

An inky blackness that seemed to call her name. Chanting. And dizziness. A dizziness that followed her out of the dreams.

Standing, floor cold against her skin, Naomi made her way to the bathroom. She splashed cool water on her face and stared at herself in the mirror.

Who was she? Why was she?

For years, Naomi had made time in her day for a run. She craved the ritual of it—felt it deep in her bones. It got her out into the city she loved and set her focus for the day. But today was different. She needed the routine, needed the city, and today she needed to clear her brain. And decide what she would do. What would become of her life?

Sleep had come hard last night. After waking from a nightmare, she had finally made her way back to bed only to toss and turn. Every time she closed her eyes, she saw Sam's face. Saw him lying still in the aftermath. And even past those thoughts, past the images of her partner, she had misgivings. Maybe, just maybe, she was not cut out to be a cop.

So now, she needed the exhilaration and ultimately the exhaustion that a run would afford her. Maybe later she would nap. God knows she could use it after last night.

The run felt good, normal. The day like so many others. The air was crisp with an acrid scent of car exhaust. On the second mile she hit her stride. She loved this part. Her entire existence centered on the sounds of her breathing and the slap of her treads on the pavement. Shooting between rushing pedestrians and honking vehicles, she didn't slow. Didn't think.

When she turned the corner and headed into the park, the sounds of her footfalls changed, moving from cement to packed earth. A mile into the green of the park and a motion caught her eye. Something sat in the middle of the trail that had her running in place, catching her breath.

A squirrel, she thought. When it moved in a disjointed hopping motion, she changed her mind thinking it might be a large rabbit. Maybe a jackrabbit. Had she ever seen such a large rabbit in the city? Even in the park this would be an uncommon sight. Taking a few steps toward the animal, she stopped with a gasp when it lifted its head and looked her way.

What the hell? she thought and, squinting, studied the peculiar animal that barred her way. It was even larger than she had believed when there was some distance between them. Its pelt, which she had thought was a short, upright hair, now proved to be spiky. It looked like it would cut if touched. When it rose on its haunches, nose moving in her direction, she was again reminded of a rabbit. With a start, it bolted off the path and into the cover of some trees.

Curiosity had her now, and she sprang after the strange animal. Seeing movement ahead of her, Naomi bent and twisted to get by a patch of briars. A few steps more, and a moment of vertigo stopped her. With her hand upon a tree, nausea came quickly, surprising her. Naomi took two deep breaths, then bent at the waist. Releasing the bark, she moved forward, and the nausea left as soon as it had come. She straightened and took another quick breath. Putting the incident behind her, thinking maybe it was something she had eaten, she scanned the area looking for the rabbit thing.

Unable to locate the animal, Naomi moved back the way she had come.

She walked for some time but couldn't find the running trail. Stopping, she looked at the sky, assessing where the sun was, but something seemed off in the park. She kept an eye and ear on her surroundings, ever watchful for what it could be. Cop's instincts on high alert. In the far distance, the low rumble of thunder touched her awareness.

The sun seemed brighter, the trees and grass greener, she realized. Sounds sharper. The air smelled fresher. Try as she might, Naomi couldn't put her finger on what exactly caused her disquiet. Turning in place, she tuned in to her environment. Thinking maybe it was her, her perceptions changed by yesterday, she continued.

She was just thinking she needed to swing back, that she had missed a turn or clue within the forest, when a scream echoed in the air. It was closely followed by a cry for help, making her come to a halt.

Where did that come from? she wondered.

Slowly, she turned in a circle, keeping her breath slow and quiet and her eyes open.

When a strange whistle came from the trees and another answered, her gaze shot up. Continuing to pivot, watchful, her senses expanded. Another call had her spinning—trying to locate where it came from.

When the bird took flight and winged past her, the cry for help was momentarily forgotten. Shock filled her body, and she tracked the animal, unable to believe her eyes. What was happening in this park?

Brightly plumed, the animal was like no bird she had seen before. About the size of a crow, its body was elongated with a bowed neck. On the neck sat a small head with three—yes, three—large, orange eyes. It had no beak, but when a warble came from afar and again this one answered, she saw its mouth was a slash under the head where it and the neck joined.

Naomi blinked rapidly, shook her head, and looked again.

Alit on a branch, the bird stared back at her for a moment and then, with a gangly hop, once again took flight. Naomi turned to watch it, sure she must be dreaming. Perhaps she was still snug in her bed, yet to wake up to her alarm.

The animal was disappearing from her sight when another cry for help came to her on the wind. Her mind shifted gears, and she looked in the direction of the sound. Turning, her hand dropped to her hip, expecting to feel the reassurance of her service pistol. Only then did she remember she was in running shorts and a spandex bra, armed only with pepper spray clipped to the belt of her shorts. Knowing there was nothing she could do about that now, she headed in the direction of the cry.

Naomi stayed within the cover of the trees. Shadows seemed deeper within the brush, and again, in the distance, she heard the odd bird whistle. Ignoring it, she continued through the timber. The sounds of a commotion came to her from ahead. She slowed her pace, stepping lightly on the underbrush.

"What's 'e got there?"

"Thievin' dwarf. Can't trust any of them."

Naomi peeked around the trunk of a tree. Beyond, in a small clearing, were four figures. Three of the men surrounded one that, for a moment, she thought was a child. She was just about to step forward when he moved, and she realized it was to him the men referred. He was smaller than the others but looked to be grown with a full, dark beard and lines on his face. Obviously afraid, he cowered from the three, his arms protecting his head.

"I bet it's 'im who took it."

The three held her attention. They were dressed in course fabrics—like nothing she had ever seen—but what caught her attention was the large blade sheathed on one of their belts.

An illegal blade.

"Where is it?" One of the men stooped and punched the smaller man on the side of his head, dropping him to the ground. The hit cut his head, adding a flow of blood to what was already running from his nose and lip. In the next instant, the man who appeared to be the ringleader pulled his blade, the metal bright in the morning sun.

Reaching into her waistline, Naomi palmed the pepper spray and stepped from the shelter of the trees.

"Halt. Police," she called.

At her words, four sets of eyes swung toward her.

Naomi gasped and stopped in her tracks. Their eyes were black, like ebony marbles. At her distance, she couldn't make out any variation of color in their irises.

"Who are you? What you want?" the one with the knife asked and turned, stepping toward her. "This ain't your business."

At their momentary inattention, the captive scuttled between two of the men and took off toward the opposite tree line.

All three turned to him and with a gruff, "Get 'im," the leader turned back to her. The two underlings, quick to comply, ran after the fleeing prisoner. Naomi was just stepping forward, intent on stopping them, when the armed man spoke.

"Now . . . what was you sayin'?"

Pulling her eyes from the chasers, Naomi faced the man with the knife.

Stepping closer, he brandished his weapon and again addressed her. "Girlie, what business is this of yours?"

"I'm a police officer. Drop your weapon."

"A Po-lice Of'cer?" Taking another step, the man regarded her with a cock of his head and a narrowing of eyes.

Behind him the two men who had chased the fleeing prisoner reentered the clearing, a struggling man between them.

Raising her voice, she addressed the two.

"Hey. You there. Let him go."

When the man with the knife took another step toward her, she shifted her attention back to him, lifting the canister of pepper spray. Halting, he regarded her raised hand, shifting his gaze between her eyes and what she held.

"Got magic there?" His eyes squinted, chin raised.

"Magic?" Her brows drew together, and she studied him.

Magic?

When he dared another step, she reached farther with the hand containing the pepper spray.

"Stay back. And drop the knife."

A small smile curved his lips as he indicated his weapon.

"This?" He raised it with his inquiry.

"Yes. Drop it and turn around."

Instead, he advanced on her. When he was within six feet, he brandished the weapon, his eyes taking on a decisive gleam, and a large smile split his face.

Naomi shot him in that gleam and smile with a full spray from the canister.

Dropping the knife, clenching his face, he fell to the grass, rolling and wailing. With his cries, his two comrades let loose of their captive and rushed to assist him. As soon as he was released, the little man again took off for the forest.

Naomi didn't stop to think. She broke into a run, following the fleeing dwarf. As she passed the three, she stooped and snatched the knife from the ground. Leaving the wailer and his cohorts behind, she picked up her speed.

She entered the forest in the exact spot where the other had disappeared and crashed through the branches, pushing them away with her hands. Realizing she had lost sight of the man, she stopped. Her heart beat so hard that she felt it in her neck. She listened. When a crash came on her left, she pivoted and sprinted.

Naomi thought to call out to him, but worrying that the

three might be following, she didn't want to give them any idea of which direction they had gone.

When another crash came to her and a small cry sounded, she again picked up her pace.

The ground disappeared beneath her, and her stomach flipped. For a second, she was falling, flailing her arms and legs. The ground rose to meet her, and she hit it—hard.

"Oomph."

Her feet, knees, and hands landed one after the other on the rough terrain. Momentum pulled her and she somersaulted. Head over feet, she had the foresight to tuck and roll. When she came to a rest at the bottom of a hill, Naomi gingerly stretched her limbs and lay stunned on her back. She took an overall assessment of how she had fared. She touched a sore spot on her forehead and stared at her fingers in disbelief. They were coated in blood. When she pushed to sit, a moan escaped her lips, and she rested her head in her hands. Giving in to the weakness for a moment, she again lay back, her eyes closed. When she opened them, she gazed upward, blinking rapidly.

Lazy white clouds floated across a crystal-blue sky. The sun was bright but didn't shine directly into this spot at the bottom of a hill. Even without direct sunshine, the day was warm. The smell of earth and green came off the forest to plume around her. On the distant horizon, just at the edge of the tops of the trees, two white orbs hung in the sky. They were close. So close, she could see evidence of craters on their surfaces. One of the planets had two distinct, but sparse, rings around it.

"What the . . . ?"

Naomi pushed to her feet, stooped, her eyes locked on the spectacle in the sky. She straightened and held her hand to the wound on her head.

When a moan sounded behind her, she turned toward it, but her attention was drawn immediately back to the objects in the sky. She studied them, not sure what she was seeing. They were beautiful, but fear filled her belly.

She knew what they were—moons. But they shouldn't be there.

Again, a groan issued, followed by sounds of movement. Tearing her eyes from the heavens, confusion filling her mind, Naomi turned to see the dwarf stand and pull himself from a bramble.

Putting thoughts of the objects in the sky to the back of her mind, she hustled to him, grasped his arm, and assisted him to stand.

As if just noticing her, he wrenched on his arm, but she tightened her grip.

"Let me go. Let me go!" he cried, pushing at her restraining hand.

"Now you wait just a minute," she said, giving him a small shake. "I have some questions for you."

"I have to leave." The little man spun his head on his neck, looking left and then right. "They'll be coming. They'll be looking for me." And again, he pulled against her.

"What's happening here?" Naomi bent at the waist to look the man full in his face. Pointing with a slightly shaking hand, she indicated the two objects. "What are those, and . . . and where are we?"

The little man's gaze followed her aim to the sky, a look of confusion on his face. Glancing at her, he spared no time for her questions but began walking forward, towing her with him.

"Wait—" she began, but he cut her off.

"We have to move. If you won't let me go, then you'll be coming with me." He continued to walk, taking her with him. Naomi gave one more searching look toward the skyline and then, releasing the man's arm, followed him into the brush.

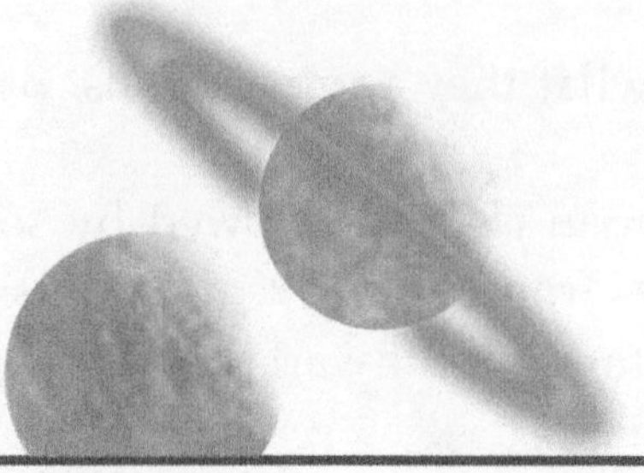

CHAPTER THREE

It was nightfall before the man stopped. For hours she had fixated on the two moons and what that might mean. She kept looking back over her shoulder to catch a glimpse of them.

Now she was tired, and with the sun's passing, the night had grown cold. Her frame shivered and she ached all over. Falling down a hill and the forced march had her body crying. They had traveled for hours, and she was even more confused than before. Not once, all day, did she see evidence of civilization. But she kept reminding herself that she had been in a park in the middle of a thriving city. And the little man was no help. No matter how many times she tried to talk to him, he ignored her and kept walking.

The bird-like things. The rabbit-like thing.

The men's eyes.

The two moons high in the sky.

The miles and miles of unending forest.

What was happening? Where was she?

She didn't understand any of this. All she did know was that she wasn't safe and happy, asleep in her bed. She wasn't going to wake from this dream. She needed to get back to her life—her world. But she didn't know how to get there. Hell, she didn't even know how she got here, and the only person she knew was the . . . dwarf? Even that was odd. Okay, she could see he was a dwarf. How long had it been since she heard people use that term? It just wasn't politically correct. Shouldn't she be thinking 'little person'? But considering that the guy who said it had black eyes and carried around an eight-inch knife, she guessed there were weirder things to worry about.

When the man halted, Naomi didn't notice, her mind still preoccupied, and she almost ran into him. She was so tired when she skidded to a halt, she barely stayed on her feet. Swaying, she watched him.

Out of a pack she hadn't noticed, the man pulled a cloth, perhaps a cloak. He wrapped it over his shoulders, then slipped under the low branches of an old pine tree and lay down. Naomi squatted to study him. His eyes were shut, and he seemed to already be asleep or doing a very good imitation of it. She moved in a circle, looking everywhere. Now what was she supposed to do?

The night continued to chill, and in her limited clothing, she was acutely aware of it. Pacing from foot to foot, Naomi rubbed her arms to generate some warmth. Exhaustion hit her hard, but she was afraid to fall asleep. Afraid the man would leave her, afraid the other men would find them, afraid of everything unknown in this strange world.

Finally, unable to stay on her feet, she moved away a small distance to sit with her back against the aged bark of a tree. Immediate warmth flowed to her from her contact with the timber. So exhausted, she was unable to school her thoughts and they circled in her mind. Striving to understand what was happening, she shifted on a hip and laid her hand upon the tree. Warmth. Pulled in by this touch, she laid her cheek against the wood and wrapped her arms around the tree's trunk. Comfort filled her, and at last her mind and body shut down.

* * * * *

The sound of running water had Naomi waking to push to her feet.

"What the hell?"

The dwarf stood next to her tree, his back to her, urinating into the forest.

"Wondered when you were gonna wake."

"There isn't anywhere else you could be doing that?"

Incensed with the rudeness of his act, Naomi walked away from him, only then realizing she could do with a little morning privacy of her own. Stepping behind a screen of bushes, she quickly emptied her bladder. When she again entered the small clearing, the dwarf was just doing up his britches.

"Where are we?" she asked.

He looked her over with disinterest.

"*We* aren't anywhere. I'm here." He pointed at his feet. "And you're there," he added, pointing at where she stood.

"Don't be difficult."

"I've got no interest in you comin' with me."

"But I don't know where I am." Her tone turned pleading. Naomi moved toward the little man, dropping to one knee to bring them more eye to eye. "If you could help me, I'd be so grateful."

"Not interested in your gratitude."

"Well then. I'm sure I could make sure you're well paid for your services."

The dwarf's eyebrows rose at this, and his chin lifted. "You have gold on you?"

Naomi dropped her eyes and scanned the ground between them. Gold? she thought. "Well, no . . ." And the dwarf stepped back from her. "But I know I can get you some."

"Uh-huh. From who?" He studied her for a moment. "Looks to me like you're all alone."

"Well, no. No." She jumped up to step near him. "I'm not all alone. I know you, now, don't I?"

Ready to try again, Naomi stuck out her hand.

"My name is Naomi. What's yours?"

"N'omi?"

"N-A-omi," she corrected.

"N'omi. What kind of a name is that?"

"Um, well." Dropping her hand, she gave a shrug. "Just a name. And yours?"

"I'm Paxton Re."

"Paxton Re," she repeated, rolling it around on her tongue. Again, sticking out her hand, she smiled and said, "It's good to meet you, Paxton Re."

The dwarf stared at her hand for a moment and then, turning his back on her, began to stuff his cloak into his pack. Naomi dropped her hand. Stooping, she brushed the soil from her knee. She glanced back at the tree where she had spent the night. It looked ordinary except it was covered with the most vibrant leaves she had ever seen. Catching her eye, the dwarf moved into the woods, and Naomi followed him. He didn't look back and didn't say anything to her.

It was a few hours and a few miles later when Naomi again spoke.

"Is there anywhere to get some food around here?"

As if she hadn't spoken, the man continued.

"Hello . . . Paxton Re . . ." she called, but he didn't answer, didn't turn.

Heaving a deep sigh, Naomi jogged up to her companion. She grasped his arm to spin him around.

"What?" he yelled; his brows pulled toward his nose.

"I'm hungry. Is there anywhere we can find something to eat?" Dipping her finger into a small pocket at the hip of her shorts, she pulled out a bill. "I have some money. I can buy us food."

Paxton Re took the money from her hand. He opened the bill and studied the paper. "What is this?" He looked from the paper in his hand to her.

"It's money. US dollars." Standing upright and stepping

back, Naomi's brows crinkled. "What do you mean, 'what is this'?"

Paxton Re tossed the bill to the ground and turned from her to march up the next hill.

"Hey wait," she called. Naomi picked up the bill, stuffed it back into her pocket, and trotted to catch the dwarf. "What do you mean throwing my money away? I can buy us some food with that."

Again, Paxton Re turned to study her. He opened his mouth as if to speak but shook his head and turned away.

CHAPTER FOUR

For the remainder of the day, neither Naomi nor Paxton Re spoke. The dwarf kept them moving, and it was all she could do not to fall behind.

Along the way she watched for anything edible, but not knowing the land and flora, she figured she could go without. They passed a stream that provided fresh drinking water. After swirling it around in her mouth, she risked a couple small swallows. When the dwarf stopped and ate something he had found, she joined in hoping it was safe for her. Toward nightfall, Paxton Re began gathering deadfall so she joined him in that, too.

When he found a spot he liked, the dwarf cleared an area and built a fire. When it was burning, Naomi moved closer. She held her hands out, rubbing them together, comforted by the warmth.

"Where are we going?" she asked.

The dwarf said nothing, staring into the fire.

"You have to tell me something. I need to know what's happening." Her tone, between assertive and whining, made her cringe.

Paxton Re gave a deep sigh and looked at her over the flames. "The town of Abster is about a day away."

Naomi sat forward, her gaze intent on the dwarf.

"Abster," she muttered to herself, trying it out. "And?" she asked when he didn't say anything further.

"And . . ." He sighed again. "I know a man there."

Naomi thought this was like pulling teeth. "And what does that mean for us?"

"He owes me. I'm sure I can get some supplies from him."

Naomi sat back, nodding in agreement. "Okay. That's great. Then what?"

"Then we'll circle around the valley. Get you back to where you started."

Naomi's head dropped between her shoulders, and she expelled a giant sigh. "Thank you, Paxton Re."

Dismissing her thanks with a wave of his hand, the dwarf stared off into the distance. "Only way I'm gonna get rid of you. Crazy like you will follow me to the end of my days."

A little laugh escaped Naomi. Finally, something was going her way.

"Anyway, I pay my debts. You came to my aid with the sprogs—seems like the least I can do."

"What's a sprog?"

"What's a—" The dwarf studied her, sure she wouldn't last a day. "A sprog," he said as though speaking to someone of less-than-stellar intelligence, "is what those guys are. A sprog is very bad."

Naomi nodded, taking in everything he said. She didn't even get offended by his tone. She needed all the information she could get.

Squinting, Paxton Re searched the horizon. "Looks like a storm brewing."

Naomi realized the dwarf was right. Large black clouds were gathering over the mountains in the far distance. As she watched, lightning flashed, and a moment later wind blew through the tops of the trees. With the coming storm, darkness was falling fast, and with it came the cold. This time, when Paxton Re pulled the cloak out of his pack, he threw a second one at Naomi. Grateful for the protection, she put it on and scooted closer to the fire.

"Where are we?"

Paxton Re pulled his gaze from the fire. For a moment, he stared at her before turning back to the flames. With a stick he pushed at the logs, causing embers to float upward on the breeze.

"You're an odd one, that's for sure."

"I'm not from here," she answered. "I don't know how I got here, and I don't know how to get home again."

"Well, wherever you're from, someone is probably missing you. When we get back to where you showed up, I'm sure we'll find someone searching for a lost woman."

It was Naomi's turn to gaze into the fire. No one would be looking for her. She had no one in her life. For some time, maybe for her entire life, she had been essentially alone. Chilled, she pulled the edges of the cloak around her legs.

They were both just settling in when, without warning, Paxton Re jumped to his feet. Pulling a branch from the stack for the fire, he faced the darkness. Startled by his abrupt move, Naomi stood warily, pulling the knife from her waistband.

"Who's out there?" the dwarf yelled.

For some time, no answer was given. Then, from the darkness, a lady, stooped and wrinkled, came into the firelight.

"Ho," she called. "Gooden eve."

"Oh, for the love of . . ."

Naomi looked from the old woman to the dwarf. Without saying more, Paxton Re threw the branch into the fire and walked away.

"What?" Naomi began, her gaze jumping from the dwarf to the old lady and back again, but Paxton Re just gave a backward gesture and kept walking.

"Hello, Naomi."

At the use of her name, Naomi gave a start and looked closer at the old woman.

"Do I know you?" With a half step back, she put the fire

between herself and the stranger.

"Not yet, my dear, but I know of you." The woman moved toward her around the fire.

Naomi kept even with her, keeping the flames between them. When they had made a circuit of the fire, Paxton Re came back into view. As he approached the women, he spat to the side. He took a seat, then gestured to them.

"Well, let's get on with it."

Naomi's gaze moved again from the dwarf to the old woman. Not sure about their visitor, she took a seat by Paxton Re. The fire still between them and the woman.

"I'm called Maude," she began.

"Among other things," the dwarf muttered.

"What do you want?" Naomi whispered.

Maude looked from the dwarf to Naomi, a small smile on her lips.

"I'm not the only one who knows of your coming." She lifted her hands, indicating the very air. "Can't you feel it? Charmot wakes."

"What's a char—"

Before she could finish her question, Paxton Re jumped up, moving around the fire. "What do you mean, Charmot?" We ain't got nothing to do with the likes of him."

"Well, Paxton Re," Maude answered, "he has something to do with you."

CHAPTER FIVE

The castle pulsed with power.

All around it, the Varatin Mountain remained silent. No animals ventured nearby. No birds flew in the skies or called among the trees.

The castle had been in this land for longer than anyone could remember. No one recalled who built it. How the stones were lifted to create the massive walls and its high tower. The old ones said, one day there was nothing, and the next the tower stood.

It had once housed wizards. Within, they had worked their magics. The more they worked, the darker the magics became. Thinking they could control the power they meddled with, they continued to chant and dance, brewing their concoctions and calling on the spirits.

In a moment's time, they were gone. The vacuum they had created pulled everything in. All light. All sound.

With an audible crack, the vacuum released, and all was as it had been, but nothing alive remained within the walls. There was nothing but an ebony stain. Black as the darkest night. Void of even a hint of light.

Over the ages, the stain grew. It pulsed and it fed, and it expanded in the air and moved across the stones. Finally, running out of space within the walls of the castle, it radiated into the world, coloring the castle and tower with its darkness.

Somewhere along the way, the stain became sentient. It thought and it hungered. It gave itself the name Charmot. Once it had been men. Foolish wizards; pulled with pieces and parts of many of them, and many other things. Its largest memories, memories dark with violence and subversion—were of these wizards. These practicers of magics. Their desires all turned dark and powerful. Turned into something different.

Darkness, thrown from windows, doors, and the very cracks of the stone could be seen for miles—if anyone ever came near enough to see. Now, the only living beings to venture near the fortress were the sprogs. Created by the dark magic. Called by the stain. Once men, they were humanoid in appearance, but the blackness of Charmot filled their minds. And their hearts.

Now, the time was ripe for a becoming. New sprogs would be born to join the forces—for the battle to come would be mighty. Charmot knew he must grow his strength. His desires knew no end. Not only would he take this world and all its bounty, but the next, and the next.

The three from the forest were here. They had heeded the call. A call unheard by man, dwarf, fairy, or beast. A call from the master, Charmot, to its followers.

Mik, the leader of the three, knew this time something was different. He had been present to many becomings. He was one of the first. But this new beckoning—there was an intensity he'd never felt before. Something else was coming . . .

Or it was already here.

CHAPTER SIX

"What's a charmot?"

Sitting beside Maude, Naomi pushed aside her uneasiness. She needed to know what the woman knew. She needed to get home, but now it sounded like it wasn't going to be that simple.

"What's a charmot?" she asked again and laid her hand on the woman's forearm.

"Well, go ahead and tell her." The grumbly baritone of Paxton Re filtered through the dark. "You started this—might as well end it."

Maude stirred the embers, causing sparks to rise into the night. Naomi followed them with her eyes until they faded from her sight. There were no moons yet this night, only the distant flash of lightning over the mountains. When Maude again stirred the fire, the sparks rose and began to dance. Moving together they drew Naomi in. They spun to show the story the old woman told.

So low Naomi had to strain to hear, Maude began her tale.

"Before he was Charmot, he was once a king. A mighty elven king. Ruler of a great land."

"Elven?" Naomi asked. "Like . . . elves? Pointy ears and all?"

Maude stared at her for a moment, and in her eyes was a look that made Naomi regret her interruption.

"An elven king, girl. A mighty king. But he was never a good king. Once, he might have been. A wife and child were his, but even they couldn't withstand his craving for power."

Paxton Re moved toward the fire, his eyes on the old woman. Sitting, he watched and listened, not adding any more comments or complaints.

"In the time before Charmot, the king's only wish was to be greater than any others, even greater than himself. At his use, he had many wizards. The wizards did all sorts of black magic in his name. He pushed them, forever straining the boundaries of what should be done.

"For a time, he couldn't move past the knowledge he had gained. Even with his wizards, his boundaries seemed set. But with their aid, the king elongated his life. With this eternity, he searched years and lifetimes for the means to be the greatest king of all. To rule the greatest kingdom. The more he found, the more his wizards learned, the more powerful he became, the more the evil ate at his heart. The souls of other elves, men, and dwarfs became fuel for his madness."

An owl hooted in the darkness and Naomi jumped. She scanned the area, unable to see more than a few feet past the light of the fire. Paxton Re's eyes reflected the glow of the flames, making him appear as if he came straight out of the old woman's tale.

"Blood sacrifices."

A shiver ran down Naomi's spine.

"Blood sacrifices made him even more powerful. In his hunt for more, he had become something other. No longer an elf. No longer man. In a joining of the magics, a great rupture occurred. The king and his wizards were sucked into the black magic they had conjured. Almost nothing was left.

"Almost.

"But evil is hard to kill. It has a will to live like nothing else. And so, he was preserved. Kept alive within the magic, fused with his wizards. A being unknown before. A shadow of himself.

A wraith. Less and somehow more. And this being, this apparition, needed to feed. Needed the life forces of others to stay alive. To stay powerful. The more he feeds, the more he hungers. Now he seeks other worlds to conquer. Other worlds to feed upon.

"He seeks a talisman. And a sacrifice. Something that will finally give him all he wants. Allow him to be all he wishes. It will give him the ability to move between worlds. With the coming of the red moons, he will bring endless night. He will be all-powerful, unstoppable."

Maude ended her story. The silence was absolute. Naomi was afraid to move, afraid to say anything. It was as if the night were alive, ready to pounce. When the old woman again spoke, Naomi started.

"This is where you come in, my dear. The talisman he seeks is the one you also seek. If you can get to it before him, not only will you go home, but you will have the means to stop Charmot from becoming."

With a whisper, barely able to get the words past her lips, Naomi said, "What is this talisman? Where—where do I find it?"

Old Maude leaned in, taking Naomi's hand. Turning it, she ran her fingers along the woman's palm. A tingling began at the tips of her fingers, moving inward toward the center of her hand.

"You must find Darklin Vale. Only when you find Darklin Vale will the endgame be revealed to you. But remember, magic is fickle. It will show you what it wants and needs and take no consideration to yours."

Seeming to mutter to herself, the old woman said, "A hammer to strike down evil."

Like a knife thrust, the old woman stabbed the center of Naomi's palm with a crooked finger. The nail cut and blood flowed. A sharp pain exploded from Naomi's hand, doubling her over. A scream burst from her, and the fire leaped to a blaze as she lost consciousness.

*****

When Naomi came to, Paxton Re sat next to her, her head on his lap. A bloody cloth was wrapped around her hand. Sitting, Naomi put her other hand to her head.

"Where is she? What happened?"

"Damn spirits," the dwarf spat. "Always bringing trouble."

"Spirit?" the woman asked, looking around the darkness. "Where did she go? What did it all mean?"

With a shrug the dwarf stood and stepped away from her.

"Paxton Re, can you tell me what we're supposed to do?"

"We, huh?" And he stared at her. It only took a moment for Naomi to become uneasy.

"Yes," she said, "we. You and me, right? We're in this together." But she didn't even sound sure to herself.

"Yeah," he said but didn't look at her. "You'd best get some sleep. I'll take the watch." And then he wandered into the night.

CHAPTER SEVEN

He was gone when she woke up. The smell of old smoke filled the clearing, making Naomi's head ache. The morning sun was just rising, and its intensity did nothing to help.

She shouldn't be surprised. It was obvious Paxton Re was going to bolt. Never friendly, he didn't plan on becoming part of the danger she was in. Then how come she felt so betrayed? Standing, she walked around the firepit, searching the area for any evidence of which way he had gone.

Nothing, she thought. All he had left her was the cloak on her back.

Okay, she decided. Time to assess. She had the cloak and a knife. The pepper spray, what little that might help against what might be a dark god. No way to make a fire, no real way to hunt for food—even if she knew how. She was pretty sure the twenty-dollar bill in her pocket was just as good as paper. Her hand hurt, the cloth replaced during the night with a better fitting, and cleaner, bandage. And she had no idea which way she was going.

She dropped to sit on the ground as desperation filled her. Tears pushed at the back of her eyes, and for a moment the world swam with them. Allowing herself this moment to feel sorry for herself, Naomi took a deep breath. And then another.

She was better than this, she berated herself. Yes, she hadn't done anything of any importance on her own—and inside, just under the surface, her father's voice told her she wasn't good enough. Was she so weak as to give up without even trying? And really, did she have a choice?

"No," she said. Pushing back the tears before they could fall, she shoved to her feet.

The sun was rising—was it the east? Figuring it really didn't matter as long as it was consistent, Naomi gave another scan of the clearing.

Darklin Vale. She would navigate with the sun. She would look for water and follow it to people. Didn't people always settle around water? She would get a job, work if necessary. She would get supplies, and she would ask about Darklin Vale. Someone had to have heard of it. Where it was located. Yes, it might take her a while, but she wasn't going to think about that. Just like the police academy. One day at a time. Do your best every moment.

Relieved to have a plan, her heart lighter, Naomi headed into the forest.

She had no sooner left than Paxton Re walked into the clearing. Approaching the burnt-out fire, the dwarf scanned the area. Easily picking up the woman's trail, the dwarf broke into a trot.

Now where could she be going?

Paxton Re stayed out of sight, trailing the woman. Interested in where she would go—what she would do.

He had to admit, he was subtly impressed when she kept to a straight line.

The sound of running water came to him. A few moments later, her head came up from where she watched her path. The woman crept through the brush toward the sound, the dwarf on her tail. When she stooped at an eddy in the stream, filling her hands with fresh water, he smiled.

Just as Paxton Re made to move forward, to make himself known, Naomi's head came up, searching the far shoreline. The sound of a heavy body came through the brush just as the woman stood up.

Paxton Re broke into a run. He didn't know what was coming, but it couldn't be good.

He crashed through the brush and vines hit Naomi at the waist, taking her down to the ground. Just as they hit, the forest on the other side of the stream erupted. Leaves, bark, and dirt were thrown in every direction.

Paxton Re looked over his shoulder and couldn't believe his eyes.

He thought they were long dead. Where had this one come from?

Naomi didn't know what hit her. First, she was crouched, drinking cool, refreshing water and then the world turned over.

She was laid out on her front, a weight across her back. On the far side of the stream, where an explosion had come from, there was movement. With this weight holding her down, she was unable to turn over or rise. She was helpless. There was no way to defend herself in this position, and she couldn't see what was coming behind her.

"Umph," she grunted, pushing to dislodge the weight.

"Quiet, now." Naomi froze. She knew that voice.

"Paxton Re?"

"I said hush. You'll draw the beast's attention."

"Beast?" She tried again to turn. "What the—"

But he cut her off, shoving her flat again.

"Damn it, Paxton Re." But push as she might, she couldn't dislodge the dwarf. Just as she was getting ready to shove him again, a mighty roar blew over them. With a small squeak, Naomi curled in a ball and covered her head with her hands, for now, happy for the cover Paxton Re's body provided.

When the splashing of water came to her, she heard Paxton Re mutter, "Oh hell . . ." His weight shifted and she was being pulled backward. Naomi looked up, her hair falling into her face. Through the tresses, she couldn't believe what she was seeing. Coming at them, moving fast, was a beast—Paxton Re was right about that. She had never seen anything like it.

Walking on its hind legs, it resembled a shaggy dog. A real mean, angry, large shaggy dog. Its back hunched, it reached with long arms tipped with claws. Its head dipped down between massive shoulders. Its maw, ridged with sharp teeth, opened, and another roar issued forth. Just before she gave in to panic, Naomi noticed the beast was wearing trousers.

Naomi turned, scrambling away. Paxton Re quit trying to pull her and had to worry about keeping up with her. When they reached the tree line, they scurried to put the timber between them and the animal.

When the beast moved into the tree line, Naomi and Paxton Re circled a small stand of trees, keeping the trunks between it and them.

Around they went—

Once.

Twice.

When it stopped, so did they.

Naomi could smell it. Musky and wet from the stream.

She could hear it. With every exhale, it made a small whine.

She looked around for an avenue of escape, perhaps a tree to climb, when the beast let out a whimper. Its head moved as it sniffed in her direction. Something about its demeanor made her sad. Not sure what she was doing or why, she stopped her mad scramble around the tree.

The beast came closer and she stood still.

"Naomi," Paxton Re whispered, his gaze locked on the animal, "what are you doing?"

"Shh . . . Just give me a second." She sounded brave, even to her own ears, but quakes of fear rocked her frame.

Heavy treads pounded into the soil as the beast moved closer. Dirt puffed up around him, and again he issued a whine.

The closer he got, the more violent Naomi's body quaked, terror filling her, but still she stood firm. When his massive head was within inches of her face, he sniffed again. Paxton Re stayed behind her, seemingly too afraid, or too smart, to run.

Naomi looked the animal in the eyes, waiting to see what it would do. Hoping she hadn't made the wrong decision.

"N'omi." It spoke, and to do so seemed to hurt him, so painful did it sound. Low and raspy, the sound was so strange, she barely understood. Eyes widened and her mind went blank. She couldn't respond. Shock had shut her senses down.

"N'omi," he said again.

"Y-yes." Her voice quivered, puffing out of her lungs. She was lightheaded, her breathing heavy. No animal called in the forest. It was as if the entire world waited to see what would happen.

"What. Are you?" The beast asked the exact question of her that she wanted to know of him.

"What am I?" Her gaze roamed from his head to his large feet complete with curling claws. "What—what are *you*?"

Paxton Re shifted from behind her to move alongside. His bravado back, he gave a sniff of disdain, looking the animal up and down before stating, "It's a werebeast."

At his words, the animal dropped his head and turned his back on them, moving back toward the stream.

"A werebeast?" Naomi looked from the creature to Paxton Re, a question in her eyes.

"Bloodthirsty last I heard. Looks like this one's been tamed."

At his words, the beast spun around, issuing a roar of such volume and force, the dwarf stepped back and sat down hard on his backside.

"Well," he muttered, "maybe not so tame."

"Be nice," she said to the dwarf and turned to follow the beast. "Um, Mr. Werebeast . . ."

The creature spun around, a low growl on his lips. Naomi jumped back, ready to flee. When he again turned to walk away, she glanced at Paxton Re. The dwarf only shrugged.

Naomi's mouth pursed at this lack of advice, and she scowled in the dwarf's direction.

Moving toward the animal, she tried again. "Um, excuse me."

This time when he turned, he seemed ready to listen to her. At least to converse without undue aggression.

Leaning forward and taking another sniff of her, he repeated the inquiry. "What are you?"

"I'm a woman. Human."

"Human." He nodded as though confirming something in his own thoughts.

"What are you?" she asked quietly.

"A werebeast," he said, "just as the dwarf said."

"Why are you here? What do you want?"

"I had a visitor. Last night." His gruff voice, low in his throat, ached. He should not be able to speak. His jaw structure didn't allow him to form the words and yet he did.

Naomi was sure each utterance caused him pain. She moved closer to him. He seemed to be in such turmoil. Such conflict. She had the urge to reach out, to lay her hand upon his arm. If she knew how to give him comfort, she would do it. But he was foreign to her. So far beyond her experiences, she had no idea what move was right and what was wrong. It would be better to do nothing.

"We also had a visitor last night."

At her words, the werebeast's head came up and he studied her.

Gruff and low he told her, "Maude found me. Told me to come to you."

At this, Paxton Re stepped forward, putting himself between the creature and Naomi. "You always do what that old spirit tells you to?"

A low growl came from the werebeast. "Your mouth, dwarf, will get you in trouble one day."

Paxton Re swallowed hard but didn't back down. "Why would Maude send you to us?"

"To her." He pointed at Naomi with a claw. "Maude bade

me come to her, not you."

"Well, I'm with her, ain't I?" He thrust his chin in the air as if daring the animal to contradict his right to be here.

"It would seem you are."

Naomi moved around Paxton Re, putting herself closer to the creature. "Do you have a name?" When he looked surprised, she added, "If we're going to be traveling together, we'll need to be able to call you something."

Searching the distance, the creature was silent for a time and then he said, "Once upon a time, I was called Adalard." The name came out with an accent she couldn't place.

"Adalard," she repeated.

The lines softened on the werebeast's face, his mass not so threatening.

"You're welcome to join us, Adalard." Naomi looked at the dwarf, including him in the decision. "And we'll be lucky to have you, won't we, Paxton Re?"

"Humph," the dwarf voiced and then added, "Well, we're heading to the city of Abster. Gotta get outfitted for a trip. Obviously can't take you into a town with us. You'll have to stay away. Catch up to us when we leave town."

"Abster?" Naomi asked. "How far until we get there?"

"Just a couple hours. If we're to find this Darklin Vale like Maude thinks we need ta, we're gonna need supplies. I know a man in Abster. He owes me a favor."

"Well, okay," Naomi said, smiling at each of her companions. "We'll get outfitted, and maybe someone can point us in the direction of Darklin Vale."

CHAPTER EIGHT

Naomi couldn't believe her eyes.

Or her ears.

The last time she had heard a cow low was when she was ten years old and her grade school class had gone to the zoo. They had watched, spellbound, as the attendant milked the cow.

She hadn't been able to drink milk since.

Now, standing in the stable while Paxton Re and another man discussed something in low, secretive tones, she had to step aside as the brownish cow shifted. At least, she thought it was a cow. Instead of two horns, this one had four. The usual two and then another set lower on the face. And its color was peculiar. Along with a brown dirt color was a hint of purple. The bovine was almost a light lavender. And big. She couldn't see over its back. Were the cows in her world really this large? When it shifted, if she stayed where she was, it would have knocked her over—or stepped on her. At least, as she remembered, the smell was pleasant.

Naomi touched the haunch of the large animal. Warm. Prickly.

With another lowing, the cow swung its head to stare at the startled woman. Caught in the gaze, Naomi could only tip her head and stare into the large, soft brown eyes.

"You done communing with the cow?"

With a start and a sheepish look, Naomi watched Paxton Re lead the other man toward her.

"This here is the man I told you about. We'll be getting supplies from him." Turning from her, Paxton Re spoke to the man. "She'll need clothing, too. Serviceable. Strong."

The man didn't speak to her. Simply looked her up and down, gave a nod, and moved away.

"Soon as we're outfitted, we'll head down to the local tavern. Lots of travelers. Maybe we can get a bead on the location of this Darklin Vale." The dwarf stared off into the distance and shook his head. "Don't know. I've traveled most places. Never heard of this vale."

"There must be someone who knows something about it."

Paxton Re simply nodded at her, watching as his friend reentered the stable. Taking the bundles from him, the dwarf handed a rolled-up cloth to Naomi. There were also foodstuffs, bladder canteens, and weapons. Naomi took the clothes, her attention on the weapons.

Seeing where her gaze lay, Paxton Re looked from her to the armaments. Shooing her off, he said, "Go and change. We don't have time to lose."

Nodding, she stepped into a back room and shook out the clothing. Pants that cinched at the waist, a short-sleeved tunic, and a belt. Underclothes, too. A wrap-type bra that she tightened over her breasts and soft, cotton underwear. Boots that fit surprisingly well and were very comfortable. Stuffing her workout clothes in her sneakers, she returned to where the two men finished preparing them for their journey.

Seeing her, Paxton Re bent to retrieve a belt and scabbard. Roughly, he placed the belt around her waist and tightened it over the belt she already wore. He grasped it, moving it back and forth to seat it on her hips. When he was satisfied, he turned to take a short-bladed sword from the pile on the floor and slid it into the scabbard.

"I don't know how to use that," she said.

"No matter. If you need it, it'll be there."

Naomi slid the knife she had been carrying, since she first met Paxton Re, into one of the belts. Catching sight of the stolen knife, Paxton Re removed it from her belt to study it.

"I got that from the . . ." At this she hesitated and, glancing at the owner of the stable, lowered her voice to finish, "From the men you were with when we met." Paxton Re gave a humph and, without another word, returned the knife to her belt. Stepping back, he gave her a once-over. Nodding as though satisfied, he handed her a pack.

When she stuffed her shoes into the pack, he said, "You might want to leave those here. Carrying any extra weight is going to be noticed right away."

Naomi looked longingly at her things. Leaving them felt like she was admitting defeat. As if she would never again need them or anything like them. With them she could convince herself she wasn't mad. Without them, she was well and truly in this world.

"Okay." She nodded and turned to the back room. Placing her shoes and clothes gently on an upper shelf, she told herself she would be back for them, but she wasn't so sure. Leaving her things brought her predicament back to the forefront of her thoughts.

What was she doing? Where was she? How did this happen?

"You comin'? We need to be leaving."

When Paxton Re yelled for her, she once again moved forward into the moment. Figuring out how this happened would have to wait. Right now, she needed to deal with the here and now, and how to get home. The only lead she had was in the information she had gotten from Maude.

She had to find Darklin Vale.

CHAPTER NINE

So far, she had met a dwarf, sprogs, and a werebeast. When Naomi and Paxton Re walked into the tavern, all eyes turned toward them. She felt as though she were witnessing a scene from *Star Wars*.

When they first cleared the door, two individuals growled, making her and Paxton Re take a step away from them and into the room. At first, she thought they would be werebeast like Adalard—they even wore trousers—but these two looked quite different. Not shaggy, their skin looked thick and tough, orange like a Hunter's Moon.

A large group of seven or eight clustered around the serving area. She perked up when she thought them men, but hearing them speak—clicks and chirps like a bird—dissuaded her of that notion.

In the back of the room, Naomi saw two dwarfs at a table, mostly in the shadows. They acknowledged Paxton Re with a slight raise of their chins but immediately went back to their drinks, their heads close in a hushed conversation.

Paxton Re led her to one end of the bar where he turned to observe the room. His eyes shifted over the patrons, never staying too long in one place. When the bartender came to them, Paxton Re told him, "Two ales," and they were served quickly.

Naomi took a drink. It was cold and frothy, but not as she

expected. Sweeter than any beer she had ever tasted. And thicker, too. But good.

Sniffing it, and taking another longer drink, she was surprised when Paxton Re said, "Take it slow. The ale here is strong. I don't need you drunk."

She regarded him with a scowl but then thought perhaps he was right. She hadn't eaten much in the last few days, and in this strange world, drunk wouldn't be a good place to be.

The ebb and flow of conversation happened around them as they kept quiet and listened. When the bartender returned, Paxton Re declined another drink for them both.

"We're looking for a place called Darklin Vale. Might you 'ave heard of it?"

The bartender shook his head, and before he moved off to serve a group farther down the bar, Naomi got a good look at him. Of average height, his skin was dark and appeared rough. He wore a well-worn cap. What she had at first thought were curls, proved to be a cluster of tentacles. They had moved when he shook his head, swaying to and fro like they had agreed with the bartender's assessment. When he glanced at her, she noticed that his pupils were elongated and ran up and down in the center of his eyes. She watched him walk away and, took a gulp of her ale.

They hadn't heard anything. A couple more sips and Naomi worried this was a waste of time. She was just about to mention this to Paxton Re when a character, tall and lanky with a head full of bright-red hair, sidled up to the bar. Naomi studied him. A grown man, she thought, but barely. He seemed to be no more than a boy. Looking around, he leaned into them.

"Lookin' for a guide?"

"Might be," Paxton Re answered.

"Hear you're looking for Darklin Vale."

"Might be," Paxton Re again answered.

"Well, I might know someone who can help you." And he searched the room as if keeping an eye out for something.

All Naomi's cop instincts screamed that this guy wasn't to be trusted. She put a hand on Paxton Re's shoulder, but he kept his eyes on their visitor.

"And who might that be?" Paxton Re asked.

"There's this guy. He's been places most others wouldn't dream of going."

Paxton Re turned to fully face the man. "And where might we locate this guy?"

"Well . . ." And the stranger gave a chuckle. "'e keeps mostly to himself. Kind of an unfriendly sort, you know."

"Hmm," Paxton Re muttered. "Some folks are like that."

"Yeah, so, this guy, he lives up in the Backaroon Mountains."

Paxton Re glanced at Naomi. "That's a fair piece."

"Yep. But like I said, he's been places. Probably be able to take you right to this Darklin Vale."

"What's this guy's name?"

"Now just wait up a minute, mister." Naomi couldn't determine what he might be, but the stranger took a step back. "Seems to me there might be a finder's fee, or something associated with this."

"Finder's fee." Paxton Re's voice was loud enough to draw glances, and he stepped up into the stranger's space. "We don't even know if what you're saying is the truth, or if you're just out to get something. Why, in the name of all the gods, would we give you a finder's fee for nothing?"

"Okay, okay." The man put his hands up in a pacifying manner, stepping back. "I get ya, friend."

"I'm no friend of yours."

"Yeah, I see that." The stranger looked Paxton Re up and down, then turned his attention to Naomi. "Here's what I'll do for you." He maneuvered closer to her. "I'll give you a name, and I've already told you where—"

"In a whole mountain range," Paxton Re interrupted.

"Yeah, yeah, all right." And he again gestured to calm Paxton Re. "I find lately I'm a bit tired of this here town and these folks.

What I'll do is come with you. Lead you right to the man, as it were."

Naomi laid a hand on Paxton Re's shoulder. "Um, Paxton Re. I don't think—"

"I'm a real likable guy . . . once you get to know me. Good guy to have in a scrap. And I can hunt. Help you with the trip in lots of ways."

Paxton Re stepped back, his eyes narrowing on the stranger.

"Paxton Re . . ." Naomi whispered behind him, but the dwarf held up a hand to her, silencing her protest. He knew a larger party would be safer on the road. It would be better to have this man with them in case the guide wasn't as easy to locate as they hoped. He would just always have to be on his guard.

Decided, Paxton Re nodded. "You can come with us." The man's face split in a large smile, and he clapped his hands together. "But I'm watching you." At this the man sobered, nodding solemnly. "I expect to get to the Backaroon Mountains in the fastest way possible. I expect to find this man you talk of immediately." The stranger nodded again.

"Now." Paxton Re settled back; his thumbs hooked in his waistband. "What's the man's name?"

"Zulrajas," the stranger said, now more than happy to give up the name.

"Sounds like a troll name to me." Paxton Re gave a squinty look at the man.

"Well, yeah." He looked off into the room. "Kinda does, don't it?"

Voice rising to a shout, Paxton Re stepped up to the man. "You're telling me this guide is a troll?"

Once again attempting to pacify the dwarf, the man patted him on his shoulders. "But he's a great guide. I'm tellin' you, he's been everywhere."

Muttering, Paxton Re stomped off into the room, swung around, and stomped back. All he could think to do was head to the next town, days away. And even there, they couldn't guarantee they would have any success. This was the best option, the quickest option.

"And . . ." Paxton Re scanned the stranger. "What's your name?"

Relaxing, the boy smiled, looking between the two of them. "Nyabingi. But folks call me Bob."

"Bob?" Naomi and Paxton Re asked at the same time, looks of confusion on their faces.

"Sure." Bob smiled at them.

"Well, okay then." Paxton Re put a hand out to the newest member of their company. "Bob. Welcome."

When Bob grasped his hand, Paxton Re gripped hard and pulled the man into his chest. The dwarf was short but barrel chested. Bob, being wiry, easily bent to look the dwarf eye to eye. "Remember what I said," Paxton Re growled at him.

Nodding vigorously, Bob pulled back, extracting his hand from the dwarf's grip. He opened and closed it a few times.

"Get what you need. Meet us at the stable within the hour."

Bob nodded his way backward. Turning at the door, he shoved it open to hustle out.

"Do you think that was the best idea?" Naomi said from behind the dwarf.

"Maybe. Maybe not," Paxton Re answered her. "I guess we'll find out soon enough." Turning back to her he added, "Let's get out of here. We'll need to be ready to leave when Bob shows up."

CHAPTER TEN

Mik had his orders. He knew what he was supposed to do, and he knew what he was going to do.

They had put him in charge of a battalion of soldiers. Some of them were experienced. Most of them were newbies. Brand new sprogs. Like colts on wobbly legs. Eyes open in wonder, not sure of their surroundings or what had been done to them.

Mik thought back to the ritual.

Bloody, it was never a pleasant experience for the soon-to-be turned. Most came to the castle against their will. Captives, the lot of them. Best way to grow an army was conscription.

They were herded into the main hall. With its ceiling open to the floors high above, the footfalls of all those below echoed into the rafters. As they settled, a quiet fell over the tower. The floors above housed Charmot. At first, the recruits didn't know anything was coming. The inky black inching down the walls did so on silent feet. When the first of them noticed the approaching darkness, he called attention to it, and panic soon set in.

Scream as they might, rail against those holding them, it benefited them nothing. The barriers kept them in place. Soon bathed in the essence of Charmot, the screams became whimpers. Where once there were bodies and minds, hale and hearty, now there were sprogs. Stronger than before, their bodies would heal quicker, move faster, and battle harder. But those minds, now were full of only the ability to obey Charmot or those who served him.

That made them Mik's to command.

As far as he knew, not one of them had his master's ear quite like Mik did. He had been in Charmot's service the longest. And his master had needed a sprog with the ability to think and reason.

Now, he had his orders, and with a complement of soldiers, he would do what was necessary to fulfill them. And fulfill them he would. There was no question. To fail would be to fall. Charmot would tolerate no defeat. Once human like all sprogs, Mik had lived a long life equal to many lifetimes of a normal man, and he wasn't ready for it to end.

Charmot had a plan, something going on that he didn't tell anyone, even Mik. Maybe especially Mik. All Mik knew, all he needed to know, was they were to go and see an elf, a very particular elf. And that elf would help Mik locate a girl. Mik kept information to himself. Information about a girl. He didn't know if she was the same girl that his master sought, but he believed she was. He had seen her. Spoke with her. Been on the receiving end of her magic potion. She had gotten away once, but he swore she wouldn't again.

CHAPTER ELEVEN

Getting back to the area where Adalard waited for them was easier than Naomi had thought it would be. She seemed to be aligning with this world, understanding where things were.

As they walked around the last bend in the stream, a gust of air blew behind Naomi, throwing her hair over her shoulder. Before she could react, a high-pitched scream pierced the silence. Spinning, she saw Adalard crouched, Bob under him. It was from Bob that the shriek came.

She and Paxton Re arrived behind the werebeast at the same time. Naomi leaned over Adalard's shoulder, peering at the terror-stricken face of their newest member.

"Bob," she said, "meet Adalard." She turned to the werebeast and added, "Adalard, meet Bob."

Without releasing the paralyzed Bob, the werebeast looked in her direction. As nonchalant as she had sounded with the introductions, her heart gave a lunge at the look delivered to her.

"You've included another?" How could she have forgotten how gravelly that voice was?

"Um, well . . ." She looked toward Paxton Re for assistance. The dwarf, this time, was silent. "Well, yes. Bob has assured us that he can lead us to an individual who is sure to know where we can locate Darklin Vale."

Adalard's head spun back to face the prone man. Bob's eyes were squeezed closed, his face puckered up. A low growl sounded from the werebeast, and a small whimper came out of Bob.

"Adalard." Naomi tried to get his attention. He ignored her. The boy shifted and the werebeast again growled, his lips pulling back from fangs. A drop of saliva landed on the boy's forehead, and Bob began to quake.

Placing a hand on one shaggy shoulder, Naomi again called his name.

"Adalard."

This time the werebeast took two paces back, letting the sun fall upon the new traveler. Bob cracked an eye open. Seeing the beast had moved, he slowly got to his feet. Giving a humph, Adalard turned to walk away. Bob raised his chin as he straightened his clothing.

"Told you I could handle him." He stretched his neck first one way and then the other.

Paxton Re shook his head and turned to follow the werebeast to the woods.

Naomi stared for a moment longer at Bob, at a loss for words.

"Well, come on then," she said and followed the dwarf and beast. With a hand held out to steady himself, Bob took a tentative step after her. Assured his legs were working, he picked up his pace and followed the group.

CHAPTER TWELVE

The early-morning sun filtering through the trees fell upon Naomi's face. She stretched, arching her back and reaching above her head.

Across the small clearing where they rested, the sun reflected off a flame-colored tree. She had noticed it when she lay down to sleep, but with nightfall coming so quickly, she hadn't been able to study it. Naomi's sleepy mind focused slowly on the beautiful tree. Long branches swayed gently. A soft humming, almost like a song, floated in the air. When a breeze blew through the clearing, the tree burst. At first, Naomi thought they were leaves and then she thought perhaps butterflies. Leaving behind a tree that Naomi recognized—like the one she had slept against the first night—the fluttering fliers swooped on the wind currents closer to where Naomi lay.

Curious what they were, Naomi stayed still. When they flew overhead, a couple came closer, and she saw they were small humanoid beings with beautiful flame-colored wings. One hovered in front of Naomi's face, seemingly as curious about her as she was about them. She reached slowly for the flier, entranced by this strange and lovely vision. It watched her for a second and then, with a blink, it was gone.

Naomi took a deep breath, reveling in the beauty of the moment. It was a good thought in her mind as she prepared for another day.

The day before had been long. They had a good jump on the trip to the Backaroon Mountain range. Bob told them even by the most direct route, it would be a couple of weeks to reach the far side of the valley. Even knowing that, it felt good to be doing something. Going somewhere. Although they were steadily moving farther and farther away from where she entered this world, it seemed that this was the way to get home.

Naomi threw off her blanket, but when she went to push herself to standing, her weight fell on her injured hand.

"Ouch," she said and sat back down.

"What?" Paxton Re came up behind her.

"Oh, my hand is still hurting me." Naomi waved dismissively, and leaning on her uninjured hand, she stood and began gathering her belongings.

"Let me see." Paxton Re approached her, putting out his hand.

"No, I'm fine." And she moved away from him.

"Naomi," he said, his tone low. When she turned to look at him, his scowl darkened even further. "Give me your hand." He thrust his out toward her again.

"Oh, for the love of Pete . . ." Naomi dragged her feet until she stood before the dwarf. "I told you it's fine."

"Perhaps. It won't hurt to be looked at."

Naomi thrust out a hip, pursed her lips, and heaved a sigh. She could feel the bandage being unwrapped from her hand but refused to look.

When Paxton Re's grip gave a jerk, and he muttered, "What in the world?" she found herself looking over his shoulder at her palm.

"What the—"

"Just be still." The dwarf gave her hand a yank to place it back where he had it.

Naomi stared. In the center of her palm, right where the spirit Maude had stabbed her with her nail, was a starburst of angry red. Overlaid on the red were lines, like the branches of a spider's web. The lines pulsed and then quieted. And then pulsed again. Each time, a tingle went from her fingertips up her arm.

Grasping the dwarf with her other hand, Naomi pulled herself closer to the appendage.

"What in the world?"

"What did Maude say?" Paxton Re let go of her hand and swung about to confront her. "Before she stabbed you." His eyes intent, the dwarf advanced on her, causing Naomi to step back. "You remember. What did she say?"

"Jeez Paxton Re. You were there. She was saying a lot of stuff."

"No." He waved her off. "Something about a hammer."

The more Paxton Re drove her back, the louder his voice grew. He was getting himself worked into a frenzy when Naomi backed right into the werebeast. Surprised, she jumped forward and ran into Paxton Re. Sidestepping, she moved out from between the two of them.

"What is happening?" Adalard asked.

"Nothing," Naomi said. "Just nothing. Let's get going." She turned back to her pack and blanket. Shoving the blanket into the pack, she turned her back on her companions.

"What has you afraid?" Paxton Re said from behind her.

"Afraid?" She spun at his words. "You know what I do for a living? It would take more than a little spirit mark to make me afraid."

"Show your hand to him," Paxton Re insisted.

When she kept her hand to her side, it was his turn to thrust out a hip and purse his lips.

"Fine." Naomi stomped by the dwarf. Approaching the werebeast, she shoved her hand at him, palm up. Even though she had seen it once, the mark held her attention. The beast brought one claw up to touch the underside of her hand, drawing it toward him. Giving it a sniff, he glanced at her.

"What is it?"

"I don't know." Her voice came out with a squeak.

Paxton Re pushed himself forward. "It's a mark from Maude. She stabbed Naomi with her nail."

Giving it another sniff, Adalard dropped her hand. It hung in the air for a moment before Naomi curled her fingers over the stain and pulled her fist to her chest.

"Your way is before you," Adalard's rough voice whispered.

"Ha." The dwarf slapped his thigh and spun around. "I told you. The old spirit did something to you."

Opening her palm again, Naomi peeked at it. "I'm sure it will help when we need it. It might even get us where we need to be." Stepping into the bright sunlight, Naomi studied her palm. Again, the lines pulsed, only this time, the red mark in the middle brightened momentarily. "Freaky," Naomi whispered.

Behind them, a sleepy voice said, "What's happening?"

Paxton Re spun around. "Bob," he said. "I'm sorry. It looks like your services will no longer be necessary." The smile on his face negated the apology in his words.

"What?" Bob jumped forward. "I'm part of this. I'm going with you." He moved from one of them to another, pleading his case. "You need me. I'm the only one who can get you to Zulrajas."

"Is that a troll name?" Adalard's gruff voice questioned.

"You know you need me," the lanky man continued. "I'm a handy guy to have around. I told you I can hunt. I'm good at keeping a camp. Well, well . . . I can . . . I can even sing." And he broke into an off-tune refrain of an old song.

"Good lord," Paxton Re said and turned away.

"Bob." Naomi tried to talk over the volume of the song, but Bob just got louder.

When the werebeast hmphed and coughed, Naomi turned on him. "Don't you dare start howling!"

At this, Paxton Re started to laugh. And Adalard let out a howl.

The louder Bob sang, the louder the werebeast howled and the louder the dwarf laughed. Naomi stepped back, looking at them.

Her companions.

Glancing down at her hand, she again curled it into her chest.

What would become of them all?

CHAPTER THIRTEEN

Two days later, the mountains came into view. In the distance, they looked purple with splotches of greens and browns. At their apex, fierce winds blew swirling snow about the summits. When the sun rose to peek its head over them, the colors were vibrant against the clear blue in the morning light.

The company of four had fallen into a routine of sorts in the last few days. That first morning, with all of them together, once everyone calmed down and it was determined that Bob would indeed be allowed to accompany them, they broke camp and headed out. In his pack, Paxton Re found an old pair of gloves with the fingers cut off that he gave to Naomi.

"Best to cover that up," he said with a gesture at her hand. "We don't want some stranger to get curious."

Naomi put on the gloves, not looking at the mark on her palm. She tried to forget the feeling of the old spirit's nail stabbing into her hand. Tried to forget the image moving on her hand, but a weak, persistent warmth coming from the area kept her mind in tune to what Maude had done.

At first, traveling was simple. The land was lush with wild grasses and a variety of trees, some familiar and some—like the one of her first night, generating its own heat, drawing her close—not so familiar.

On one of the first days, the company came upon a small stand of bushes. Like nothing Naomi had ever seen, they were purplish in hue. As she neared, Naomi realized the leaves were what gave off the purple stain, the branches being blood red. Around the base of each leaf, a small cluster of three to five berries appeared lush and juicy, just a shade darker than the leaves. Naomi was just reaching for them when a hand jerked on her arm.

"I wouldn't do that." It was Bob, now moving to block her path to the bushes.

"They look delicious," she said, peering over his shoulder, her gaze on the berries.

"That's what they want you to think."

Now, Naomi looked at the young man, her brows drawn in. "Want me to think? What do you mean, the berries?"

A gruff voice came from her other side, and she looked down to see Paxton Re staring at the bush with loathing.

"Damn Bendal Berries." And he spat to the side. "Carnivorous is what they are."

"Carnivorous?" Naomi gave a small laugh and turned to Bob for confirmation.

"Oh, aye," he said, nodding. "They'll even digest the bones."

"Oh, come on! What is this, some kind of a joke you play on people?"

"You don't believe us?" Paxton Re muttered, looking around the area. "I'll show you and hope I'm not sorry." After a moment the dwarf walked away, returning with a long, thick tree branch. Holding the branch out in front of him like a sword, Paxton Re hesitantly approached the Bendal Berry bush. Once near, he gave the plant two swift jabs from the wood.

Naomi's breath caught as long tendrils shot out of the bush, wrapped around the branch and, almost jerking Paxton Re off his feet, pulled the bough back into the thicket of the plant.

"Wha—" she began, only to be pulled backward by a rapidly retreating Bob.

"Once they get you, they sink barbs in. Heard say it stings like a swarm of bees, but soon enough you can't move."

"And it kills you?"

"Yep. But not quick enough. You'd be half eaten before taking your last breath." The boy pulled her along, and glancing back, Naomi saw Paxton Re hustling to join them.

"Suppose it's hard for you to understand about a meat-eating plant," Bob said.

"No." Naomi shook her head. "We have carnivorous plants in my world, just not man-eating ones." Moving away from the dangerous bushes, Naomi kept glancing over her shoulder until they were well away.

Naomi ran her palms along the tips of the lush field grass. It was a way of grounding herself in this world. She hadn't ever lived in the country in her world. Never was around fields planted with grain, but this felt familiar. She kept her eyes open, her senses alert, and most often, it was the animals that drew Naomi's gaze. They were everywhere. The land was bursting with life. Small ground dwellers—animals resembling rodents, rabbits. And larger fauna resembling deer. Often, she saw the odd bird creatures of before, though they weren't the only things in the sky. Twice, she saw small vibrant shapes, like those from the previous morning. When she pointed them out to Paxton Re, he grunted and mumbled, "Pixies."

Naomi wanted to ask him more. What did he mean, pixies? Were they real pixies? Were they intelligent? Could she speak with one? But Paxton Re moved away too quickly. Just when she was going to yell out to him, Bob moved up beside her.

"Pixies can be dangerous," he muttered. "Best just to leave them be."

"Dangerous?"

When he didn't volunteer any more, she turned toward him and walked. "What do you mean, dangerous? They're pretty tiny."

"Yep." He nodded in agreement. "You'd think that, wouldn't

you? But they'll ambush you. Nasty little buggers."

Naomi glanced back to watch the small flier until she could no longer see it. Catching up to the group, she let the subject drop, but it stayed on her mind for most of the day.

An occasional stream gave them the opportunity to pause and drink. The larger ones they had to decide how to cross, but fresh water was always welcome.

Each time Bob got close to Adalard, the werebeast would growl, once even snapping at the man. Curious, Naomi questioned him, leaning in as they walked side by side. "Why don't you like him?"

"His smell is off," the gravelly voice answered.

"Off, how?"

"Don't know," he growled, giving the lanky man a sideways glance. "Don't know what he is."

Naomi hadn't given a thought as to Bob not being human. He could pass as one in any drawing room in her world. Now, she found herself watching him and giving more consideration to what he might be. Realizing she didn't even know all the options—elf, dwarf, werebeast—she filed Adalard's opinion away for further consideration.

Time passed and distance did, too. Long days of walking fostered an atmosphere of intimacy among the party.

Naomi found not only Paxton Re seeking her out, but Adalard, too.

One day as dusk approached, she screwed up her courage and asked him about his origins.

"What do you mean?" He glanced at her, his face thrown into part light, the sun setting at their backs. He was inscrutable at the best of times and now, in the gloaming, he seemed more beast than ever.

"Well," she began, not wishing to offend him, "in my world, there are myths of individuals like you." She walked a bit, trying her words in her head before voicing them. "These individuals begin as humans."

When his head swung again to regard her, she paused. "A human who had an encounter with another werebeast—or werewolf. They're bitten. And changed."

His quiet response came to her. "I have not always been as you see me."

"Would you tell me your tale? I'd like to know more about you."

Adalard sneezed and shook his head. He didn't answer her, didn't look at her again. A moment later, he wandered away and she regretted offending him.

Paxton Re took his place by her side. His thoughts were more utilitarian.

"Need to find a good spot to spend the night. Sun's going down fast."

Naomi nodded in agreement, searching the area ahead of them.

"You notice the storm?"

Turning as she walked, Naomi searched the far sky. "That storm?" She gestured with her chin.

"Yes, that storm. Might break tonight. We'll want shelter then."

Naomi scanned the darkening sky off to the back and right. Distant bolts of lightning flashed, but the sound didn't reach them.

"How long do storms last in this world?"

"This one?" he asked almost to himself and rubbed the side of his nose, squinting at the evening sky. "Maybe forever."

Deliberately not looking at him, she asked, "It's like the storm the night Maude visited us."

"I guess so."

"Char . . . What was it? What did she say?"

"Charmot." His tone was sharp, the word clipped.

"Yes, Charmot."

The dwarf spun to her, causing them both to stop. His voice rising, he pointed at her. "Don't take Charmot so lightly. He's very powerful. He's either killed or enslaved thousands. If he knows you're here and he wants you, I don't know how to stop that from happening."

Naomi stared at the dwarf, at a loss for words.

Paxton Re spit to the side, looking left and right to see Adalard and Bob closing in on them.

"And these two"—he gestured at their companions—"their being here won't make a bit of difference. We could have an army, and it would do no good."

"Well, what then, Paxton Re?" Naomi threw her hands up. "What should we do? Are you telling me not to even try?"

Now she advanced on him. It was her voice to rise, and him to shrink back.

"I can't do that. I won't do that."

Gesturing back the way they had come, she said, "If you want to leave, then fine. I thought you'd left me once before, and I decided to go on. Just do what you want." She turned to stomp away, Bob and Adalard parting and moving quickly out of her way.

Hustling forward, Paxton Re said, "Now wait, Naomi. That's not what I'm saying at all."

As they passed between the two, Bob looked at Adalard. "Did they say Charmot?"

With a dismissive grunt, the werebeast followed Naomi and Paxton Re.

"Naomi, wait!" Paxton Re yelled, hustling to catch the woman.

Ignoring him, she splashed across a small stream. Paxton Re waded in behind her.

"Damn it, Naomi." Grasping her arm, he spun her around. "That's not what I'm saying, and I think you know that."

"What do you mean then?" Hands on her hips, Naomi's temper flared.

"What I'm saying is just maybe, you don't want to admit how much danger you're in. Maybe it's a little more than you can handle—with everything else."

Naomi always thought, though you might lie to others, you should never lie to yourself, so she stopped and thought about what he had said, her temper calming.

Considering everything that had happened in the last few days, she thought she had done pretty good. Okay, the thought of an all-powerful, magical being with thousands of henchmen at his disposal, searching for her had her freaking out, but short of leaving this world, there wasn't anything she could do about it.

Her solution: Her salvation lay in Darklin Vale. It seemed it was her only passage home.

And, she felt, her liberation from this world lay with these three individuals. Paxton Re, Adalard, and even Bob would have a role to play.

At the sounds of splashing, she looked to see the werebeast and man crossing to join her and Paxton Re.

Calmer now, she faced her three companions. They stared back at her as if she had all the answers, but inside she was uncertain and scared, and she knew less than each of them. Finding herself in this new world, no way home, and knowing no one, she had done the best she could.

Naomi allowed herself to study her companions for another moment and then put her hand out to Paxton Re. When he gripped it, hand to elbow, she gave him a nod.

"We've got this, Paxton Re." She looked to Bob and Adalard. "We've all got this."

Paxton Re released her arm, turning to scan the area next to the stream. "Let's gather some wood and get a fire going. This place is as good as any to spend the night." The dwarf turned away and, picking up sticks, obeyed his own orders. Adalard and Bob followed his lead silently. For a moment, Naomi stood where she was, uncertain about the future but glad her argument with Paxton Re was at an end. She needed him—needed all of them.

*****

Naomi's mind spun as she watched the embers of the dying campfire float into the air where they disappeared against the black backdrop of the night sky. On her back, wrapped in her cloak, she was torn.

They were all so brave. All so willing to see her through to the end of this journey. She would need to be braver. Stronger than she had ever been. She would need to make sure none of them came to any harm, and if it seemed they might, she would need to be brave enough to continue alone.

She couldn't be the cause of their deaths. She couldn't be the cause of anyone's death.

CHAPTER FOURTEEN

It was two days later when they entered the forest.

Almost immediately, sounds changed. The tones. The volume. Birdcalls halted entirely. The vast abundance of wildlife that she had become acquainted with, now ceased to be. No wind moved through the tops of the branches to whistle above their heads. Gaping her mouth in an imitation of a yawn, Naomi tried to make her ears pop, feeling as though she had crested a large mountain range. Studying the area, she soon realized altitude wasn't the problem. They were shut in, as effectively as a door closing in a windowless room.

The sounds of their footfalls came to them loudly in the heavy air, and even the mundane, everyday noises they made—clearing of throats or sighs—were loud. When Bob yawned, his jaw cracking, Naomi jumped. The very air was expectant.

"No one said we had to walk through this forest," she whispered.

"No one knew it was here," Paxton Re said.

"How long do you think it'll continue?" Naomi asked no one in particular, and having no answer, no one replied.

* * * * *

They walked for what seemed like hours, with the forest never changing. Wisps of fog trailed between trunks of the trees. It floated upward where it thickened enough to block the light of the sun. Because of it, the day was colored gray, as were the trees and grasses. Naomi worried that if they stayed too long, they would become gray, too.

The day darkened, slowly. When it became difficult to find their way, they stopped as one to glance around them.

"Maybe it's nighttime?" Bob said to no one in particular.

"It's something," Paxton Re rumbled in a low voice. When a moment more passed and no one had anything to add, the dwarf moved toward a small grouping of brush, causing the others to follow.

"We might as well try and get some rest. I'll take first watch." With a shrug he dropped his pack. Pulling his short sword from its scabbard at his belt, he moved away from the three to kneel at the base of a large tree.

Naomi waited for a moment and then, with a large sigh, she slung off her own pack. Sitting next to Paxton Re's bundle, she pulled a thin blanket from her bag, leaned back against his pack, and closed her eyes. When she heard a rustle, she cracked her eyes to see Bob and Adalard getting comfortable on either side of her. Thankful for the company and protection, she pulled the blanket up to her chin and was soon asleep.

* * * * *

When she next opened her eyes, the day had regained its hazy, gray cast. Seeing her two companions still on either side of her and still asleep, she sat up to search out Paxton Re. He sat still at the base of the lone tree, but now he was slumped, his head bent forward on his neck. Naomi rose, absently noticing that neither Bob nor Adalard stirred at her passage. Approaching the dwarf, Naomi grasped his shoulder and gave him a small shake.

"Paxton Re."

When he didn't wake, she crouched to his level and firmly shook both shoulders.

"Paxton Re," she said louder.

Alarm began to filter into her senses when he didn't wake. Grasping his face between her hands, she tipped his head up and looked into his countenance. Holding him under the chin, she slid open an eyelid and almost dropped his head back down. Checking first one pupil and then the other, she confirmed that both were clouded. Fogged over like this forest.

"Paxton Re," she said and slapped his cheek. The crack of skin to skin echoed among the trees. A hint of color came to his skin where she had struck him, but the dwarf didn't stir. Naomi watched him for a moment longer and then, gently, laid him out on the forest floor.

Standing, she moved back to Bob and Adalard who still slept where she had left them. Worry filled her as she kneeled before them. Checking their eyes, she wasn't surprised to see they, too, were clouded over. The gray a match for the color of this place.

Unsure what to do with her companions, at a loss for what was even happening, she paced between them, her mind in a turmoil.

When the faint gurgle of water caught her attention, she raised her head, listening to determine from where the sound came. Decided, she dug in her pack, coming up with a bowl of sorts. After pulling her knife from her belt, she moved in the direction of the water, marking a rudimentary arrow in each tree as she passed. With a silent hope that these trees didn't heal quickly, she continued.

It was the motion of the water that finally caught her attention, showing her where the stream lay. She scooped up a cupful, bringing it to her nose to smell. Nothing—not good, not bad. Taking a sip, Naomi swished the water about in her mouth and gave it a small prayer before swallowing. She waited a few moments and then refilled the cup. She headed back the way she had come.

Returning to the cluster of bushes where her companions still slumbered, she studied the three of them. With a small internal shrug, Naomi stood over Bob and then, kneeling, threw the cupful of water in his face.

The young man lurched up, catching his breath.

"What the—"

Naomi had already dropped to her knees in front of him, clutching him in a hug. Patting her shoulder awkwardly, Bob wiped his hand over his face and pushed water out of his hair.

"Naomi, what's happening?"

With an effort Naomi released the young man, sitting back but keeping him at arm's length.

"Do you know, Bob? Do you remember anything?"

Bob started at her, his brows drawn in. Turning his head, he surveyed the area, taking in first Paxton Re and then the large body of the werebeast beside him. Again, he wiped where a bead of water dripped from his wet hair.

"Remember? Remember about what?"

Naomi gripped the boy's forearms. Her desperation caused her to give him a small shake.

"Bob," she breathed. "You, Adalard, and Paxton Re have been in some kind of a trance. They still are." She tossed a hand out toward the dwarf and werebeast. "I just threw water in your face, and you woke up, but you were out. Your eyes were grayed over." Saying this out loud seemed to remind Naomi of her desperation and she again wrapped her arms around the young man, her breath hitched.

"Well, now Naomi." He gave her shoulder a pat. "If the water worked with me, I just bet it'll work with Adalard and Paxton Re."

She raised her head with a nod, sitting back from him.

"Yes, yes, I hope it will. I was just so relieved. You sit here. I'll go back to the stream and get some more water."

"I can do it, Naomi." Bob was quick to offer.

"No." She stopped him with a hand. "We don't know what effect the trance had on you. Sit here and rest a moment. I'll be right back."

Back to the stream Naomi went, once almost losing her way before locating her arrow on a tree. When she returned to their campsite with the cup of water, Bob watched intently as she threw it in the dwarf's face.

"Well, what did you do that for?" he said, sputtering and wiping his face.

Naomi gave him a big smile but didn't answer as she turned to again head to the stream.

"What's going on here, boy?" he prodded Bob, studying the fact that he, too, was wet. When Naomi stepped from the woods and approached the werebeast, Paxton Re rose to his feet. With fascination, he watched her throw the water on the beast.

Adalard blinked up at them, like a sleepy kitten, not startled in the least.

Smiling, her face about to burst, Naomi spun in a circle, staring at each of them in turn.

"Now that you've woken us all, and in an unpleasant fashion, you wanna tell me what in the world is going on?" Paxton Re stood, his hands on his hips.

Naomi approached him and bent to give him a hug, a slight giggle coming from her. "You were all in a trance. Your eyes were glazed over with a gray fog. Gray like this forest. I didn't know how to wake you." She took a deep breath. "But the water worked."

"A trance?" the dwarf said. "But not you?"

"What?"

"Not you? You were awake?"

"Yeah," she said. "I guess I was . . . I mean, I was asleep. But I woke up . . ." Her voice trailed off. "I wonder why it didn't affect me."

The three stared at her for a moment and then Bob offered, "Maybe it's what Maude did."

Naomi brought her gloved hand up. "What do you mean?"

"Well? I don't know. But it's magic, right?"

"Right," Naomi agreed hesitantly. Something just didn't feel right about that explanation, but perhaps Bob was correct. She sure couldn't claim to be an expert in all things magic—even in some things.

"Well, we're awake now," Paxton Re stated, his tone gruff and no-nonsense. "Let's see if we can get out of this forest before darkness falls again."

In silent agreement, the company picked up their packs and allowed the werebeast to lead them into the dense forest.

* * * * *

The day progressed with little change. No indications for direction or time passage came to them. Relying on Adalard's sense of smell, they followed trustingly at his back. Throughout the day, they heard rustling or crashes within the jungle of woods but saw nothing.

The time spent within the woods began to wear on the company. Senses meant little in such a place. Sight perceived only shades of gray. Even they had begun to wash out—clothing taking on an ashen color, skin paling to a sickly shade. Smell came in small bursts, but even that was muted. Dull, almost dirty, but even that was welcome for without it, there was simply an absence.

Naomi found herself rubbing her ears, attempting to pop them. When she became aware of her behavior, she noticed the others. Adalard shook his head. Bob tapped the side of his head near his ears. Paxton Re jawed in an exaggerated fashion. Like the land after a heavy snow, this world was muffled.

Having become aware of the impact of this place, Naomi swished water from her canteen in her mouth before swallowing it. True, water had little taste to begin with, but this liquid seemed not to even be there. Nothing. It didn't quench her thirst. It didn't even wet her throat.

Passing trees, she reached to touch the rough bark only to jerk her hand back. Naomi stopped, bringing her hand closer to her face, rubbing thumb to fingertips.

"What is it?" Paxton Re said.

Glancing up, she saw the trio had stopped and turned to her.

"Numb." She held her hand out to them.

Returning her look with one of quizzical impatience, Paxton Re stepped toward her. "What do you mean?"

"Haven't you noticed?" When he just shook his head at her, she glanced at the others only to meet the same perplexed expressions. "Our skin is numb. We can't hear, taste, touch, or even see right. We're all turning gray," she finished, her voice rising a little in hysteria. "We have to get out of this forest."

"Hey, you," Paxton Re said with a gesture at Bob. "You're from around here. What do you know about this forest?"

Bob shifted foot to foot, unable to meet the dwarf's eyes. When Paxton Re grabbed his arm and gave him a shake, the man let out a small squeak.

"What aren't you telling us?"

Barely opening his mouth, his eyes averted, Bob muttered, "Heard tell, this forest is haunted."

"Haunted?" Paxton Re shook him again. "Like with ghosts and spirits?"

"Hungry ones." The boy began shivering and dropped to his knees, forcing Paxton Re to release his hold of him.

"How much longer can this forest go on?" the dwarf asked, spinning in a circle. He studied the surrounding terrain. "Let's keep moving."

* * * * *

The day darkened around them, throwing trees and scrub bushes into shades of gray and black. At first, like the day before, the setting of the sun was hardly noticeable, but between one step and the next, Naomi realized she couldn't see the path in front of her. Hurrying, she caught up to the dwarf. "Do you think we should stop for the night?"

Paxton Re turned to her and seemed to think. "I hate to, but I don't suppose we have an option."

They moved on a bit farther, letting Adalard lead them through the semi-dark. He moved quickly, unhampered by the fading light, and they soon lost sight of him.

"Adalard," Naomi whispered, searching the surrounding area.

"Damn it." Paxton Re stomped his foot. Scanning the area, he added, "We'll make camp here. When he realizes we're no longer following him, I'm sure he'll circle back around. We can't go on without him—it's just too dark. Who knows what hole we'll fall into?"

Naomi, Paxton Re, and Bob spread out to locate firewood. They couldn't go far. The sounds and the quickly disappearing light were so odd, they worried about getting turned around and lost. They found the lack of dry fall didn't matter though. When they tried to light a fire, even with tinder, it would not catch.

As the last of the light faded, the wind picked up, driving a cold shaft through each of them. Huddled together, they strove for warmth but found none. They could only hope to make it until the day lightened and a small bit of warmth made it through the mists surrounding this forest. Then, they would be able to continue.

*****

Naomi awoke with a start, surprised she had found sleep. Groggy and still half asleep, she started when a howl sounded.

Realizing it was that which woke her, she sat up.

"What was that?" Paxton Re mumbled in her ear.

"I don't think it was Adalard," she whispered.

When the howl came again, followed by another, this one of a different tone and volume, Bob sat straight up beside them.

"Wha—what was that?"

"Shh, Bob. Stay quiet."

She couldn't see him in the complete darkness but felt his body quake against hers. On her other side, Paxton Re sat up straighter, and she heard the scrape of his sword sliding from its scabbard. With no light to the night, Naomi's other senses expanded. Every little noise sounded like an explosion.

When, in the distance, there came the sounds of many footsteps nearing, sniffing, and a low keening, the trio pulled back together.

"Hurry, you two. Arm yourselves." Grabbing them, Paxton Re pulled. "Stand back-to-back." The dwarf took command as Naomi climbed to her feet, pulling the boy with her. She had no idea how to use the short sword she had been given, but she pulled it from the sheathing at her waist. She had seen Bob's knife in his belt, and she felt him pull it, pushing himself between herself and the dwarf. His shaking rocked her body, the muffled sound of his crying filled her ears, and she could smell his tears.

"Quiet, you," Paxton Re threw over his shoulder at the young man. "We need to hear them coming."

Bob quieted, but his gasping breaths moved him against her.

"When they attack, strike to kill."

"What are they?" she whispered, but he didn't answer her.

The quiet spun out before them. Had she reached, Naomi felt she could have touched it. The black was absolute. She blinked but stared, unable to locate even a hint of light to focus on.

Straining, she picked up the sound of a bird passing overhead.

Then, the snap of a twig, crushed by a heavy foot.

Her hands were sweaty, and she tightened her grip, fearing

she might inadvertently let loose of the hilt of her sword. When she heard the smallest of movements, perhaps just a displacement of air, she swung out. She struck something large, her sword slicing into it above the level of her head. With the impact came a cry of pain, and whatever it was pulled back, almost taking her weapon with it.

The shriek was like nothing she had heard before. It hurt her ears and constricted her brain. Her mind spun, striving to understand what could create the sound.

Then she was too busy to think. Thrusting and hacking, a splash of wet and sticky washed over her face and chest. With a gasp, she tasted something tangy, and her stomach churned.

Bob was pulled from beside her. Reaching blindly she wrenched him back into their midst.

Though she couldn't see anything, she kept the touch of Paxton Re on one shoulder and Bob on the other. Around her she could hear the whistle of weapons, animal cries, and the breathing of her and her battle mates.

Time passed. Slow and without measure. The constant battle—swing, thrust, hack—the smell of blood, the cries of whatever it was they fought. Naomi forgot about anything but living another moment.

How many of them were there? Her arm leaden, it was sheer will that lifted her sword. Where she feared she would drop it at the beginning, now she was sure she would never be able to release it. Not only the paralyzed cramp of her fingers on the steel, but her skin was glued to it with the flow of muck cut from those who attacked them.

Paxton Re stumbled and she thought he went down, thought they had lost him, only to feel him fight back to stand heavy again guarding the rear.

How long had they battled? It seemed an eternity, and still the enemy came with fresh resources. The three of them could never win, the odds far against them, but still, they couldn't give in. Couldn't rest.

* * * * *

At first, Naomi thought her mind was playing tricks on her.

Movement in the blackness.

But no. There again. The night was lightening.

She thought to call out to Paxton Re and Bob. Thought to bolster their flagging courage with the promise of sunlight. The hope that they might win this night.

Then, a cry next to her and Bob was gone. She reached, shifting to find him.

"Paxton Re!" she screamed. "Bob, Bob's gone!"

A blur flew past her, a whirlwind pushing her back, her hair bloody strands in her face. She couldn't see. Couldn't find him.

Screams came to her. At first, she thought them from the boy, but these couldn't be from any being she knew. Shrill, unintelligible, they were like nothing she ever hoped to hear again.

Then Bob was back. Injured, bleeding, but alive. Their attackers were pulling back. She could hear the battle rage, and as the day continued to lighten, she recognized Adalard.

He had come back. He was fighting against the horde. Holding them back, blood ran down his back and arms. Almost too fast for her to track, they rushed in on the werebeast. Large and shaggy was her only impression.

"Adalard!" she cried.

Paxton Re grasped her arm, pulling her away from the battle.

"Wait!" she yelled, resisting his pull. They had to help. Adalard was all alone.

Paxton Re continued to pull her. As they passed Bob, laid out on the ground, she grasped him by the ankle. Digging her fingers in, she held on as the dwarf pulled her and now Bob back toward a rocky crest.

Paxton Re stopped and collapsed. Naomi dragged Bob the rest of the way to where Paxton Re lay, his back against a stone wall. Bob was unconscious, blood oozing from multiple wounds. When she looked to where she had last seen Adalard, there was nothing but the torn ground, bloody with body parts scattered about. A war zone.

Pulling the young man to her, she sat next to Paxton Re, an arm around Bob's chest. With the stone at their backs, they scanned the field looking for Adalard, watching to see if their attackers would come back now that the sun had risen. Part of Naomi wanted to see them in the dim light of this day, and part of her preferred they be relegated to the midnight hours.

Her body calming, her breath smoothing, she hurt from multiple wounds. Scratches and even what she thought might be bites oozed blood and flared with pain. Stretching her arm, her breath caught in a hiss, she studied her arms, hands, and even legs. The more she looked, the higher her eyebrows rose. She didn't remember getting any of these injuries.

Paxton Re stirred next to her, sitting up straight.

"Here comes the werebeast," he mumbled.

From out of the fog, Adalard's large body appeared. His fur was coated with blood, and she had good reason to believe it wasn't all his.

He stopped in front of them, weariness covering him like a shroud.

"Come," he said and, bending down, lifted the limp body of Bob to place him upon his shoulder. Turning, he walked back into the mist.

As quickly as possible, with their aches and pains protesting, Naomi and Paxton Re assisted each other to stand and follow the werebeast.

*****

Naomi's body promised to shut down if they continued their trek. It was impossible to rate the passage of time within this forest. All she knew was she was close to total collapse.

Then Adalard cleared a stand of trees, and they were in

the sun. It was as if someone had turned on a light. Squinting, blinking rapidly, Naomi stopped and shielded her eyes with a hand. The warmth of the sun seeped into her, heating her skin and comforting her mind. Glancing at the others, she was startled to see life leaking back into them. Like a babe taking its first breath, their skin was warming. Color coming back to them.

Paxton Re passed her, moving to Adalard where he dropped Bob by the edge of a small stream. A moan came from the man drawing Naomi's attention. She hustled to him, then dropped to her knees and took his hand.

"Bob," she called softly, watching for any movement. When he moaned again, she ran a hand along the side of his face.

"Bob." She was rewarded with a fluttering of his eyelids. "Paxton Re, wet a cloth for me."

The dwarf sat as if he hadn't heard her but then with a moan of his own, he again pushed to his feet. Dropping the pack from his back, he pulled out an extra shirt and wet it with water from the stream. Naomi took the shirt, rang it out, and placed it across Bob's forehead. At the cool wetness, the boy's eyelids again fluttered.

"It's okay, Bob. We have you."

Naomi ran her hands down his body and extremities looking for wounds or broken bones. She found a couple of bite wounds and cleaned them with another shirt.

"How is he doing?"

Naomi looked over her shoulder to see Paxton Re closely watching her ministrations.

"I don't really know." She shrugged at the dwarf. "He's regained consciousness a couple times but hasn't said anything. Any bleeding has slowed or stopped." Scanning the area, she stood and walked to where Adalard sat.

"Do you know what they were? Are their bites dangerous . . . other than being a bite?"

For a moment Adalard didn't answer. He was exhausted; after giving a sigh he said, "I don't know anything about them. I was looking for a way out of the forest. I knew I'd lost you three but also knew I could travel faster alone. I thought I'd find an exit and return to you before dark, but I got turned around and lost my way. By the time I knew where I was, you were under attack."

"We all need a chance to rest and heal. I don't want to hurt him more, but I'd like to move farther away from the forest before nightfall. Can you carry him farther away from here?"

The werebeast nodded slowly, every move taking effort. Picking up the young man, Adalard waited for Naomi to precede him and pick her way through the bushes and brambles, moving up the length of the stream. Paxton Re followed them silently.

Not far ahead, the small stream entered a lake. At the other end they could see the water filtering out of the lake and into another stream.

"This'll do. Let's move up to the lake."

Adalard carried Bob, and Paxton Re followed Naomi. Toward the head of the lake, near where the stream entered, was a small beach. The sand was edged with long, soft grasses.

"Here, Adalard. Set him down." Indicating the grass, Naomi took off her backpack and spread her cloak.

The werebeast lay the boy down, gentle for one so large.

Stepping into the lake, Naomi rewet the shirt she had used to clean Bob's wounds. When Adalard stepped back, Naomi moved to sit by the young man. As if sensing her presence, he opened his eyes.

"Naomi," he said and then had to clear his throat and swallow deeply.

"Here." She jumped up. "Let me get you some water." From where they'd laid their packs, Naomi grabbed a canteen. Opening the lid, she again sat by the man. When she lifted his head to aid him in drinking, he gave out a deep moan but took the water.

"I had the worst nightmare," he said, staring into her eyes.

"You're okay now, Bob. Everything is okay now."

"I was in a whirlwind. And there were animals flying around me."

Nodding, Naomi opened his shirt, wiping down his neck and chest.

"Every time one of them flew past, they pulled a piece of me off. I was so scared that I would be all gone before the storm went away."

"You're okay now, Bob. Nothing is going to hurt you."

Seeming to take comfort in her words, the young man relaxed, closing his eyes. In a moment he was asleep, breathing deeply.

Naomi sat next to him, studying his face. She wouldn't have said she particularly liked him before this. He was a bit of an irritation. Talking too much, too loud. Now, she felt as if she would do anything to keep him safe. When he had been pulled from their group, yanked away and she couldn't find him, she had thought her heart would break.

She could see now, he . . . all of them . . . were her responsibility. They had each left their lives. And did she even know what they had given up? She had never spoken with them about where they were before they met her. Did they have families? Responsibilities that they had put aside to help her?

The weight of it pushed on her. How was she to ensure they each came through what was ahead of them. And what was ahead of them?

The forest and its denizens came as a complete surprise. They were ill-prepared to defend their lives. They would need to plan. To be more equipped. It could only make them stronger.

Naomi watched from the bank, sitting with Bob as the sun sank in the sky. Their preparedness needed to begin right now.

CHAPTER FIFTEEN

Mik stopped and, with him, the battalion he led.

He scanned the area from the tree line. This was where it happened. This was where he had the dwarf. Where he lost him. Lost him to the girl. Would they still be together?

He imagined the grasses were still bent and broken from the scuffle. This was the beginning. It was from this point he would send his soldiers out. They would locate the dwarf. There was no doubt in his mind.

And the woman. He had his questions about her. And he would ask them, but first he had to find her. And it wasn't only his curiosity. Now he knew his master knew of her. Knew of her and wanted to know her location.

Don't stop her, was the directive. But to know where she was, he must stop her. Must question her. Maybe he could split two hairs with one chop.

With a fierce growl he cut the battalion into three. They knew who they searched for. They knew what to do when they found them.

He wanted them, and he wanted them alive.

His sprogs marched past him—a ragtag band, but deadly. Like hounds, they would sniff out his quarries.

After his army passed, after the noise of their footfalls had died down and the dust had once again settled, Mik headed out after them. He would travel slower, no need for speed. Always on the lookout for sport, he would take his time and do what he wanted until word came to him that the two were found. Then, he would have his answers.

CHAPTER SIXTEEN

The clang of steel against steel rang through the cool air of early evening.

The dwarf only came to the woman's shoulder, but he was strong. Each night, after camp was set and dinner consumed, the three companions took turns teaching Naomi to fight. Some, like swordplay, had rules and a finesse to them. Naomi thought it was like dancing.

And some—knife fighting, for instance—were about cunning and trickery.

Just last evening, when practicing with Bob, she had cut him. She felt bad. Of course she did. He was just finally healing from his ordeal in the forest. But a small part of her was ecstatic. He was very wily. Hard for her to even keep up with, let alone best. To have cut him, even just a little, was a victory of sorts.

And then there was Adalard. Physically powerful, his brand of fighting was to plow through an opponent. Due to her size, this wouldn't work for Naomi. What he could teach her was how the body worked. Balance. Where to hit to bring down an enemy.

Put together, these skills promised to make her formidable. She needed to be able to protect herself and to be more of an asset to the group if they were again confronted.

Naomi refused to consider losing one of her friends. She would do whatever she could to protect them. And to protect herself.

*****

Naomi swung again, driving Paxton Re back. She had to utilize a two-handed grip, her muscles not sufficient to swing the blade with one arm. This was a disadvantage in many ways, and she worked daily to become stronger. Life in her world had filled her mind with exercises and strengthening techniques. She employed them now. And she had begun to run again. Every morning, rising before the others, she ran. It felt good, like reacquainting with an old friend. For the first time in this new world, Naomi felt like the woman she had been. But different, too. Better. Stronger. More observant. Focused.

Darklin Vale was her destination, and she had every intention of reaching it. She would find what was needed—do what was needed. And with these successes, she would get herself back home.

Back and forth across the clearing the woman and the dwarf battled. Paxton Re knew she was not yet good enough for him to use his full force against her, and he felt he didn't have to worry that she would get the upper hand.

Then he remembered that just yesterday she had cut Bob, and he focused his thoughts. The last thing any of them needed was to become seriously injured.

From the corner of his eye, he saw Bob and Adalard watching them. The young man moved his body with them as though he were part of the play-by-play. Oomphing and slapping, he dodged and weaved while keeping his gaze on the combatants. Paxton Re made a mental note to include him in their sparring sessions. It would benefit Naomi to have another opponent. Rarely did just one fighter come at you but they came in twos and even threes. She would need to be prepared for that, also. And she would soon learn his style of fighting. She needed to know fighting changed with the fighter.

Seeing the tip of Naomi's weapon droop, Paxton Re called a halt. He could see the exhaustion surround her like a fog. When he called for them to stop, raising one hand, Naomi dropped her arms, weapon aimed at the dirt at their feet. Bent at the waist, one hand on her thigh, she took deep breaths. When she straightened, she smiled at the dwarf.

"Was that all right? I think I'm getting better. Stronger."

"You are." And he nodded. "You're doing very well. Learning fast."

"Well, I'm motivated. I don't ever want to be unprepared again."

The two walked side by side to the camp and their companions. The sun, low in the sky, shot its last rays over the land, coloring it in red, orange, and yellow.

"You know," she said, "it's like weapon training in my world. You're more of a danger with some form of armament and without training, than with no weapon at all."

When they reached Adalard and Bob, Paxton Re stopped before the young man.

"Would you like to train with Naomi and me?"

A smile spread across Bob's face. "Really?"

His gaze jumped from Paxton Re to Naomi. Seeing the truth on their faces, he jumped in the air and gave a loud whoop.

"You bet, I wanna!"

He did a little jig across the grass and back. Suddenly, he stopped, his grin dropping away and his shoulders sagging.

"Now what?" Paxton Re asked.

"I don't have a sword. The only weapon I have is my knife."

Paxton Re put up a hand and shook his head. "Don't worry about that. You can use mine."

"What?" He again did the jig. "Thank you, Paxton Re. Thank you. I won't let you down."

"Relax, boy," the dwarf growled. "It's just a lesson."

With another whoop, Bob raced to where Adalard sat with his back against a tree.

"Did you hear that, Adalard?" When the werebeast nodded, the man told him anyway. "I get to practice with Naomi and

Paxton Re." Feigning a sword, Bob struck a pose. He sidestepped across and back a small area as if fighting an opponent.

Paxton Re walked by him on his way to their camp, his head shaking. Naomi was right behind him, smiling. As she walked past Bob, her head turned to watch him. She spun to move backward.

"You've got some pretty good moves there, Bob."

The boy stopped and stared at her. "Good moves? Whatcha mean?"

"Oh." Naomi had forgotten, just for a moment, where she was and what her circumstance was. Of course Bob didn't know what she meant by that.

"It's just an expression. From my world. It means you move well. That you'll do good." She turned back around, moving past Paxton Re to their camp.

* * * * *

She stoked their fire, adding more fuel before sliding under her blanket. They would be up and moving early tomorrow morning, and after sparring, she was tired. She felt good though. She had always considered herself to be in shape. She ran, did some weight training, watched what she ate, but after the first day training with the sword, she could barely lift her arms. Her back and core ached. Her legs hurt. Even the other training—knife and grappling—and the forced march were using muscles she didn't know she had. Now, days later, the ache had receded to be replaced with strength. She had never felt so good. Even her mind was clearer. Sharper.

Thanks to Adalard's hunting skills, the group ate well. Paxton Re and Bob showed her which plants were edible and which to stay away from. As they walked, each kept an eye out for anything they could add to the meat Adalard supplied to make a complete meal.

This world had lots of water—streams and lakes. In fact, the more they walked, the more waterways there were, so coming by fresh water was no problem.

Naomi's only concern as she drifted off was that it didn't seem as if the mountains were getting any closer, no matter how many days they trekked.

CHAPTER SEVENTEEN

The sun shone hard and bright above the city of Abster. In the center of the square stood an old tree that was used by the villagers as a signpost. On it were directional arrows to the most popular places in the town. Taverns, city hall, inns, all of them blazoned with their names.

Turn Your Head Alehouse. Known for its commonly good-looking waitresses.

Rest Your Bones Inn. Famous for the softness of its pillows.

Hang 'em High Courthouse and Shop. Known to ignore the loudest plea.

Today a body hung from the post, partially obscuring some of the more well-known locations. It slumped. Blood that had run from various wounds coated the body and pooled beneath it, and now, having begun to dry, insects stuck and the body emitted a faint, but foul, odor.

Mik glared at the remains. The man had given him very little by way of information before giving up and dying.

"Bring me another," he yelled to the sprogs waiting behind him, keeping an eye on the villagers. The remainder of his subordinates in this group were burning the town to the ground even now. By the time they left, there would be nothing to tell you a town had thrived. Just a scorched spot on the road.

Behind him, a soldier grabbed a young woman. Her scream

made the corners of his lips turn up. Even as he was anticipating her torture a man ran up, blocking her advance.

"Sir, please sir."

When Mik didn't answer, the man continued, falling to his knees in supplication.

"Please sir. I have information."

When Mik's gaze shifted to the man, he pleaded, "Please don't hurt the girl. I have information for you." Without looking up, the man thrust a bundle at Mik.

With a crick of his finger, Mik had the sprog releasing the girl and grabbing the man to haul him forward.

"The man you're looking for . . ." the villager began even before reaching Mik. Again, he fell to his knees, hands clasped, eyes pleading.

Mik stared down at him, dark eyes unreadable. The man swallowed hard, wet his lips, and began again. "The man. The man you're looking for. He was here." In his hands, the villager held a pair of modern running shoes.

Slowly, like blood seeping from a wound, a smile spread across Mik's face. He leaned into the man to run a hand almost lovingly across his cheek.

"Tell me everything," he whispered.

CHAPTER EIGHTEEN

By the time the company of four left the scrub and timber behind, Naomi had become proficient with sword and knife. She worked every day to get where and what she needed to get home, but without her realizing it, that old life moved further and further from her thoughts.

Stepping from the wood line, she took no more than two paces before her feet sank into swampy grassland. Reeds grew waist high, and at first glance, it wasn't obvious that they covered a marshland. The smell though. The smell should have warned her right off. Ripe with an odor of moist rotting things. The buzz of insects filled her ears and drowned out the sound of the others behind her.

Stepping back, she pulled her boots free with a sucking sound and a fresh bloom of stench. "Can we go around this?"

Paxton Re moved to stand beside her, pushing his toe into the ground. He created a hole that quickly filled with a green, brackish water.

"Morlon Bog," he said with a wrinkle of his nose. "We certainly aren't going through it."

Adalard stepped forward and immediately stepped back as he sank into the soft earth. His clawed feet made loud squelching sounds as he pulled them from the quagmire. He leaned forward at the waist and sniffed suspiciously at the land before them.

"It'll add days to our travels." His voice came out in a low growl.

"I don't suppose that can be helped," Paxton Re responded.

Naomi looked around the two of them to catch Bob's eye. The young man shrugged.

"Okay, then, I guess we go around," she said, adding her shrug to theirs, and moved down the semi-dry line of earth between the bushes and the grasses. Two paces more and seeing a long branch about the size and width of a mop handle, she stooped to pick it up. She poked into the ground before her and, where slick, kept herself from sliding into the soft earth.

As she continued, even with the aid of the stick, Naomi had to pull her feet from the bog time and again. She would think she was on stable ground and then, in a split second, she slid into the mire. She wasn't the only one unable to keep a firm grip on her step and heard the three behind her grumble about the traveling conditions.

"This is ridiculous," Paxton Re mumbled.

"I can't feel my feet—they're so cold." Bob's voice came out like the whine of a small child, but Naomi couldn't fault him. Her feet had lost feeling some time ago. It was hard to tell how much farther they would need to go to get past this swamp.

"It's getting evening. We should find a place to camp for the night," she said to the group.

"Well let's move up away from the wet," Paxton Re answered.

Agreeing, Naomi kept going for a ways, picking up dead fall along the edge of the timber. Once, she happened to glance back to see the others following suit.

When she located a break in the scrub and timber, she left the land division. A small circle of grasses welcomed them and soon they had camp made.

*****

Naomi's eyes popped open, her senses alert without yet knowing why. Was it a sound? Lying still, she opened her perceptions to the night around her. The smell of wood smoke came to her, the fire they had lain long since burned out. A bird passed overhead—busy in its night's hunt, and although she knew it was no flying creature she would recognize, in her mind's eye, she saw something akin to an owl.

Turning her head, she studied her three companions. Each slept in their own personal way.

Paxton Re, like a roly-poly, had his head tucked to his knees. She wondered what followed him into his dreams.

Adalard lay on his back, arms and legs akimbo. Occasionally, a twitch would move a limb, like he was chasing hares in his sleep.

And Bob. Enigmatic Bob. What did she or any of them really know about Bob? He appeared human—as human as herself, and yet there was something about him. Just as she watched, he shifted in his sleep, throwing one arm over his forehead. His voice, slurring almost to the point of incomprehension, floated across the remnants of the fire.

"Rrrunnn . . ."

A shiver passed down her spine when she realized what it was he said.

"Rrrunnn . . ." he repeated, his eyes rolling under their lids.

Concern for him moved her. Shifting from her bedroll, she slowly closed the distance between them.

"Rrrunnn . . ." he intoned, his voice low and guttural in his throat.

Nearing the boy, Naomi squatted beside him. She touched his shoulder and gave it a small shake.

"Bob," she whispered. The young man took a deep, cleansing breath, and although he didn't wake, he seemed to settle deeper into his sleep. For a moment, Naomi watched him, uncertain if she should wake him to chase away the nightmare, or not. When a low crash issued from the forest, Naomi's head jerked. She waited, almost holding her breath in anticipation of she knew not what.

Again, the crash sounded, and this time she was up and moving toward the sound. Snatching her sword by her bedroll, she brandished it toward the tree line.

She entered the forest slowly, footfalls light, sliding between the trunks of the dense foliage. When she saw a light, she stopped, scanning the area. The night, quiet like never before, beckoned her forward, and she heeded its call, slipping closer to the light. At the edge of the forest, almost in a small clearing, Naomi realized the light came from one of the moons that seemed to weigh heavily in the night sky.

Spellbound by the looming presence of the orb, she was startled when motion at the edge of the clearing caught her eye. A stag, immense and with a coat the color of old Roman coins, stepped into the lunar light. Naomi's breath stopped, so stunned was she by the beauty of the buck. Before she could fully take in the spectacle before her, two additional stags joined the first. Each was colored in shades of gold, shining in the luminous night.

They glowed, still as statues.

As one, they raised heads, heavy with antlers, to peer into the light. When a beam intensified, Naomi squinted, straining to keep her eyes open. Blinking heavily, she strove to clear her eyesight only to realize it wasn't her—it was the light. Intensifying even further, the light split into three parts and pulsed downward. When the illumination returned to normal, three beings stood in the clearing. From this distance, she couldn't tell if they were male or female or if they were even defined as such. They stood slightly shorter than her own diminutive height and were colored the blond of the light from where they had come.

As the bucks moved to meet them, the three began to dance. No music filled the clearing, but Naomi heard it in her head. Soft, pulsating, it moved her blood. Around the clearing the six moved together. To Naomi, they seemed to be celebrating. Was it the night? The season? Or simply being together?

She didn't know, and it didn't matter.

When a tear dripped from her face to land upon her hand, she startled. Glancing down, light glinted in the glowing droplet. When she again looked toward the clearing, she was alone.

CHAPTER NINETEEN

Blinking, Naomi squinted into the sun as it crested the far hill. She didn't have any memory of making her way back to the campsite, or her bedroll. Now, lying in the frost of morning, she wondered if it had all been a dream.

"Get up, sleepyhead." Paxton Re gave her a soft kick. "We need to make some distance today." He turned to look in the direction they had been heading for days, his voice soft. "Those mountains don't seem to be gettin' any closer."

Naomi rolled out of her bedding, bundling it together to strap it to her pack. Her mind was on what she had seen the night before—she couldn't make herself believe it had been a dream. How would her mind even come up with the beings that came down from the moon? *Had* they come down from the moon? Ridden on a shaft of light? And the stags. Stunning. Really not like anything she had seen in her world.

Naomi tossed her pack over her shoulder, pushing the other arm through a strap. She fit her sword into its scabbard and, jogging a little, caught up with the others.

They hadn't gone too far when Paxton Re looked over at her. "What is that?"

Brows furrowed, Naomi asked, "What's what?"

"That you're humming."

Surprised, Naomi paused for a moment and then resumed

her steps. She hadn't even realized she had been humming. There was no need to question, though. She knew. She was humming the melody from last night. The song that the stags and beings had danced to.

"I don't know. Just a little tune I heard somewhere."

"Kind of familiar."

Naomi hustled to catch up to the dwarf.

"Familiar?" She walked beside him. When he didn't answer she tried again. "Did you say it was familiar?"

With a dismissive air, Paxton Re shrugged. "I don't know. Maybe."

Unable to let it go, Naomi pressed him. "Do you know where you've heard it?"

Paxton Re stopped and squinted, studying her. "I don't know. Is it important?"

"No. No." She turned to follow the others. "Just curious."

"Seems more than just a little curiosity. What's going on?"

Naomi watched the ground in front of her as she continued to follow Bob and Adalard. She didn't know what to tell Paxton Re. She had thought to keep the episode in the clearing to herself, but she wasn't comfortable with out-and-out lying to the dwarf.

"I just heard it somewhere. Wondered if you knew it."

Paxton Re gave a nod and seemed to let the subject drop with her answer.

They hadn't walked too far when Paxton Re came to a stop.

"Hey, boy," he yelled. Glaring at Bob, who hadn't heeded him, Paxton Re again bellowed, "Yo . . . Bob!" At this, the boy jumped and, with a smile, turned in the direction of the dwarf. Seeing his scowl, Bob's smile immediately faded.

"How much longer until we get to those mountains?" Paxton Re gestured in the general direction of the Backaroon Mountains.

Rubbing his chin, Bob glanced at the peaks in the distance.

"Well, now . . ." And he seemed to be thinking.

Paxton Re took a step toward him, and Naomi put out a hand to grasp his shoulder. When he spun to her, she smiled.

"I know," she said with a shake of her head. "But give him a moment."

"Seems to me . . ." The boy again stopped in thought. "Seems to me, I never been to the Backaroon Mountains."

"For the love of . . ." Paxton Re walked away from the group, muttering under his breath.

*****

By midday, they left the Morlon Bog behind. The change came slowly, the land becoming firmer and the reeds dying out to long wavy grasses.

Naomi stopped and scanned the area. Her companions kept walking, and as she spun in a slow circle, they moved past her. Behind them on one side lay sparce trees becoming denser the farther back her eyesight went. On the other was the bog. Turning back to track her friends, she saw miles of grassland. The grasses were tall and golden, reaching almost to her waist.

Seeming to sense her hesitation, her three companions turned, putting the setting of the sun to their backs. With the lighting and the distance between them, Naomi couldn't make out their features, just shapes. Each unique, she easily knew which was which.

Paxton Re, short and stocky. His pack rose above his head, high on his back.

Bob, tall and lanky. Even standing in one place he seemed to be in constant motion.

And Adalard. Large, broad. His dense coating of hair gave his silhouette an uneven shape.

How had she come to care for these three so deeply in such a short time? It had never been her way to allow herself close relationships. When you opened yourself to others, you left yourself susceptible to pain and loss. In her experience, it was hard, if not impossible, not to disappoint other people.

From where she stood, the mountains weren't visible. Walking now in a low swell of the land, if you didn't know there were mountains in the distance, you would never see them. This day had few conversations, everyone seeming to be wrapped up in their own minds.

As Naomi caught up with the group, Bob couldn't take it anymore. Turning to her, he said, "So, Naomi, you've never been here before?"

Naomi stared at him for a moment, unsure if he was being purposely obtuse, or he really didn't get that she was from another land.

"Uh, no, Bob. I haven't." They continued to walk. Bob didn't ask any more questions. Naomi watched him as they moved through the long grasses.

"Where did you grow up?" she asked him. She had her curiosities about him, too. Was he human? If not, what was he? Adalard told her Bob smelled "funny," and she still didn't know what he meant by that.

"Oh," he answered, his gaze drifting away from her. "It's a long way from here. Along the base of a mountain range miles away."

Nodding as if she understood, when in fact she didn't, Naomi let it go as he seemed to want her to.

Thoughts turning in as she walked, Naomi considered her life and if she would make it home. She hoped she would. She missed a latte in the morning, the sounds of the city, and dinner out at a busy bistro. She had been in a crisis with the shooting and Sam's injury, but she knew her life back home was made up of more than just this one grievous incident. If nothing else, this journey into another land had opened her eyes to the whole of her life. She had never really given it any thought before this; she'd taken it all for granted.

If seen now, by people who knew her in her former life, even those who knew her well, they wouldn't recognize her. Her time outside in the constant elements had darkened her already warm brown skin. Her hair, grown long, was its true black color four inches down from the scalp. Beyond that the length was a lighter brown. She had highlighted it, not happy with the deep shade, but now she didn't even think about her hair other than to bind it back when sparring.

Unhappy with the cut of her tunic, she had taken her knife to it. Now, it was sleeveless and came to rest an inch above her waist. Using part of the cutaway tunic, she created a headband that kept the sweat from her eyes. Its lower strands were braided into her hair and the rest hung down her back. These alterations were better for fighting and ease in day-to-day movement.

She had never been truly confident. Always thinking she wasn't quite enough. She now moved with an assurance she didn't have before. With weapons training, and time in a dangerous environment, a predatory confidence flowed through her veins and was visible in her manner. A confidence she didn't even know in her conscious mind. A confidence that had become a part of her.

As they crossed the grasslands, she continually scanned the area, watching and waiting—for what, she didn't know but knew this lull couldn't continue. They were out in the open, victims for any number of dangers.

Following the three, she opened her hands and brushed the tops of the long prairie grasses. So sharp they almost cut, she was careful not to grasp them.

"How far is it across this valley?" she called.

Paxton Re turned to her, then studied the area around them. With a shrug, he said, "Who knows."

"Good answer." She nodded as she moved past him. "Informative."

Not one to take offense, Paxton Re followed her, keeping his thoughts to himself.

When they had left the trees behind, they had left their shade.

Now, the sun, high and hot, beat down on the small party. They moved along, occasionally taking sips from their flasks of water, each aware they were on rations until they reached the mountains.

"I wish I had my sunglasses," Naomi muttered.

Bob stopped, turned to stare at her, and raised his eyebrows. "Your what?"

"Sunglasses." Now she stopped, wiping sweat that trailed down from her temples. "They're something you wear that sits on your nose and hooks on your ears. They shield your eyes from the sun."

"Sunglasses," the young man said with a nod, seeming to take in the idea.

Naomi shielded her gaze with her hand, studying the horizon.

They needed to get to the mountains, and if getting to them meant making it through this valley, then that's what they would do.

"Oof." The air expelled from Naomi's lungs as she fell hard on the valley floor. On her way down, she had grabbed at anything; the long grasses made small slices on the flesh of her hands.

Sitting, she turned to see what she had tripped over. There, buried in the forest of long grasses, was a hole. It wasn't very large. She supposed she should be glad she hadn't fallen into it, but her foot had caught on the edge, bringing her down. She scooted forward on her rump, studying the crater. It looked to be covered with a weaving of grasses and some white substance.

Leaning toward it, she caught a scent that had her nose wrinkling.

"Pew," she muttered.

She pulled back and stood. Staring at the hole for a bit, she reached with the toe of her boot to push at the rim of it. There was a small give and the odor intensified.

"Icky."

"You okay?" Paxton Re faced her, waiting.

With a wave of her hand, she urged him on.

"Yes, I'm good. Just tripped."

Throwing one last look over her shoulder, she hurried to catch up with the others.

*****

For two nights and days, the foursome traveled across the grassland. It seemed to be never-changing. They needed to find water soon, or they would be hurting.

Two nights later Naomi flopped down beside Adalard. Paxton Re and Bob sat across from them, each wrapped in a blanket. As hot and unrelenting as the days were, the night had grown chilly. With no trees, that meant no wood. No wood meant no fire, and no warmth.

Sleep was going to come hard and, most likely, would not be restful. It was unfortunate. They could all benefit from a hot meal and restful sleep.

For another day they had made good time, gotten even farther into the valley. The timbered area was long behind them and no longer visible, and the mountains always seemed just out of reach. The company had taken to using the sun to navigate.

She continued to see more of the grass-covered holes in the ground. Even though she asked, no one seemed to know what they were. It was a barren land devoid of food or water.

"How long do you think before we cross this valley?"

She asked the group, hoping for an answer, but none was forthcoming.

Paxton Re, staring at his feet, said, "Don't know if the rest of you noticed, but there's no game. Nothing but the never-ending grasses. The food we're carrying isn't going to last forever."

"Maybe tomorrow we'll get closer to the mountains." Adalard's voice was low but filled the night. On the tail of his words, a low rumble sounded in the distance.

Naomi tilted her head, listening for anything else, but the

night was silent.

Totally silent.

"No night birds." Her voice was a whisper on the breeze that stirred the grasses.

She waited to hear the usual night sounds. Birds, small animals, insects. Nothing came to her. After a time, she wrapped up in her cloak and lay down, but sleep was a long time coming.

* * * * *

Naomi awoke sometime later, not sure how long she had slept. She took some comfort in the group's small snores and the shifting of their bodies. Turning to her back, she studied the night sky and was again surprised she couldn't recognize any of the constellations she had known in her other life. Glancing about, hoping, she looked for the Big Dipper—but it was nowhere to be seen. With a deep breath, she acknowledged her homesickness. Desire for the past flared, and if she could have a wish, she would be transported back to where she came from.

Her gaze at the sky blurred as a tear rolled down the side of her temple to drop into her hair. Her life was so confusing, and in so much turmoil. She yearned for the normal. She was just falling back to sleep when a shifting of the earth had her sitting up. Eyes wide, hands splayed to each side of her, she searched the darkness.

An earthquake?

When none of the others awoke, she scanned the area. Had she been dreaming? Or maybe her body had jumped as she fell asleep.

Yes, that was it. She almost had herself convinced of it. Slowly, she lay back, her body stiff. It was some time before she again slid into slumber.

CHAPTER TWENTY

It was later the next day when they saw the people.

Pulled by an ox, the two-wheeled cart carried a man and a woman. In the woman's arms, a small child slept. Naomi couldn't tell if it was a boy or girl, androgynous in that way of the very young. Behind the cart came what looked to be another family, all walking. A mother, father, and two adolescent boys, followed by an ancient dog. Lagging behind, an old man walked, a rein in his hand. Attached to the rein was an old swayback horse pulling another two-wheeled cart. This cart was full to the brim with some type of husked plant. Corn, Naomi thought, or the nearest thing to it in this land.

Naomi and her companions spotted them early in the morning, moving on an intersecting path with them. Neither group swerved, and when they met, the couple in the front cart seemed cordial if a bit lost.

"Heyo," the man yelled, raising an arm in welcome. When they pulled their cart to a halt, stopping those behind them, the two in it got a good look at Adalard. Eyes wide, jaws dropped. Though neither said anything, either too polite or too frightened to draw attention to his differences, they continued to stare.

Uncomfortable with the attention, Adalard turned his back to the strangers.

"Hello," Naomi greeted them, stepping forward. "Where

are you traveling to?"

With the stopping of the wagon, the child woke, first fussing and then crying with loud wails. A look of long-suffering came to the man's face. After wrapping the reins around a brake lever, he jumped off the wagon to land next to the group.

"We left from the town of Magora some days ago." He gestured to those in his company. "All of us, and now we seem to have lost our way."

Naomi turned to Paxton Re, her eyebrows raised.

"Magora?"

Paxton Re nodded, kicking the dirt at his feet. "Yeah, small town north of here."

When the child's fussing abruptly cut off, Naomi glanced that way to see the babe suckling. This act, along with the small clicking noises the woman soothed her child with, made Naomi relax, too.

"Where might y'all be traveling to?" the man asked.

Naomi faced the man again. "We're heading to the Backaroon Mountains." At the man's confused look, she pointed with her chin. "Just east of here. Where are you heading?"

"Yeah, that's pretty near to where we're goin'. Got off course, I guess."

"Ahem," Paxton Re said and turned. He gestured with his head for her to follow him. Naomi smiled at the man and followed the dwarf.

"Paxton Re? What's up?"

"They say they're heading to the mountains."

"Yes," she agreed.

"Only problem is, there ain't nothing in or around them mountains. Certainly nothing you'd be taking women and children to."

"Well, why would he tell us that?"

"Don't know. Got their own reasons, I suppose. Just think we should be wary."

"I was going to invite them to travel with us. Do you think

that's a mistake?"

"No, no." The dwarf shook his head. "Not saying that. Maybe havin' them with us would be good. Better to keep an eye on them."

She nodded to him and, turning back, walked to the man.

"Well." She glanced at her companions. "Since we're all traveling the same direction, if you'd like to travel with us, that would be fine. Safety in numbers and all that."

The man smiled and looked toward the woman who still sat on the cart. Without consulting those in his company, he said, "Well, thank ye kindly. We'll take you up on that."

"Okay." Naomi nodded at them all. "That's decided, so let's get going. See how far we can get before it's too dark to see."

*****

They felt as though they had made good time by the setting of the sun, though all they could still see were the long waving grasses, and the mountains in the distance were like a tempting mirage. Settling down for the night, the company of four and the newcomers covered with blankets as the evening turned colder.

The man's name was Jacob and his wife, Bess. The child, a boy, they just called Sonny. The family's surname was Offen, but they didn't offer anything else. They stayed to themselves, preparing for the night farther back from the rest. The old man with the horse the others called Paps. Naomi didn't know if that was his name or a title, like grandpa.

Seeing the lack of food Naomi's group carried, Jacob and Bess shared theirs with them. Naomi hadn't realized how hungry she had become living on limited rations. Everything was eaten cold, as there was no fire, but it was like a feast.

Finishing, Naomi lay back, again studying the night sky. The moons shone like beacons, one after the other, so that visibility was high. The rotation of the moons in this world was much quicker than on earth. Every few days and the full moons again lit the night sky.

The others settled, and soon she heard their deep sleeping breaths. Comforted, she, too, slept.

* * * * *

The next couple days passed without event. To Naomi, it was as if she were experiencing the same day over and over. The never-ending fields of grass, the stretch of her muscles as she walked, the blast of the sun as first it shone in her eyes and heated the back of her neck. Even conversation had ground to a halt. There was nothing to talk about because nothing happened. Each day leaked into the next and then the next, and still the mountains did not grow nearer. And nothing happened to confirm Paxton Re's worry about the band of travelers.

In the middle of the third day, with the sun straight overhead, Naomi stopped and slowly pulled the glove from her hand. The others continued, passing by her without speaking.

At first, she didn't study her palm, just letting it fall to her side. She straightened, arching her back and stretching her muscles. It seemed, in this continuous flow of grain, that the focus of their journey was being forgotten, diluted.

Relaxing, her shoulders slumping, she looked at her hand. There, just as every other time she looked, was the mark from Maude. This time, however, it seemed just a bit faded.

Is that possible? she thought. Could the magic be fading?

"Paxton Re!" she yelled. Breaking into a trot, she hurried to where he waited. "Look." She thrust her hand at him.

"Yep." He nodded. "I've seen it."

"No, look." She shoved her hand under his nose. When all he did was raise an eyebrow at her, she said, "Doesn't it look faded?"

Paxton Re looked again but didn't answer.

"Well?" she insisted. "What do you think? Can it be fading?"

Without looking again, the dwarf turned and began to follow the others. Over his shoulder, he answered, "I don't know. You'll have to ask Maude."

Naomi watched him walk away. Then she again studied her palm. Her gaze moved from her hand to the dwarf and back again.

"Whatcha lookin' at?"

Startled, Naomi jumped and turned. Bob glanced over her shoulder.

"Oh, hi Bob. It's nothing."

"Seemed pretty important."

Looking at him again, Naomi shrugged. "I was thinking that the mark from Maude was fading."

She jumped again when Bob grabbed her wrist, pulling her hand toward him. Bent over, he studied her palm.

"Hmm. Maybe. You never can tell about magics."

He released her hand, and she pulled her glove back on.

"Yep. That's a good reason to have me around."

When she stopped and looked at him, he stared off into the distance. Mumbling to himself he repeated, "Yep . . . good reason to have someone around who knows how to get you to where you're wantin' to go."

*****

Naomi knew she was in a dream, but the emotions were real. The images true.

She was back in her world. In the convenience store. Back with the young man right before he pointed his weapon at her partner.

Don't do it.

The words she had yelled that day, but like that day he took the stolen firearm and fired it.

The shock of seeing her partner go down rocked her. The blood seemed to surge out of his body, covering the ground between them. Another jolt shook her body, making her stumble and flounder.

Another quake jolted her even harder, and she came awake, springing from the dream.

The violence followed her into wakefulness as the earth trembled beneath her. Great quakes moved the ground as if it were a living being trying to knock her off its back.

Looking around, Naomi shook her head to clear it. Around her chaos reigned.

In the partial light of the waning moons, bodies ran. Like wraiths, they streaked by and around her.

Naomi sat, startled, her head swinging back and forth, her gaze trying to settle on something she recognized. When three shapes appeared out of nowhere, she froze. She didn't even breathe. Still sitting, the shapes were larger than her, and their appearance, even in the misty night, had her heart thumping. Their silhouettes didn't look like anything she knew.

When a scream issued from the far side of where their camp was situated, the three shapes twisted and rose as if on tiptoes. In a blink they were gone.

Her breath expelled from her, and for a moment, she felt faint.

What in the world was that?

"Naomi."

When Paxton Re grabbed her arm, she almost pulled her knife before she realized it was a friend.

"Paxton Re. What's happening?"

"Hard to tell in the dark, but it's not good." Pulling her arm, he moved her to her feet. "C'mon. We need to get out of here."

"Where is everyone else?"

"Don't know. At this point, it doesn't matter. We need to move."

"But Paxton Re . . ."

"No." He pulled her with him. "We can argue about it later. For now, we're moving."

Naomi resisted for a moment more, but soon she was running alongside the dwarf. Shapes she didn't recognize passed them in the night, but they didn't slow. Stooped, she kept her eye on Paxton Re's back and kept up with him.

When nothing followed them and the scattered screams fell behind, the two of them dropped down to hide in the long grasses. Pushing to her knees, Naomi peered back toward the camp.

Just then, the clouds parted, and the moon's light shone down. It looked like a battlefield. The ground around their camp was torn up. It was turned over as if something enormous had pushed its way up from beneath the earth. Lots of large things. One cart was overturned, its contents of vegetables spilled about the area, crushed and scattered. In the dark, the horse screamed. Then it was cut off. Some distance from the wagon, the ox's carcass sank into a hole in the ground, its blood pooling to wet the grasses.

As she watched, something pulled the bovine from below. A hard yank had her jumping and falling back into Paxton Re only to quickly push back to her knees. When the animal was yanked again, the force broke it in half, and the body was wrenched beneath the ground.

"Paxton Re, what in the world have we walked into?"

When he didn't answer, Naomi pulled her gaze from the carnage and spun to the dwarf. Behind her, he watched the campsite. He shook his head.

"I don't know, but we shouldn't be here."

When Naomi spun back to the site, a group of raiders skittered across the field, stopping near her bedroll. They paused, three of them again, seeming to study her belongings, one reaching out with a hairy leg to shift the sleeping area.

Spiders.

Naomi's mind told her what they were, but she couldn't

grasp it. Waist high, gray, and hairy, they chittered back and forth.

Were they talking? Discussing her location? Had their dinner gotten away from them?

A chill ran down her spine made worse when sweat followed it.

"My God."

"Shh." Paxton Re grabbed her arm and yanked her down. Face down, side by side, they stared at each other. Eyes wide, heart hammering, Naomi's mind was blank, but out of concern for her companions.

"Adalard. Bob," she whispered.

When the grasses stirred, Paxton Re put a hand over her mouth and a finger in front of his. The panic in his face made hers even more acute. The crunch of grass made her heart pound. When sweat dripped from her forehead to land on the ground next to her, quaking began in her shoulders and traveled down her body. She was certain whatever it was that waited just beyond the stand of grasses could hear every sound they made.

Could it smell them? Smell the fear pulsating from their bodies?

When it shifted, she thought for sure they were found out but then it moved down the hill.

Paxton Re rose to a crouch. From the ground, Naomi stared up at him, trying to determine whether he saw anything or if their spot was safe. When he bent to her, she rose to meet him halfway.

"Looks like they've moved on."

"What are they?" Her voice quivered, and try as she might, she couldn't stop it.

"Not too sure." He popped up to double-check nothing was sneaking up on them. "Heard about things like them, time or two. Always thought it was fear and imagination."

"Now what do you think?" And her teeth gave a small chatter. Tightening her jaw, Naomi placed a hand over her mouth, though whether it was to keep her teeth from chattering or from a moan escaping, she wasn't sure.

"Now, I think we need to get out of here." Again he popped up to scan the area.

"What about Bob and Adalard? Do you see them anywhere?"

Already shaking his head, Paxton Re didn't look at her. "I don't know where they are. I don't think we can hang around to find out."

"But we can't just leave them."

"We can if we must," he shot back in a hiss. "Right now, our survival is more important than finding those two.

"Besides," he muttered, "I've never met two more likely to make it through something like this."

Naomi didn't want to even contemplate what might have happened to their companions. When Paxton Re took her arm and pulled her up, she allowed him to lead her away from the site of destruction. Only once did she pull from him.

"What about our things? How can we go far without any of our belongings?"

"Jacob told you about the town of Magora. We'll need to backtrack, but it's not too far from here. We'll make our way there and pick up what supplies are available. It's not gonna be safe to get our things."

Knowing the only weapon the two of them had was the knife attached to her waistband, Naomi hoped they didn't run into any of the spiders.

They had walked for hours before the moons set and the sun began to rise. The morning light was diffused in the mist, and Naomi found herself jumping continuously at the moving and shifting fog.

They realized they had missed Magora in their headlong flight. Not sure where they were or what to do, they just kept walking, certain that something would come up.

CHAPTER TWENTY-ONE

Bob had been standing watch when the spiders attacked. Later, he thought that he might have dozed. Might not have heard them coming, but he didn't think so. He knew the others' safety was in his hands when watch was his responsibility, so he didn't think he had forsaken that.

When they overran the camp, he had jumped up, weapon in his hand. He had even wounded one initially, but there were just too many of them. He'd dropped to the ground, getting run over by them. His breath was pushed from his lungs as the many-legged creatures stepped on him, but Bob kept his teeth clenched and any noise inside. His life had taught him to be quiet when necessary.

It was calm for a few seconds, the marauders moving on, before he gingerly pushed himself to his hands and knees to peer about. They seemed to have passed by where he lay, seemed to have moved on to the camp. In the distance, he heard scuffling and a scream that was quickly cut off. It sounded like a woman. For a moment, thinking it might be Naomi, Bob contemplated giving her aid. But he had seen the one he had wounded, and fear filled his head and heart.

Shaking his head and telling himself no, Bob began to crawl through the grasses away from the main body of the camp. He had his head down and pushed through the weeds. He didn't even realize he still carried his short sword. Facing backward, he pulled it with.

When he came upon one of the holes in the ground, he shuffled back from it, surprised to see hairy legs creeping through the opening. His breath caught when a smaller version of the spider pulled itself out. Panic had him jumping up to slam his sword into the spider's body. A small cry came from the creature, and it collapsed under his weight, the weapon skewered to the ground by a kind of sticky substance seeping out and along the dirt. Bob fell back from it, landing on his backside and pushing himself along with his feet. When his hand touched another of the holes, he shrieked and pulled back from it. Jumping to his feet, all subterfuge gone, he raced away from the area. He didn't know where he was going, and he didn't care. He just had to get away.

Bob ran on through the night into the early morning hours. The stars faded and the moons set, but he didn't notice. Each time he tripped and fell, he pulled himself back to his feet. Nothing tracked his flight. Nothing realized he had left, but still he ran. Alone, miles between him and another living thing, and still he ran.

Finally, he fell, and exhaustion kept him down. Once, he pushed to his knees. He held the pose, a quiver moving through his frame, only to drop. His face hit the hard ground, but he was already out and didn't notice.

*****

When Bob woke up, the sun was high in a clear blue sky. Sweat coated his body, leaving stains on his clothing. With a moan, the boy turned to his side, his hand coming to rest on his face where pain radiated out. Gingerly, he touched his nose only to pull his fingers away covered in the partially coagulated blood that coated his lower face. With a moan, he sat to look around. At first, he thought there was nothing but more of the grasslands, then he squinted. There in the distance, appearing nearer, was the shape of mountains.

At last. He had come within sight of the mountains. Standing, slowly, the pain pulsing through his frame, the young man looked back where his trail led. For as far as he could see, the broken line of grasses ran from his current location. Knowing if something did decide to track him, it wouldn't be hard, he decided to get going toward the mountains. He didn't know where the rest of his party were but hoped they would continue this trek. If they had survived the night. The thought gave him pause, and for a moment, he again looked back the way he had come.

Perhaps he should go back. Perhaps he should see for himself if any of them made it. An image of the group filled his mind, centering on Naomi. He had committed to aiding her on her quest to get home. He had given his word.

Bob took one step, intent on heading back, when another vision entered his mind. The spider as it crawled from its burrow in the earth. A shiver again ran down his spine, and his stomach gave a lurch. He stopped in his tracks knowing he couldn't go back. Couldn't return to the place of the raid by those creatures. Torn, he forced himself to again think of Naomi. Guilt filled him, but along with it was a sense of panic. With a shake of his head, he swiveled to face the other way, to see the mountains in the distance.

He gave a moan and spun toward the way he had come.

"No!" Furiously shaking his head, he slapped himself in the face and began to cry, tears running down his cheeks.

He just couldn't do it. He was a coward. He knew he was a coward, but the thought of the spiders kept him from moving in that direction. He would continue to where they were going and hope they caught up with him. That was all he could do.

And look on the bright side, he thought as he headed out. Without water and food, he might not make it anyway.

*****

Bob walked all the next day and the next, resting little and eating nothing. Twice he came upon small streams to quench his thirst, but with no vessel to carry water in, he had to leave it and hope for more.

Partway through the next day he came across the remnants of a wagon and thought perhaps his luck had changed. Scouring through the pieces of what was once someone's life, he began to make a small pile outside the wreckage.

He gathered anything he thought might be of use. Soon he had a pile that consisted of a suitable vessel for water, two moth- and rat-eaten blankets, a dull, rusty knife, and some vegetables that were dried and shriveled but still edible. He squatted within the sparce enclosure gnawing on the meal, such as it was.

When he heard the movement outside the overturned wagon, he froze. Sitting perfectly still, only Bob's eyes moved. They twitched back and forth as if they could see past the wood barrier to what lay beyond. For some time, no other sounds came to him. Long enough that he thought he might have imagined it. Just as he was relaxing, his shoulders sagging, and his breath becoming normal, a man stepped around the wall of the cart.

"Well, well. What do we have here?"

Bob jumped to his feet, scanning the ground for the old, rusted knife—his only means of defense. When he saw it, half buried beneath one of the blankets, he made a move for it, but the stranger was quicker. Kicking it away from them, the man placed a hand on the middle of Bob's chest and gave him a shove.

"Now you just hold on a minute, bub. Where you think you're goin' in such a hurry?"

Bob thought to speak. He tried, really tried, but all his saliva had dried up. His throat moving in a large swallow, Bob coughed under his breath.

"What was that?" the man asked, moving until he was so close, Bob took a step back.

"That's right, boy." The stranger nodded. "You just keep in mind who's in charge here." Studying the pile of Bob's belongings, the man kicked at the pile. "What is all this?" Looking from the pile to Bob, the man moved even closer. "You got anything of value on you, boy?"

The man's breath was intense, and Bob stifled a gag. Keeping his eyes lowered, Bob's legs trembled. He was afraid that if he didn't sit, he just might fall, but he was too scared to move. Bob's mind flew; he needed to get away from this man. Nothing good could come of being here. But before he could try anything, the man grabbed Bob's arm in an iron grip and projected him out of the cover of the overturned wagon. There, on the other side, stood two additional men. His odds of getting away just plummeted.

With a push, the man thrust Bob in a direction away from the wreckage.

"Come on," he said. "Start walkin'."

Bob moved out ahead of the three men, continuing to look over his shoulder as they followed him. He didn't know where they were going, and he didn't know how to get free. What would they want from him? Part of Bob wanted to know so bad, he almost thought to ask the man, but another part of him knew it might be safer not to know.

The four of them, the three men and Bob, walked for hours. Whenever Bob faltered, the man who had found him would kick and hit at him until he moved quickly enough to make him stop. Though the three of them drank frequently from waterskins, they never offered any to Bob.

By the time the sun began sinking in the distance, he felt lightheaded and weak. Sheer force of will and self-preservation kept him upright and moving.

They had entered a small covering of sparce pines when the man called a halt. With thanks, no longer caring what might happen to him, Bob sank down by a tree. Through slitted eyelids, he watched the three men gather dry fall and start a small fire. They pulled foodstuffs from out of their bags and soon had a meager meal cooked. Again, they didn't offer to share any with him.

Overcome by thirst and hunger, his pride silent, Bob scootched up to the fire.

"What you want, boy?" the man who had captured him asked.

Bob had to swallow twice before he could speak. "Could I have something to drink? Maybe something to eat?"

The three men stared at him long enough that Bob began to second-guess his decision to draw attention to himself. When the man threw a skin of water and a hunk of bread in his direction, Bob lunged for it. Taking it, he again scooted to put his back to a tree. He gnawed on the dry bread and sipped the water, his eyes wide as he watched the men.

Bob began to plan his getaway. When the men fell asleep, he would sneak off. He could be stealthy. He would be gone before they knew it.

*****

When the man kicked Bob awake, the sun was just peeking over the horizon. Bob sat up and looked around. He should be miles from here. He didn't even remember falling asleep.

The men stomped the remnants of the fire apart and picked up their belongings. The leader, the one who captured Bob, grabbed him by the arm, bruising an already bruised appendage. He again thrust him in front of them.

*****

It was midday when Bob smelled wood smoke. At first, he thought he was imagining it and then when it continued wafting in and out, he hoped for a prairie fire. Perhaps in the confusion, he could use it as a distraction to get away from the men. When he spotted the flickers of many fires and heard the hum of many voices, Bob realized his wishes were not to be answered.

Bob and the men behind him broke through the woods, and before them was a camp of about fifty men. Some headed toward them, and some watched with suspicious eyes. Near the center of the camp stood cages. They were constructed of metal bars bound with ropes. From within, men, women, and children watched. Bob was afraid the same desperation in their eyes showed in his.

Bob started as two men came from behind him, grabbed an arm each, and practically carried him through the camp. The cage was opened, and he was thrust inside to fall among the other captives before he had time to think. Coughing, he pushed from where he had fallen. He faced the door, only to see a large angry man latch it and click home a large seal. He was effectively locked in.

Bob looked at the others around him. Some stared back, but most averted their gaze. They were a beaten lot—starved, dirty; the very air about them reeked of hopelessness.

Pushing to his feet, fighting a bout of lightheadedness, Bob made his way to the front of the cage. He grasped a bar in each fist, the solidity of it giving him pause. How was he to escape this situation?

CHAPTER TWENTY-TWO

The morning sun wasn't even shining over the horizon when Bob gasped, sitting straight on his pallet. Men and horses moved around the cages, and the people within began to get to their feet.

Unsure what was happening or what to do, Bob rose gingerly, stretching his back and neck.

"What's happening?" he whispered to one of the old-timers.

"Best keep your head down and your mouth shut," was the only answer given to him.

When the cage door opened, and no one volunteered to step out, one of their captors came in. Pushing and kicking people, he got them moving out of the cage and toward a large wagon. When a whip cracked, Bob and half the people cringed—thinking they were soon to be beat. Straining in their tack, four oxen pulled the wagon forward, the mass of captives slowly following.

They hadn't gone far when they came to the foothills of the mountains Bob had seen his first day alone. Here, a structure had been built into the side of the mountain. When men jumped down from the wagon and opened the large door of the structure, Bob craned his neck to get a look at what was within. All he could see was a pit of blackness.

"What's this?" he whispered, but no one answered him.

"All right, you heathens," one of the men from the wagon

yelled as he approached them. "You work and you'll be fed. You don't, and we'll use you as mortar to strengthen the mine."

People began to file past him, dragging their feet, heads hanging as they approached the door of the mine. As they passed two men who stood just outside, they were handed a shovel, and a small bladder container was hung around their necks. At Bob's turn, he couldn't help but shrink back from the man, his fear almost absolute. With an impatient jerk, the man grabbed his arm, slung the bladder around his neck, and shoved the spade into his hand. When Bob reflexively took the tool, the man gave him a shove toward the entrance.

Squinting, Bob tried to make out some feature of the interior, but all he saw was darkness. He was some feet within the structure, jammed in with the other captives, when his eyes adjusted enough to pick out small spots of light farther along the tunnel. For a while that's all there was.

Then, Bob thought he heard something. Just the faintest of sounds. Like a distant birdcall, or a small baby's cry.

He noticed movement down the tunnel. The others saw it now, too, and they murmured. Shuffling their feet. From behind, two of the captors pushed through the middle of their mass. Shoving them to the sides, they yelled, "Get back now. Get back!"

They were pushed against the sides of the tunnel, all gaping mouths and wide eyes when what came from within the mine came into view in the barely lit tunnel.

People. People just like them.

"Holy gods," he heard someone whisper, but all other sounds had ceased. Except for the occasional small moaning sounds coming from those exiting the mines.

They were dirty, but that didn't even begin to describe it. Black with whatever came from within this mountain, Bob couldn't tell which were men and which were women. He was sure, like his group, when they had gone in, they were all different shades—palest of peaches to darkest of night. Now, they all looked the same. The only way he identified children was due to their size.

As the group exited, all heads turned to witness their passage. Thoughts running through to what would become of them now, and what would become of this group. Just as he thought the procession done, there came the squeak of wheels. Two carts, pushed by others like their captors, moved past them. Piled with bodies, Bob couldn't see where one ended and another began.

Soon, their captors were herding them together and down into the mine. Once, Bob glanced back and saw the small rectangular opening full of a sunlit day. His eyes soaked up the sight knowing he may never see it again.

CHAPTER TWENTY-THREE

The smell woke Bob.

He didn't know if he had been asleep a moment or a day. Time here passed at its own speed. In the first couple breaths of wakefulness, he aligned himself with his predicament.

He was in the mine. Still in the mine. Forever in the mine.

After being herded down the shaft, they had come to a rudimentary elevator. Five at a time, they were lowered even deeper into the darkness of this grave. When the jailers had them together once again, they moved them forward. By the light of small flames set into the walls, everything looked black. The light reflected off every surface except the people. When the illumination fell upon one of the damned, it seemed to soak into them. Bob was sure this was true with him, too.

When they came to a juncture in the lower shaft, they took a left. Not too much longer, the space opened into a large cavern. Lying in the center of the room were bundles. Blankets. Beds? Were they to be down here that long? He wanted to take a drink from the canteen slung around his neck, just a sip to wet his throat, but he was afraid once he started, he wouldn't stop. And he didn't know if he would be getting any more.

One of the jailers stepped forward. He pulled a bulk from the floor.

"See this?" He shook it at them. Bob moved forward with

the group in an attempt to discover what the man held.

It was a cross piece of wood, maybe two feet long, with ropes threaded through it at far points. Attached to each of the ropes was a bucket.

"Get him," the man said with an indication of one hand. Two of the captors jumped forward and grabbed a man who had the bad luck to be standing in front. The man put up a small protest, but after a sharp rap to his head, he calmed down.

Facing them, his head down, he allowed their captor to sling the bucket over his head and rest the board upon his shoulders.

"Everybody gets one of these." The boss stepped closer to them and pointed back at the man. "If you don't fill your bucket and bring it to the lift often enough, you'll be proving you're not worth us using good food and water on you." He stepped closer again, peering into their scared faces. "Understand? You'll work, or you'll starve."

One small boy took a step forward, his hand in the air. The man looked at him for a long moment and then, with an incline of his head, said, "What?"

"Um, what—" Losing his speech in a dry throat, the boy cleared it and tried again. "What do we fill it with?"

"Well, now. That's a good question. You might be the brains of this here group." Turning, the man pointed down into the long darkness away from where they had come. "What you'll find down there is Juice. Powerful. All the lands pay a hefty price for it. So, you . . ." He grabbed the boy by a shoulder and shoved him toward a pile of the buckets. He turned and grabbed another, a woman. "And you." And then another. "And you." When he reached for another, the man moved before he could be grabbed to willingly follow the first few. Once the dam had broken, they all moved like sheep to gather their buckets.

With a hearty belly laugh, the boss watched them. Then he yelled, "All of you will dig until you die. You'll bring me the Juice."

* * * * *

The smell of sweat, fear, and death was a constant presence in his nostrils. Bob picked up his bucket. He had learned that water was brought to them. He didn't know how often as there was no time down here. He didn't know where the water came from, and he didn't care, but he understood it wasn't fresh. It, too, smelled of old, and awful, things.

Rations of food were also sparsely doled out. His body quit being hungry some time ago. They all existed on the bare minimum. And some of them didn't even do that.

How many had died? He didn't know and couldn't find it within himself to care. He was still alive and that was all he knew. Sometimes, he dreamed of the light and warmth of a sunny day. The freshness of a new rain. But these dreams were becoming more and more infrequent. They were darkening, fading, like all of his memories until soon there would only be the now.

To assist with the digging, he had only a shovel. With it, he was able to break away at the walls of the mine. When he had enough loose soil at his feet, he filled the two buckets on his yoke. Then it was time to go to the lift. Fill their larger buckets—under the watchful eyes of the jailers—and return to the hole. Over and over. Trip by trip. With no marking the passage of time, he had no way of knowing how long he had been down here. How long each trip took. Unfettered by a schedule of time, his body and mind ruled themselves.

Once, standing in the middle of the tunnel, his buckets empty so he must have been heading back into the mine, he kind of shook himself. He felt as though he had been sleeping except for the fact that he was standing. Others moved around him, small moans coming down the tunnel.

Twice he had seen light from the way they had come in. Light and small sounds, the echoes of voices. He believed their captors had other groups down here. Down some other series of tunnels, but he didn't know for sure.

Shouts drew his attention back into the tunnel. He moved that way not out of curiosity, but more a sense of preservation that still stayed with him.

At the spot where they dug, under the marginal lights afforded them, two men—at least he thought them men, so covered in the black of the Juice he couldn't tell—fought in a weak, haphazard way. Usually, the group existed in harmony, not due to their good natures, but due to their slow starvation.

One man thrust with his shovel, catching the other on the shoulder hard enough to tear fabric and break the skin.

"Ye bastard," the injured man voiced. "I'll not give you my water. I'll kill ya first."

"I'll kill you and take it," the second man answered.

Fights over food and water were rare simply because no one had the energy. Usually, the jailers stopped fights, wanting time and energy spent on digging, but this time they let the men battle it out. The injured man waded into his attacker, taking another hit on the arm. Blood ran freely from his two wounds, but he didn't seem to notice. He swung his fist. Now, Bob saw he wielded a rock. When the rock connected with the other man's temple, he went down in a heap. Straddling him, the man with the rock sat on his opponent and slowly and methodically beat the attacker's head until little of it remained.

Dropping the rock, the victor lifted the flask of water from what was left of the man's neck and, dropping it around his own, shuffled down the tunnel.

Quick money exchanged hands of the jailers, and soon they were shoving people and yelling to get back to work.

"Hey, you," they yelled, pointing at Bob and another man. "Grab that one and get 'im out of here."

Bob studied the dead man for a moment and then, with the other man, grabbed a leg and pulled the body from the tunnel. Coming up to the area around the lift, Bob saw a heap of bodies, some wrapped in linens waiting for disposal. The lift was nowhere to be seen, and for a moment, they were alone with the carcasses. As his companion dropped a leg and turned back toward the tunnel, Bob had an idea.

Would it work? Did he care? Something had to be done, or he would die in this mine.

Working quickly, Bob pulled linen from one of the bodies. Stained and foul-smelling from fluids leaking from the remains, Bob quickly wrapped himself in the cloth, wedging himself between some of the remnants. Just as he was getting himself settled, voices neared. After a moment, there came a squeaking of a wheel as the lift was lowered.

"Here y'all. Help me get this cart moved. Let's get 'em loaded before I lose my dinner."

Breathing as shallow as possible and staying limp, Bob pretended to be one of the dead. Thrown into the cart, he almost messed up and made a sound. And again, when a large body was tossed on top of him, but his deception stayed and soon the cart was being pushed back onto the lift and the lift moved.

Muffled by layers of bodies, the grunts of men and creaks of wagon wheels drifted. Bob tried to relax, kept thinking, "You are one of the dead," but his heart pounded in his chest. Fear and anticipation both rattled his bones.

When the motion stopped and then some of the weight was lifted from him, Bob realized they were off-loading the bodies. Again, his mantra, "you are one of the dead," played in his head.

Pulled feet first, he hit the ground, rapping his skull and seeing stars. Soon after, the sound of the cart moving away had him straining to hear. Fainter and fainter until they disappeared, soon he was alone with the dead. Afraid to move, afraid one or more of the men lay in wait, Bob remained frozen until the day had long dipped into night. When he lifted his head, pulling the linen from his face, the brightness of the stars hurt his eyes. He scanned the area. He was alone. A vast blankness of prairie rolled away as far as he could see.

CHAPTER TWENTY-FOUR

Bob didn't know where he was. He had pushed himself from the grave of carcasses, thirst and exhaustion fogging his mind and body. He didn't remember much of the journey but had walked until his body had given out.

Last night, he had slept in the long grasses and awoke before the sun had risen. Now, he walked in the semi-dawn—careful where he placed his feet. Midmorning, a cloud burst filled the sky and for a few blessed moments, it rained. Throwing his head back, mouth open, he took in as much of the moisture as he could. After the storm passed, Bob saw an added benefit had been a slight cleaning of his clothes and body. He didn't reek quite as profoundly.

It was hours later when he came to the wagon tracks. Well-worn, they proved people traveled through these plains regularly. With little more than a shrug, the young man changed directions to follow the ruts. He needed to locate help. He had no food, and no water, and no idea of how to get back to where Naomi and the others were. How was he to help Naomi if he died out here in the grasslands.

It was later that day, the sun sinking in the sky, when Bob saw a plume of dust rising on the horizon. He attempted to pick up his pace, but dehydration and exhaustion had his body in chains—no matter what his mind wanted.

Walking through the night, his feet catching on every obstacle on the route, he came over a ridge to find a camp spread below him.

Tinkers, he thought.

Tradesmen traveling from town to town.

The ten wagons were covered, resembling little houses on wheels. They were brightly painted, designed to draw attention.

Now, with the sun having dropped beneath the horizon and the wagons drawn into a circle, the inhabitants had a bonfire lit in the center of the wagons. Bob heard the strums of a guitar and the low voices of people sitting around the fire.

From the outside looking in, the camp seemed peaceful. If he weren't in such dire straits, Bob wouldn't have imposed upon them. He didn't have an option, though—he needed help.

Bob was just bolstering his energy to make the final leg to the wagons when a twig snapped behind him. Spinning, he saw the silhouette of someone right before a fist connected with his chin.

Not completely unconscious, his awareness pulsing in and out, Bob felt his ankle grasped and he was pulled toward the camp. Reminded of being pulled from the cart, he struggled, but soon, having used up what little energy he had, he lay limp and allowed himself to be taken. Each time he forced his eyelids open, he perceived snippets of the world around him—tall grasses shifting past as he was pulled toward the camp, the bright fire, a gaggle of voices, silhouettes leaning over him.

Bob's jaw ached, throbbing with pain.

Opening his eyes, and this time striving to keep them open, the boy shifted, glancing around at his captors.

A man leaned over him. He was large—not only tall, but wide. His black hair stuck from his head in all directions looking as if a squirrel had burrowed in to make a nest.

"Why are you tracking us?" he yelled into Bob's face.

"I—" Bob began. Working up some saliva, he swallowed hard and tried again. "I'm not. I'm lost." He scanned the inhabitants looking for a compassionate face.

"No way you're lost out here!"

"I am," Bob insisted. "I don't know where I am. I've been wandering for days."

A buzz of conversation came upon hearing this. Amid the murmurs, Bob heard a softening. Pushing himself to a seated position, he tried again.

"Yeah. I fell in with a bad lot—barely got away."

Squatting next to Bob, the man again got in his face. Everything he said was in a volume set to rupture one's ears.

"Who are you? Where are you going?"

"My name is Bob. Just Bob." Shifting to put a bit of room between himself and the leader, Bob added, "I guess I'm going wherever you are." He gave a large grin.

*****

When the wagons pulled out the next morning, a tall, lanky man walked along one side of the second wagon. Three others walked with him. He wore the brightly colored clothing of the Tinkers and looked to be one of them.

Before a mile had passed, the tall man stepped out from the others, stopped, and peered back the way he had come—back into the dark morning.

Bob knew he was heading the wrong way, heading away from Naomi and his friends. Right now, he couldn't see an answer to his predicament. To get to where he needed to be, he would have to go the wrong way.

He took one more long, lingering look toward the mountains and then, turning, he hustled to catch the wagons.

A man watched from within one of the wagons. His name was Mazition, and he was chieftain to these Tinkers. When his lieutenant brought his news of the lost man, his first instinct was to cut his throat and leave him for the animals. Then he remembered, a couple of towns back there had been talk of sprogs. More of them gathered than anyone could remember seeing before. Even the old couldn't recall having them amassed in such a way.

Maybe this man had something to do with them. Maybe not. It was true the two situations could be separate, but he didn't think so—and throats could always be slit.

So, he had told his men to feed and water the stranger. He let him come with them.

Now, he watched him stop and look back the way he had come. Yes, there was something about this stranger. Something that Mazition felt in his bones would be useful for the Tinkers. So, they would keep him, this Bob. They would keep him until he became useful.

CHAPTER TWENTY-FIVE

Naomi squinted and scanned the far horizon. When the sun broke through a cloud layer, she held the side of her hand to her forehead to shield her eyes.

It had been days since she had last seen another of their group—except for Paxton Re. She and the dwarf had been on the run since that night with the spiders.

She had tried—Paxton Re pulled her away—to locate Adalard and Bob. In the darkness and chaos, they had disappeared.

When they fled the slaughter, devastation, and noise, she and Paxton Re hadn't realized they had brought something with them.

Now, days later, they were still fleeing one of the spiders that stayed hot on their trail. Nothing they did was successful in throwing off the beast.

Naomi spun, looking back the way they had come, and surveyed the land. Below where she stood, just a few feet away, Paxton Re slept. They had begun to take turns, one on watch, ever vigilant for the spider stalking through the night.

Attempting to put miles between them and their pursuer, they had barely slept. Now, exhaustion was taking its toll. Dizzy and slightly confused, she stared unblinking at the dwarf's rolled-up figure.

With a flurry, a flock of birds lifted to the air in the distance, drawing Naomi's attention. Her gaze gone sharp, she scrutinized the area. As far as they knew, the spiders went to ground when the sun rose, but that could change at any moment.

She didn't see anything, but a tingling began in the small of her back. It shifted up to her hairline, almost as if someone were touching her and pushing her forward. Taking the hint, Naomi moved down from the small hill where she stood. Her aim centered on Paxton Re.

She hadn't quite reached him when the dwarf sat up, face sleepy, eyes unfocused.

"What? What?" he mumbled, looking around them. Seeing Naomi heading his way, he rolled to his knees and, with a small groan, came to his feet. "What is it?"

"I think we should be moving."

Taking in the intensity of her gaze as she watched all around them, Paxton Re gave small stomps of his feet to wake his legs.

"What did you see?" he asked, straightening his jerkin and hiking up his pants.

"Nothing, really." She shook her head at him. "More a feeling."

Paxton Re nodded as if he understood, and with a rub of his eyes, he headed out into the morning light.

Naomi gave one more glance to the far distance and then followed him.

The sun and forced march warmed them, and soon, Naomi was wiping sweat from her brow. Paxton Re, his face glistening, walked on, never pausing or altering his stride.

Crazy robot, she thought, wishing for a shady spot to rest. And a glass of tall, iced tea, her mind added.

Her daydream came to her full-blown—thoughts of a cool breeze drying the day's sweat. The soothing taste of tea, iced and seasoned with a hint of lemon, and the rocking motion of a porch swing. She was so far into her fantasy when the spider erupted from the ground in front of them, her mind took a split second to come back online. Naomi fell back in shock, hitting the ground and scrambling away—her legs and arms pinwheeling.

The spider, prey almost within its grasp, reared back, releasing a hiss. Front legs raised and jaws open, Naomi looked up into the fanged maw of the huge arachnid. Her mind screamed for her to move, but frozen in fear and shock, she could only watch as the spider tensed to strike.

Cringing, eyes snapping closed, Naomi jerked at a loud scrape. She popped open her eyes to see Paxton Re, hands tight on a section of log that he thrust between the spider's jaws.

Thwarted, the beast pulled back, breaking the log. It breathed another hiss and pulled back to strike again.

Rolling to the side, Naomi came up on her feet, then pulled her knife free from her waist. Seeing Paxton Re dive to the side, narrowly avoiding a hit from the spider, she jumped forward. Slicing at its front legs, she sidestepped a bite from the giant predator. Paxton Re appeared again just behind the spider. Armed only with another section of wood, he swung a mighty blow into the spider's body.

Naomi screamed her battle cry and joined Paxton Re to jump forward, thrusting her knife into the beast. It reared back in pain, a reddish, viscous fluid flowing from multiple wounds.

The creature's underbelly, sparsely covered with light prickly hair, became accessible when the spider rose higher on its back legs.

Naomi rushed forward on instinct and stabbed the creature's soft stomach. The beast released a sound close to a scream and reared back to expose even more of its vulnerable underside.

Naomi twisted her weapon, slicing from the initial wound up toward the spider's jaw. Paxton Re joined her, stabbing and thrusting with his makeshift club until blood and gore ran free.

With a final thrashing motion, the spider threw itself forward, narrowly missing its two assailants.

Panting, Naomi dropped to her hands and knees, knife falling from her grip. With the hand that held his club, Paxton Re picked up her weapon and gripped her arm, forcing her to stand.

"Come on." He led her a short distance away from the carnage. "Who knows if the thing is really dead."

Naomi looked over her shoulder at the fallen arachnid, fluid still seeping from its split belly.

"I think it's dead," she mumbled.

"Way our luck's goin', it'll probably come back to life."

When he released her arm, Naomi sat on the hillside to face the spider's carcass.

"Do you think it was alone?"

"Yeah," the dwarf answered. "I think if it weren't alone, our day would have turned out far different."

With a deep breath, Paxton Re sat next to Naomi.

"We must be coming up on some civilization soon, don't you think?" Naomi asked.

"Yeah," he breathed. "Though what we'll do with no money or anything to trade, I don't know."

Exhausted in body and mind, the dwarf and woman sat on the hill and watched the flies gather around the spider carcass. Then, as if one, they stood and kept moving.

CHAPTER TWENTY-SIX

They heard the town before it ever came into view. It sat on a rise between two branches of a river, and from what Naomi could see, fishing was its major industry—that and taverns.

When she and Paxton Re walked into town and down the main road, no one batted an eye. People of all types and sizes filled buildings and spilled out into the dirt road. Animals were as numerous as the people. Horses and dogs she recognized, and they flowed between the people. When she stopped to stare at a small cat-like creature, Paxton Re took her arm and pulled her farther down the street.

With a growl in his voice, he pulled her down to hear him.

"Don't be staring at anyone."

"Anyone? That was a cat . . . kinda."

"It's a lykbo. And they don't like to be stared at by anyone they consider to be their inferior."

Now Naomi stopped and stared at Paxton Re. When he realized she was no longer walking alongside him, he turned to find her.

"What?" he asked.

"Their inferior?" When he nodded, she asked, "And who might that be?"

"Everyone." He continued on his path into town.

Naomi blew out a breath, ruffling her bangs from in front of her eyes. With a surreptitious glance, she scanned for the lykbo. "I knew it was a cat."

Hustling, she caught Paxton Re and stayed by his side to the heart of the town. The farther they walked, the more Naomi came to realize this was more of a city than a town. Its streets seemed to go on forever, and although she watched and waited, she couldn't see a lessening of the traffic.

They had reason to believe they were being sought by the leader of the sprogs, but they had no idea where he was or how far behind them he was. Most days, different sorts of peoples didn't mingle, so a woman traveling with a dwarf might be enough to draw his attention. But then again, with the size of the city, who would even notice them.

When Paxton Re veered off the roadway, Naomi followed. He entered a small establishment. Within, they were the only ones there. A moment later, a tall, thin man approached them.

"Got something to trade," Paxton Re said.

"Let's see it."

Reaching to Naomi, Paxton Re removed her knife from the belt at her waist. Surprised, she started back a moment. When Paxton Re handed the knife to the proprietor, Naomi thought to protest. With a raised hand, he hushed her. When an amount was agreed upon, Paxton Re took the coin and led them from the building.

Naomi had just opened her mouth when the dwarf cut her off. "We need to eat, don't we?"

"Just, that was the only weapon we have."

"Yep." He nodded. "Food is the priority at this point."

The inn, when she saw it, drew her attention. People moved in and out of the entrance, coming and going on business she had no notion of—maybe, couldn't even fathom. This was the largest gathering of people from this side that she had yet to see. It seemed, everything she could imagine could be found here.

When she made to move toward the inn, her mind full of

thoughts of soft beds and a warm meal, Paxton Re stopped in his tracks.

"Where are you going?"

Her brows crinkled at his words, and she looked between him and the inn down the street. "To the inn." Her eyebrows rose, and a touch of irony heightened her tone.

"Are you dense?" he asked. "We can't be staying in a place like that. It would be the first place that sprog and his followers would look for us."

"Well," she muttered, following him as he moved toward the quiet side of the city. "I didn't know." When all the dwarf did was shake his head and continue ahead of her, she jogged up to walk beside him.

*****

After another mile or so, Paxton Re took them into a building that looked abandoned. Dark and cold, it didn't offer any of the amenities Naomi had been dreaming of.

"Really?" she said, staring at the falling-down building. "Couldn't we have just stayed out in the wilderness if this is the best we can do?"

As soon as they entered the lodging house, Naomi felt the atmosphere change. She considered this evidence that her cop's sense still worked.

The front room was full. Dark and dank, a fog of smoke hung from the rafters. Conversations played out around the room, so many people talking that it was difficult to see where one discussion began and one ended.

She and Paxton Re stood in silence at the door, taking in the confusion—not at first sure where to turn.

"Come on," the dwarf said.

"Where to?" She hurried to follow him through the crowd. "Hey, Paxton Re." She raised her voice. "Wait for me!"

For a moment she lost sight of her companion in the crush of bodies. When a group shifted, she caught sight of his mop of hair and turned her body sideways to slide through. She quickened her step to catch him.

"Paxton Re," she called, and for a second, panic filled her. Then the crowd opened and allowed her to find her friend. Thinking he was right in front of her, certain she had caught sight of his dark mop of hair, Naomi pushed past two burly drinkers. Ahead of her she found a wall. Stunned, she stood for seconds, sure she was mistaken though the barrier was right in front of her.

She must have taken a wrong turn. She spun and studied the way she had come.

Naomi didn't know which way to go. She rose on tiptoe and looked left and then right. As she again panned over the crowd, her gaze was drawn to one individual. Through the layer of bodies, this man stared back at her.

In the dim, smoky light of the alehouse, Naomi squinted to better study the stranger.

Her breath caught in her throat when she realized he wasn't a complete stranger.

The man from the woods, she thought. The man with the black eyes. And panic filled her.

She stepped to the side, hoping to move around him, perhaps lose him in the crowd, but the man moved with her. Shifting back again, she watched in horror as he mirrored her movement. Naomi dared to drop her gaze from his to sweep the room. She still needed to locate Paxton Re, but that concern had become secondary to her escape from her current predicament. As with Adalard and Bob, Paxton Re knew of her destination, and if they became separated, they could hook up again farther along their path.

Naomi gave a quick upward glance to ensure the man was where she had last seen him. With a quick move, she shifted left and then, hoping he would continue his game, ducked and dodged right. Staying to a crouch, she shimmied around the legs of men who were busy drinking—even once to crawl between the legs of one particular reveler.

She moved as fast as she could, never daring to look back.

Naomi was almost to the back exit when a hand reached to halt her in her tracks. A squeak escaped her lips, and she was already swinging a fist to free herself.

"Paxton Re," she breathed, barely able to halt her strike.

"Where have you been?" the dwarf growled. "I've been looking for you everywhere."

Now their grips reversed—his loosing and her grabbing him. "That sprog is here."

At his confused expression, Naomi began to pull him out of the room, throwing an explanation over her shoulder.

"From the forest. The leader of the three who had you. When we first met."

Naomi and Paxton Re exited the rear of the alehouse with stealth and speed. They had known all along that the sprog would be tracking them, but to have evidence of it and being so close to caught brought a whole new urgency to their quest.

Twisting and turning—down one street and up another—they kept an eye out for their pursuer. They had hoped to rest and regroup in this town, but now they couldn't. They needed, not to only press on, but to make sure they weren't followed.

When they saw a group coming toward them, black eyes obvious even at a distance, they again switched directions. A call sounded behind them, and Naomi and Paxton Re broke into a run.

They flew around a corner only to come face-to-face with what appeared to be a child—a girl of about twelve. She wore clothing of earth tones and carried a staff in one hand. A longbow was strapped across her body. The feathered tips of arrows peeked over her shoulder.

Naomi skidded to a halt, Paxton Re running into her before he could stop. Without saying a word, the girl gestured for them to follow her.

Options limited, Naomi gave a quick glance around. She grabbed Paxton Re by the arm and they hustled after the girl. They had no more than gotten the door to a building shut when the thunder of steps passed in the alley outside. Naomi halted, holding her breath, her hands pressed against the inside of the door. The building they had entered was comprised of large wooden slats. The slats fit loosely together, allowing light to streak through to the inner rooms. As the bodies moved past, the light shifted, passing over her and Paxton Re like specters. Naomi shivered, hoping this wasn't a foreboding of things to come.

By the time the sprogs passed outside, and her heart rate had returned to normal, the child was gone. With a gesture at Paxton Re, Naomi and he hurried into the next room only to see a hole in the floor with a ladder leading down. Below there seemed to be some sort of illumination. Naomi took the ladder down, hearing Paxton Re quickly follow.

Below, a tunnel lit sparsely with lanterns hanging from the wall every few feet led off into the distance. In the murk, Naomi could just make out the shape of the girl moving away from them.

"Come on, Paxton Re," she whispered and moved along the hard-packed floor.

They hurried to catch the girl, watching as, up ahead, she made a turn. Naomi picked up her speed, breathing hard in the warm, musty air.

"Hey," she called. "Wait for us!"

When they, too, made the turn, the girl turned toward them just some feet away. Breathing hard, hearing Paxton Re behind her, Naomi studied the girl and caught her breath. In the dim light of the passageway, Naomi could see she wasn't a child as she first thought. She was small in frame and stature but looked to be an adult—if a young one. She had large blue eyes, slightly tipped up at the outside, and Naomi could just make out the tops of the girl's ears poking out from her light-blonde hair.

An elf.

If this encounter had happened a few weeks ago, Naomi would have thought she was dreaming. Now, however, she had met a werebeast, sprogs, whatever Bob was, pixies, and her companion was a dwarf. The fact that the girl appeared to be an elf filled Naomi with amazement but no disbelief. She only wondered if anything in the stories from her world about elves would be true.

"Where are you taking us?" Naomi asked.

The girl looked them over for a moment and, without answering, gave them a gesture to follow before she turned away.

"Wait." Naomi halted the elven girl with a hand on her shoulder. When she turned toward them, Naomi again asked, "Where are you taking us?"

When the girl spoke, her voice startled Naomi with its sing-song quality. Beautiful, almost like birdsong.

"I've been sent to bring you before the magistrate."

"Magistrate?" Naomi looked to Paxton Re who turned blank eyes to her. Spinning back to the girl, she asked, "What magistrate?"

"He will judge you—for good or bad."

"That doesn't sound good."

When the girl turned and continued down the tunnel, Naomi didn't move. Paxton Re stood with her and watched the girl move away.

The dwarf cleared his throat and kept staring back the way they had come. "Maybe it would be best if we went back. Kept on by our own."

"I think you're right, Paxton Re. I don't like the sound of the magistrate."

This time Naomi followed Paxton Re while he led them back down the tunnel to the stairs. They had almost reached them, could see them in the musty light, when a crash came from the building above. The stomping of feet had them halting and turning toward the tunnel. Paxton Re grabbed her to whisper, "It's the sprogs," before pulling her back the way they had come.

Moving quickly down the tunnel, they extinguished the flames on the walls as they went, hoping to be beyond sight of the stairs by the time their pursuers made their way down. When they made the turn without any sounds of being followed, they breathed a small sigh of relief and picked up their pace. Before long they saw the girl again waiting for them at a fork in the tunnel. She didn't say anything, just took them down the right arm of the fork.

When the girl's speed slowed to a steady pace instead of all-out flight, Naomi kept looking behind them, ready for their followers to catch up to them.

"You need not worry," the girl said.

"What?" Naomi watched the girl's back. "What do you mean?"

"They won't follow us."

"How do you know that? How can you be so sure?"

"The way we took is masked. They will go the other way without ever knowing the second tunnel exists." The girl's gaze caught Naomi's eye, and she gave a small smile. Now turning to walk backward, she again addressed the two. "My name is Laina. What are your names?"

"I'm Naomi and this is Paxton Re," Naomi said with first a gesture at herself and then at the dwarf.

"I am very pleased to meet you, Naomi and Paxton Re." She gave a small bow, showing exceptional grace, then continued to walk backward.

"So, Laina . . ."

The elven girl swung back to walk with them, keeping her eyes on Naomi.

"What is this about a magistrate? How will we be judged?"

"I don't know," Laina admitted. "King Mallevorn had a dream. A foreboding, some are saying. He knew of your coming.

He instructed me to bring you to him, and to be judged."

It wasn't long before the lanterns affixed to the walls ended. Laina stopped them. She handed her staff to Naomi. Then she pulled off a pack she wore, squatted, and rooted around until she pulled out a short torch, flint, and a stone. Laying the brand on the dirt floor, she struck the flint with the stone. It sparked but didn't light the torch until the third strike. Laina handed the flaming torch to Paxton Re and stood after placing the flint and stone back in her pack. She donned the pack and turned to Naomi. Holding her hand out for the staff, she waited. Naomi moved to give it back to the girl but then something stopped her. She drew the weapon back. Laina cocked her head to study the woman. Then with a gesture of impatience, she demanded the staff. Naomi handed it back, but it took a tug for Laina to pull the wood from Naomi's grip. Then, with a long look for Naomi, and a jerk of her head, she had them follow.

Paxton Re kept the torch high, allowing its light to fall around them.

The tunnel's exit came abruptly. A hedge of vines covered the end. When Laina pushed them aside, scattered sunlight streamed in. Blinking rapidly, Naomi stepped from the tunnel, which opened on the edge of a deep forest. Fir and broadleaf trees twined together; ferns crowded around their bases. Birdsong sounded, and when a muted crash issued, Naomi spun to see the back end of a deer disappearing into the growth. In the distance, a mountain range—white-capped with snow—rose to the sky.

"Where are we?" Paxton Re muttered. He turned to Laina. "Where are we? I don't recognize those mountains." He gestured toward the distant landscape.

"This is the territory of King Mallevorn. It stretches for as far as you can see in every direction." When Paxton Re made a harumph sound, glancing at the mountains, Laina added, "Unless accompanied by an elf, you would not be here. It's not surprising that you've never seen the Ulerick Mountains."

"Ulerick Mountains?" he grumbled. "Never heard of them."

Giving the dwarf an indulgent smile, Laina turned to Naomi. "We have two days' travel yet ahead of us. We should be on our way."

With the torch extinguished and again stowed in Laina's pack, the three set off into the wild forest. No path marked their trail, so without the elf as their guide, they would soon have been lost.

As the sun set on the first day, Laina moved them quicker and quicker. When Naomi hustled to her side, grabbed her by the arm, and spun her around, the young elf looked frantic.

"What is it?" Naomi asked.

"We need to get across the river before darkness sets in."

"Why?"

When Laina turned from her to hurry away, Naomi put a hand on Paxton Re to move him with her.

The sound of rushing water came to them just before the night filled with high-pitched whistle. Naomi stopped in her tracks and swung around. She gave a start as the elven girl grabbed her arm to thrust her in front of them.

"Hurry!" she shouted. "Get to the water!"

The whistling—now it seemed more of a hiss—was getting louder as Naomi, Paxton Re, and Laina broke into a run. At their move, the night erupted into chaos full of noise and motion. The hissing was accompanied by growls and coughing. Figures flitted back and forth in front of them. When Naomi hesitated, she was shoved from behind by the girl. Once, Paxton Re went down—sprawled on his hands and knees. When Naomi stopped to help him, Laina was already there, pulling the dwarf to his feet with a strength Naomi would never have imagined from the small form.

Just when they came within sight of the river, Laina was taken from behind. The girl gave a scream as she was pulled backward into a swirling mass. Naomi rushed into the fray.

In the dark and confusion, she lost sight of everything. For a moment she thought she was within a tornado and then she saw the girl on the ground. She was torn and bloody but attempting to rise. Her pack, bow, and staff were nowhere in sight.

Naomi rushed to her side only then realizing Paxton Re had followed her. The two had just helped the girl to her feet when Naomi was knocked backward. In the distance, torn away from the winds, she heard her name called by Laina and Paxton Re.

"I'm here!" The words were wrenched from her by the storm.

Again, she was hit, and this time a sharp pain tore down her arm. Picking herself up from the ground, her hand encountered Laina's staff. Naomi wrapped her fingers around it, using its length to rise. One hand on the staff and the other clamped to her wounded arm, she stumbled through the storm.

Hearing a scream and guttural shout, Naomi turned in that direction only to see Paxton Re and Laina. They stood back-to-back, Paxton Re with a stone in his hand, and Laina held a knife. The whirlwind closed around them, and Naomi squinted, seeing forms in the confusion. She marched forward, determined to protect her friends. As she moved, she transferred the staff to her other hand. The fresh blood from her wound met the wood of the staff, then a bolt of energy surged through her. Her back arched, head thrown back. For a moment, it was as if she were alone in the world. In the silence of this moment, Naomi no longer heard conflict. No smells came to her. She was blinded within the brilliance of the joining.

The staff transformed. Growing longer and broader, it filled her grip as if made for her. Small branches erupted from the wood, and here and there a light-green leaf unfurled.

Coming back to herself, Naomi blinked, and the world was again in front of her. Everything was the same as it had been . . . but she was different.

Feeling the power and a timelessness course through her blood like a river, she stepped forward.

CHAPTER TWENTY-SEVEN

Adalard halted from his hunt. For days he had traveled, nose to the ground, the scent like a bright trail in front of him.

Circling, he was dumbfounded that the trail was gone. Evaporated as if it hadn't been.

Standing tall, the werebeast stretched his body to its full height. He swiveled his head, looking left and right, ready for some clue to show itself.

As the realization dawned that he had lost her trail, Adalard's hunger rose to a frenzy. He had been ignoring his body's needs. Ignoring the thirst. The hunger. The exhaustion.

Adalard had been outside the edges of the camp, outside the expanse of the fire, when the spiders attacked. Some of their fellow travelers, the lucky ones, died before they awoke. Others experienced the horror of what had come.

Seeing the ambush from a distance, Adalard raced to his companions. Although fast, he was still too slow. Getting to the campsite, Naomi, Paxton Re, and even Bob were gone. When he heard what he thought to be a woman's cry, Adalard followed it to a burrow where spiders were feasting on victims. Hoping his nose was true, he turned from them searching for Naomi. Farther and farther from the central point he circled, picking up a trace of his companions only to have it filter out in the heavy, mossy scent of the spiders.

*****

When the sun rose over the far mountains, he wasn't any closer to locating them than he had been when he started. Disheartened, Adalard made his way back to the campsite. In the light of day, he clearly saw the destruction wrought by the creatures. Torn up ground, sinkholes taking up large areas, belongings strewn about—some blowing in the morning breeze. No bodies. Adalard chose not to think of what had become of them. His aim was to locate his companions.

That morning, he had picked up Naomi's trail. Now, days later, he had again lost her.

A small animal raced across his path, and he was on it before it knew he was there. A crunch and a swallow, and the worst of his pangs faded.

He would double back. Get back to the spot where he had her scent. Turning to do just that, the wind brought a new call to him. Much information was contained within the gust. Animals, plants, births, deaths. And at the end, a whiff of Naomi.

Standing taller, nose in the air, he scented her out. There, he thought. Looking toward the mountains, Adalard dropped to all four and broke into a run.

CHAPTER TWENTY-EIGHT

Naomi moved into the battle, feeling no fear. There was nothing but the rush of blood in her ears and the anticipation of the war to come. Knowledge filled her, ancient and wise. The way of war, to defend, became a part of her. She stepped forward, confident, lethal.

The beings within the tempest didn't sense her, didn't feel her coming. As if cloaked, she waded into them. They didn't know she was there until the blunt of the staff connected with the first one. The crack of its skull reverberated through the storm, causing a hush to come to an otherwise overpowering din. She didn't even pause; her only thought was reaching her companions.

With each swing of the staff, more of their adversaries fell.

Like an extension of her arm, the staff whistled through the air. A spin here. A thrust there. When calm once more settled on the land, Naomi looked around. The beings, whatever they were, must have taken their fallen with them as no bodies littered the ground. Only Paxton Re and Laina stood witness to what she had become.

"The Bloodline," Laina whispered.

"Naomi?" Paxton Re said, and Naomi's distant gaze dropped to the dwarf. In her right hand, she held the staff, end firmly on the ground. As they watched, the staff shrank, leaves disappearing. For a long moment, it was visible. Then it faded until it was a twisted, leafy vine on the woman's skin. Running from hand to shoulder, the beautiful mark fluttered for a moment as if in a stiff breeze and then became still.

Naomi stared at him, confusion in her eyes. "Paxton Re?" she whispered and then collapsed.

*****

"What was that?" Paxton Re was practically shouting at the elven girl. He paced in front of where Naomi still lay. When she had first collapsed, he had rushed to her, checking to make sure she was still breathing. Relieved that she seemed none the worse for wear, he straightened her limbs and turned on Laina.

His glare had the young girl backing away from him. She gave a mighty shrug, her palms in the air. "I told you, I don't know."

"And I don't believe you!"

"I don't know what you want me to say."

"You said 'the Bloodline.' What did you mean by that?" When the elven girl just stared at him, Paxton Re bellowed, "Tell me what's going on." His anger seemed to have no effect on the girl as she offered no explanation.

He paced over to Naomi and squatted to recheck her. Sleeping, as far as he could tell. He again confronted the elf.

"This woman is my friend, maybe the only friend I have, and you know something about what just happened to her."

When Laina again shrugged, Paxton Re added, "It's your staff."

"Paxton Re."

At the whispered name, the dwarf spun around. Naomi was awake. Sitting up. She had her head in her hands, and as he neared her, she put one hand out to him and lifted her face to his.

"Naomi." Again he squatted, taking the offered hand.

"Am I really your friend?" she began with a small smile.

"Well . . ." And with a grumble under his breath he added, "You weren't supposed to hear that."

Naomi gave a small chuckle that broke off as she saw the mark on her arm. Turning her arm this way and that, she studied the symbol. When she glanced at the dwarf with a raise of her eyebrows, he said, "Yeah, I know." He threw a gesture over his shoulder at Laina. "And the elf won't tell me anything."

Seeing Laina over Paxton Re's shoulder, Naomi pushed herself to her feet. Approaching the girl, Naomi held out her arm.

"What is this?"

"I told him." She jerked her chin at Paxton Re. "I don't know anything about it." Before they could begin to berate her, Laina swung her pack onto her back and turned toward the river.

"We should get across the water. It's safer on the other side."

"Where is your staff?" With Naomi's question, Laina faced the two of them. Her gaze darted from Paxton Re to Naomi.

With a gruff mumble, the dwarf said, "It's in your skin."

"What?" Naomi jumped back, her arm held out to the side.

"You had the girl's staff. Fought as if you had, had it all your life." Walking up to her, Paxton Re placed his hand on the arm with the mark. "Saved us is what you did." He glanced at Laina. "Then, when the fightin' was done, the staff disappeared into your hand. Then that appeared on your arm. Soon after, you collapsed."

"Collapsed," Naomi parroted. "That's why I was on the ground."

"Yep. Been out for some minutes. Been trying to get information out of that one." He pointed at the elven girl.

"Laina." Naomi moved to the girl. "You must know something. The staff . . ." She glanced at her arm. "Is yours. What happened? Why is this here?"

"We can discuss this when we get to the city. For now, we need to move." Ending the discussion, Laina turned and moved away from them. With no choice but to go with the girl, Naomi and Paxton Re followed.

*****

Even as the sun began to set, Laina kept them moving. She set a brisk pace, rarely pausing throughout the day. They had just passed through a particularly dense stand of briars when a glow became obvious in the distance.

"There." Laina pointed. "Eldenblair. Home city to King Mallevorn."

"Is that our destination?"

Laina nodded to Naomi's question. "Come. We will be there soon."

Soon wasn't soon enough for Naomi. All she wanted, in this moment, was to sit down and rub her feet. She had passed hungry a few hours ago, as exhaustion had set in and she was no longer concerned with such mundane things. Now, all her concentration was on putting one foot in front of the other. She had been tired coming out of her stupor following the battle, but now her body was getting ready to shut down.

When they entered the city—crossing a massive wooden bridge that spanned a chasm—Naomi's spirits and energy picked up. Soldiers stood along the main avenue, armed and alert even as they stood at parade rest. Many pairs of eyes followed the trio as they moved farther into the city. When the stomp of many feet sounded and the soldiers filed behind them, Naomi and Paxton Re gave continuous glances back. And worried looks to each other. The soldiers, however, stayed back, simply following.

Rounding a corner, a large brass gate towered between them and the spires of a castle ahead.

Laina led them right up to the gates and gave three sharp raps upon the metal. The deep reverberation echoed up and out to fill the air. On the final chords of the ring, the massive gate screeched and began to swing open.

When it reached its midpoint—neither fully open nor closed—Laina stepped within. For a second, Naomi and Paxton Re looked at one another and then, together, followed the girl in.

CHAPTER TWENTY-NINE

Laina was nervous. No matter how often she told herself all would be well, her heart pounded in her chest. King Mallevorn had made his decree. Little did it matter that she was his cousin's child—he would use her at will.

She didn't know why he wanted the duo, but if his plan fell apart, it would be her he would blame. Selfish and vain, he would not take the fault himself but lay it at her feet.

She had liked the two companions right from the beginning. Their loyalty to each other, perhaps. And Naomi's reaction to the staff, and the staff's to her. She had only heard of it happening that fast and hard once before, though the fact that, that one had ended in tragedy would have no bearing on this. No matter what, bonding had to be fulfilled. Perhaps it would be better if the king did not know about it right now. Better to see what his plans were first.

Laina looked up as they neared the castle. Seeing the light in the top room of the tower, her stomach turned. The old queen—insane by any standards—clung to life as tenaciously as a wood tick. She would need to make time to see her this visit. They were family after all. She reminded herself that all would be dependent on the whims and need of a king.

"Come." She ushered Naomi and Paxton Re through the lower door. Up two flights of stairs, they passed no one. The castle gave all appearances of being vacant, though she knew that was not so. Partway down a hall, Laina pulled a cloak from a hook on the wall. She gave it to Naomi. "Put this on." Stopping the companions before entering the next room, Laina pulled the sleeve of the cloak down around Naomi's hand. "Keep this between us for the time being," she whispered. Not waiting for an answer, she turned and preceded them in to see the king.

When they passed into the throne room, the king sat on the room's namesake. Standing to the side and slightly behind him was another man. While the king was dressed in splendor, the second man was clothed entirely in black. He had the hood of a loose-fitting cloak pulled up to partially conceal his face. They both looked up at the newcomers.

"Laina," the king bellowed, his voice echoing through the chamber.

Naomi started at the loud boom of his voice but hoped her involuntary movement was covered by Laina as she moved forward. The elven girl stopped just before the dais, dropping to one knee.

"My king," she said, her head bowed.

"What have you brought me, cousin?"

The king kept his gaze on Laina, but while they talked, the second man slid off the dais and along the wall until he stood behind them. The elf was tall and thin. His frame was covered by the long, dark cloak so that all that showed were thin, claw-like hands and a gaunt visage mostly covered by long snarled hair and a ratty black beard. The beard, which hung to midpoint on his chest, had beads and feathers entwined with it.

Naomi shifted subtly as he moved to keep him within her sights. There was something about his movement—his general air—that filled her mind with images of a slimy, overgrown bog and the things that swam beneath its surface, and she didn't care to have him at her back.

"My king, at your request, I have ventured out of the kingdom and brought you back the two from your vision."

At her words, Naomi's attention returned to the discussion.

"Good, good," the king muttered. With a groan, he stood, his flowing robes falling behind, and he made his way down the stairs past Laina to Paxton Re and Naomi.

Naomi's first thought was to bow, but unsure of protocol, and seeing Paxton Re do nothing, she followed his lead.

The king moved around them as if they were on the blocks for sale. Looking them over from head to toe, he uttered a small sound of acknowledgment.

"Magistrate," he called. "Come and greet our visitors. See if they will do for our needs."

Naomi turned from the king to the magistrate, shocked to have him right behind her. She hadn't even heard him move. This close, she saw every little imperfection on his skin. This close, his pupils reflected the light, giving the appearance that they glowed from within. She wrinkled her nose, just stopping from covering her face with a hand. His smell, though far from the most unpleasant aroma she had contended with, reminded her of an old cupboard—wood rotting and a bag of long-forgotten potatoes turning to dust in the far corner.

When she stepped back, placing a hand on Paxton Re's shoulder, the magistrate followed. He kept his near proximity to her, continuing to watch her as if she were an insect under a glass.

Naomi stood her ground, though the smell emanating from him had her holding her breath between small gasps.

"You may leave, Laina," the king said, making the statement an order.

Laina looked from the two she had brought to the king and back again.

"Um." She again scanned the faces. "My king—" she began, only to have him cut her off.

"Goodbye, Laina. Do stop and visit the queen before you leave the city."

Seeing no way to refuse the king's order, Laina turned from

the throne room. She knew the two were her responsibility now, Naomi especially. She needed to know what was going on.

*****

Laina hadn't even reached the end of the hallway when she broke into a run. Long forgotten by most of the castle inhabitants were hidden spaces between rooms. Many of them overlooked select areas of the palace. As a child, Laina had located most of them—she was certain there were many more to be found. Now she knew her knowledge would come in handy.

Sliding to a halt, Laina took a quick look down the corridor. No one was coming, but that would not last forever. The castle was a notoriously busy place. She laid a hand on a stone in the wall. With a push, and an upward shove, the stone moved. And so did a portion of the wall. Laina gave another glance down the hallway and then stepped into the space.

CHAPTER THIRTY

When Laina left the room, Naomi registered it in the peripheral of her vision. Her direct attention, however, was filled with the magistrate. He still stood too close—stared too intensely. She was afraid to release her hold on Paxton Re for fear she would fall under his spell.

The king took a slow lap around her, Paxton Re, and the magistrate. When he got close, she pulled her gaze from the adjudicator and gave her attention to the king. He arrived back at the head of the room, slowly mounted the dais, and took his seat on the throne, straightening his robes around his frame. Naomi glanced down at Paxton Re and then again at the king when he began to talk.

"I have a journey for you." He gestured between her and the dwarf.

"A journey?" she asked, her brows drawing in. "We're already on our way somewhere."

"Ah, yes." The king leaned forward. "Your quest. What if I told you once you find Darklin Vale, you'll require a particular object to fulfill your desire? An object you will need to acquire before you leave our valley. Once you leave, it will be too late, and when you look for it in the future, it will be gone."

"How can you know this?"

The king waved off her question and leaned back into his

chair. "Let's just agree that I know what I know."

"Assuming you're correct"—she took a step forward—"what's in this for you?"

King Mallevorn gave a secretive smile, his gaze jumping between the magistrate and the woman. Standing, he moved toward her, again stepping down to her level. He rubbed his palms on his robe and then curled them into the opposite sleeve, cupping his elbows.

"Let's just say . . ." He again made his way around the throne room. "That this object you seek—a talisman, as it were, has a use for us before you may have it."

"Hogwash," Paxton Re muttered.

Three sets of eyes leveled on the dwarf, all with some degree of amazement.

"How dare you . . ." The magistrate started forward, obviously in violent intent, but the king waved him back.

"Let it be, magistrate. You know the temperament of dwarfs." He ended his statement with a tone that left no question to his low feelings toward Paxton Re and all his kind. Proceeding as if the dwarf had not spoken, he continued laying out his plan. "I will provide you with an escort," the king added. "Seasoned warriors. With their aid, you will get your object. You will bring it to me for my use and then you may have it."

Naomi didn't like this king. And she didn't like his magistrate. She didn't trust them. She was thinking that Paxton Re was correct when he had said "hogwash."

"I would like to talk to Laina."

"She is of no bearing. You will do this for me—bring me back what I require. There is nothing to think about. Nothing to discuss." With that declaration, King Mallevorn returned to his throne.

The magistrate again caught everyone's attention as he moved between the king and his visitors. Shifting back and forth like a snake preparing to strike, he thrust a gnarled hand out to grab Naomi by the wrist. Holding it up, the sleeve of her cloak fell, revealing the intricate marking.

"What is this?" The king jumped to his feet. Faster than Naomi would have thought possible, he made his way to her.

"Now you just wait a minute." Paxton Re attempted to slide between her and the magistrate. Stronger than she had thought a moment ago, the man pushed Paxton Re backward and out of the way.

Hustling up to them, breathing hard, the monarch made to grab Naomi's arm but pulled back at the last moment. Showing no such hesitation, the magistrate pushed her sleeve up higher and held her arm out for the king to examine.

"This is impossible," he whispered, once again reaching a finger to within inches of her skin. Getting in her face, but making sure to avoid her arm, he shouted, "How did this happen?"

Naomi—tired, hungry, confused, and just plain overwhelmed—gave the king a little smile and said, "You tell me, Your Majesty. I've got questions of my own."

Stepping back from her, the king yelled, "Guard." Four uniformed, armed men entered from the back of the room. "Take them to the south cells."

To her and Paxton Re, he said, "You will be taken to sleeping quarters, fed. Tomorrow you will meet with your escort and plan the journey. You will leave as soon as possible."

"What is the item?" When Paxton Re again spoke, all eyes turned to him. "The item we're to find."

Great question, Naomi thought.

"That will be discussed tomorrow, also."

"And your use for it?" Now the dwarf took a step toward the king. His eyes narrowed, and his voice came out in a growl. "What exactly is this talisman to you? And what do you plan to do with it?"

"My reasoning is my own," the king stated before dismissing them with a glance.

Soon surrounded, all Naomi and Paxton Re could do was move with the flow of bodies as they left the throne room.

"I don't like this," he muttered to her.

"What are you thinking?"

"I don't know. But it's not good."

Naomi didn't know what to say but kept her gaze on the dwarf.

"I've been around mad kings before, and it's never good."

* * * * *

Laina dropped her gaze from the small holes high on the wall of the throne room. Her cousin wasn't to be trusted. She had an idea what he was after—the lore of the talisman was age-old. She needed to stay in the know.

When she heard whispering, she again stepped up to the peepholes. Below her, the king and magistrate stood, heads together.

"What of the Bloodline?" the king asked.

"A curiosity, nothing more."

"And the deal we've struck. After we get the talisman?"

The magistrate scanned the empty room. Then, stepping even closer to King Mallevorn, he whispered, "The deal will hold. And perhaps we'll get even more than we know."

Taking the king by the shoulder, the magistrate ushered him from the room and into a back hallway. The door closed behind them, leaving Laina alone with her thoughts.

She figured they would take Naomi and Paxton Re to the cells in the lower level of the palace. There wasn't anything she could do tonight, but by tomorrow, she would have a plan in place.

* * * * *

Later that night, unable to sleep, Laina began to lay her plans. They needed provisions. Weapons. She climbed from her covers, her mind already in motion. Dressing in traveling leathers, she grabbed a short sword and attached it to her waist. Moving stealthily through the halls, she made her way to the armory. A guard sat by the entrance. When he gave a loud snore and a twitch, she snuck in and retrieved a short sword for the dwarf and one for Naomi. From across the room, she took a longbow and a quiver of arrows. In addition to the sword, Naomi now had the staff. She would need little else but that.

On the way to the lower cells, she dropped into the shadows twice to avoid being seen. A unit of soldiers surveilled the hall, and she couldn't get to Naomi and Paxton Re until they left. For now, there was nothing to do but wait.

The woman, though she knew little of it, was protected by the Bloodline. If and when it became necessary, she could use it to her defense. But the dwarf. The dwarf Laina knew little about—his past. His experiences. How would he react in a life-and-death situation? She would need to save him to find out.

CHAPTER THIRTY-ONE

The dwarfish kingdom of Brikenhammer had stood for as long as anyone could remember. The current king, Magnes Longbeard, could trace his lineage back through previous kings ten generations—and dwarfs lived extraordinarily long lives.

Like all dwarfs, these loved to eat, drink, and celebrate, but even more than that, they loved to dig. Mining was in their blood. Running shafts deep into the earth, they were experts at locating gems and precious metals. The King's Vault at Brikenhammer attested to their success.

The kingdom, built right into the northernmost reaches of the Backaroon Mountains, was a sight to see—towering so high clouds often obstructed the view of the highest spires, and large hunting raptors circled on the sharp air currents. The dwarfs had long ago given up on the towering heights and had sent their aim down.

King Magnes Longbeard had seven children, each with their own intentions for the throne. His eldest, a son of forty years, monopolized his father's time, driving the other siblings from the affections of the king. As eldest and next in line for the throne, Jae Laq began to plot the demise of his father. Unwilling to wait until the old king died, Jae Laq wanted to rule now.

As his fantasies turned to thoughts of fratricide, Jae Laq's gaze expanded to the rest of the family. After all, they were all a threat to his rule. Each of them had a claim to the throne of Brikenhammer. He would have to ponder this . . . and watch.

*****

Paxton Re sat on the bench next to his youngest cousin. Trilly had only been in the city for a short time. Her parents, cousin to King Magnes Longbeard, decided she was old enough, at thirty, to learn the ins and outs of politics.

"What troubles you, little one?" he asked, placing a gentle hand on her shoulders.

When she tipped her face to him, he realized she had been crying. Wrapping an arm around her shoulders, he pulled her in tightly. At his loving touch, and gentle voice, the girl broke down, weeping into his chest.

"Now, now, sweet cousin. Nothing can be that bad."

"I hate it," she muttered, barely audible against his shirt.

"Hate what, dear Trilly?"

"All of it." And again she glanced up at him, pulling slightly back from his chest. "The city! The noise, the masses of people, the politics of it all. Everyone is so false." Again she buried her face into his shirt, then muttered, "I hate it."

Paxton Re knew his cousin had been deliberately reared outside the providences of the kingdom of Brikenhammer. Her parents thought that a good foundation for schooling before being thrown into the cesspool of the monarchy, and that would help build the confidence to forge one's way. Trilly was the youngest of twelve, and for eleven children, their policy had worked. Trilly, sensitive and more than a bit naive, was not built for life in the mountain.

"Perhaps your parents would be willing to take you home. If you told them how unhappy you are."

Before he had even finished speaking, she was already

shaking her head.

"I can't disappoint them like that." She pulled from his embrace to sit on the bench and stared off into the distance. "In fact, I heard them talking last night after they thought I was abed." She stopped, and a single tear ran down her cheek. When she didn't continue, Paxton Re nudged her, giving her a prompt to continue.

"And?"

"Oh, Paxton Re," she wailed. "It's so very terrible."

"What Trilly? What's terrible?"

Shiny eyes looked up into his, and again tears spilled over. "They hope to marry me to the king."

Paxton Re didn't know what to say. It was true that the queen had died some time ago, but he hadn't heard any rumors about King Magnes desiring another wife.

"Are you certain? Perhaps you misunderstood."

"No, no." She shook her head. "I know what I heard. The king saw me at the State Dinner two nights ago. He took a liking to me, and it got him thinking about having a new, young wife. More children." With her head down, hair hanging to obstruct her face, she continued. "With my lineage, I'm acceptable as a wife to the king." She fell silent, only the shaking of her shoulders giving evidence to her continued woe.

Paxton Re had to admit it all made sense. It was common for men of royal blood to marry within their family. He didn't like that the king's gaze had stopped on his favorite cousin, though.

"Is there any way you can help me, Paxton Re?"

Paxton Re looked at the misery on Trilly's face, her eyes still swimming in tears. He would help her if he could, but there was nothing he could do. Nothing but be here for her—be a friend and a willing ear when she needed one.

He was already shaking his head, preparing to tell her the truth, but she knew it. Saw it on him. With a cry, the girl leaped to her feet, spinning to face him.

"Never mind, Paxton Re." She swept the tears from her face

with a hand that trembled. "I'll take care of it myself."

Paxton Re stood, reaching for her, but she was gone in a swirl of silk. He watched as she disappeared around the corner of the path, his mind in turmoil. He loved Trilly like a sister, but tradition was tradition, and dwarfish kings had been marrying young women of royal blood for as long as anyone could remember. Maybe he could talk to her, get her to see the positive side of things. She would be marrying a king, for the sake of the gods. She might even be the mother of the next king, though it was true that King Magnes had other children from other marriages.

Paxton Re strolled slowly down the path, his thoughts on possible topics of conversation with Trilly. Preoccupied with his thoughts, he didn't see the man who hid in the shadows, eavesdropping on his conversation with his cousin.

CHAPTER THIRTY-TWO

Trilly would never marry King Magnes. Many decades old, he was ancient to a young heart like her. Just the thought of his aged hands on her made her shudder with revulsion. In the true fantasies of a young girl, Trilly had always imagined her future husband to be a young and virile dwarf. A warrior to protect her at all times. In her dreams, she had been given a chaste kiss by her mystery man, and it had been firm, and powerful lips he had pressed to hers. Not old and shaky ones, drool seeping from the corners.

Flying about her quarters, wringing her hands until they hurt and showed red, Trilly planned her escape. And escape she would. She was leaving the mountain city of Brikenhammer. And she would go tonight.

When the knock came, expecting Paxton Re, she flew across the room and flung open her door. Seeing the scourge of her panic, Trilly stood stunned, mouth agape. King Magnes pushed past the girl and entered her room.

"Close the door, Trilly. We must talk."

Trilly gave her door a halfhearted push and turned to face the king. He didn't immediately speak but made his way across her room to a small table holding a carafe of fine wine and two glasses. Pouring wine into both glasses, King Magnes turned back to face the girl.

"Come, Trilly. Sit with me by the fire and have a sip of wine."

Still in a semi-dazed state, Trilly moved across the floor and took one of the glasses. The king took her elbow and led her across the room to where a settee and two chairs faced a low-burning fire. Seating her on the settee, the king sat next to her and took a healthy swallow of wine.

"I presume you've heard that you and I are to be married." When she only stared at the fire, he continued, "It is my wish that we become better acquainted before the festivities." When she still sat as though made of stone, King Magnes reached to touch her hand. At the contact, Trilly jumped as though being hit with an electric shock. Leaping to her feet, she dashed the glass of wine into the fire where it sizzled.

"No." She spun toward him. "No! I'll never be your wife." With these words spoken, she fled to the balcony to look down on the valley many stories below. When hands lay on her shoulders, Trilly startled, not having heard the king follow her.

He turned her around. "We will be married, Trilly. I think it would be good for you to get used to my proximity." And with that he took her into his arms.

Nose filled with the scent of him—old sweat and sour breath—she wriggled, trying to free herself. He was stronger than she would have thought, and without consideration, Trilly struggled harder, spinning on the balcony. When she at last broke his hold, she gave a mighty push to his chest to gain herself some space and fresh air.

The king stumbled backward, catching his foot on the hem of his robe, and with a pinwheel of arms, he went over the side of her balcony. It all happened so fast that Trilly simply stared for a moment before rushing to the edge of the balcony to peer over.

"Well, it looks as though you've done me a service."

Spinning from where she was, Trilly saw Jae Laq stroll out onto her balcony.

"Maybe next time you plan the assassination of a king, you should lock your door."

"But . . . I . . . I didn't—" she sputtered, unable to put a coherent sentence together.

Jae Laq walked by her to peer over the balcony at the dead king below. Continuing to stare, a slow smile moved across his face. When he turned to face her, the smile remained. In its shadow, the girl gave another shudder.

"One thing I'll say for the old man . . ." The new king took a leisurely stroll around the girl. "He had good taste."

Trilly turned as Jae Laq came around her, seeing avarice and evil in his eyes.

"Let's give it a try, shall we?" With a shove, he pushed her into her room and onto her bed.

Paxton Re heard the muffled scream right before the warning horn went off outside the main gate. He stopped and looked back the way he had come. He continued to Trilly's door a few feet in front of him.

His first instinct was to knock on the door, but instead he grabbed the knob. It turned easily in his hand, and he stepped in to close the door behind him. The scene that greeted him had him pausing for just a second and then rushing forward. Grabbing the man who lay on Trilly—even now hiking up her skirts while she struggled—he got two good hand holds and flung her attacker across the room.

Paxton Re leaned over Trilly's prone figure. The bodice and skirt of her gown were torn, her lip was bleeding, and even now, a bruise blossomed across her cheek and jaw.

"Trilly," he said gently, but her eyes were glazed and staring at the ceiling.

The sound of a sword clearing its scabbard had Paxton Re turning from his cousin to face the threat behind.

CHAPTER THIRTY-THREE

The harsh clang of steel on steel broke through Trilly's catatonic state, and she turned her head to study the room. The sun streaming though her open balcony doors obliterated some of the scene, but she saw two men fiercely battling.

Pulling herself into a seated position, Trilly raised her head and looked through the fall of hair that obscured her vision. She identified Jae Laq and Paxton Re. When she stood, weakness in her knees almost took her to the floor, but she pushed forward, stumbling into the main room of her quarters.

"Stop!" she shouted, but in the general din of the battle, the men didn't hear her. Nor would they have halted the fight even if they had.

Trilly reeled into the men, and when Jae Laq presented his back to her, she jumped on him, wrapping her arms around his neck and squeezing with all her might. As if she were nothing more than a fly, the new king spun her off, throwing her into an armoire in the corner. Her efforts were for naught, but in getting his attention, she gave Paxton Re the opening he was waiting for.

Swiping his sword into Jae Laq's legs, the blade cut deep, causing the other man to stumble. In an effort to regain his equilibrium, Jae Laq lowered his sword. Paxton Re stepped forward and ran his blade through the other man's chest.

All motion stopped. The only sound was Jae Laq gasping.

Paxton Re stared into the dying man's eyes, for the first time understanding the ramifications of his actions. As the life left the dwarf and he slid from the blade, Trilly flew into Paxton Re's arms.

"Oh, Paxton Re," she wept. "What have you done?"

With one hand wrapped around his cousin and the other still clutching the blood-soaked sword, Paxton Re didn't know how to answer her. The better question was, what was he to do now?

Trilly withdrew from Paxton Re's embrace and pulled him away from the body.

"Come with me," she said, rushing him from the room. "You must leave, Paxton Re. You must flee the city or for sure you'll be punished for this."

Studying her with eyes still glassy, Paxton Re muttered, "I can go to the king. I can explain to him what happened."

"Oh, Paxton Re." She again wrapped her arms around his waist. This time when she pulled back, she looked up into his face, hers a picture of sorrow. "The king is dead. Did you not hear the blast of the horn?"

"Dead? When? How?" His brows furrowed and he glanced about the room as if to find an answer to his questions.

"It was an accident," she whispered, casting her gaze to the floor before them.

"What was, Trilly?" Taking her chin in his hand, he raised her eyes to meet his. "What happened?"

"He was here. Here in these rooms before. I—I pushed him away." Rushing to her balcony, Trilly pointed. "I pushed him, and he tripped, and he went over the side of the balcony." As she spoke, the girl's voice rose in volume and gained an edge of hysteria. "I ran to the edge, and he lay at the bottom. Broken. Paxton Re, he was broken." With those words she broke into tears. Covering her face with her hands, Trilly sank into one of the chairs on the balcony.

Paxton Re approached the edge to peer over. A flock of

people filled the area, but he didn't see the king's body. Perhaps they had already moved it within.

King Magnes dead along with Prince Jae Laq. Both, from this room. What would become of them?

A stiff wind blew in from off the mountains to ruffle Paxton Re's hair and fill his lungs. He took a moment to relish in the quiet and peace of his mountain home. The scents and the sounds that blew in with the wind. Then with a blink, he turned.

"Come, Trilly." He held out a hand to her. "I'm going to need your help if I plan on getting out of the city alive."

*****

Now, Paxton Re found himself once again responsible for a young woman he had come to care for. Only this time, he was imprisoned and not sure if there would be any way for him to come to Naomi's aid.

He paced the cell once and then sat down to think.

CHAPTER THIRTY-FOUR

Naomi squeezed her eyes shut and gave two rapid blinks when the dawning sun hit her. The night before, she had been separated from Paxton Re. Protesting did no good. The guards ignored her, and shoved her into a room. Just before her door clanged shut, she saw Paxton Re as he was thrown into a room across the hall.

The room—cell was more like it—was in almost total darkness. One small candle sat on a shaky table at the back of the room. It illuminated the space just enough for her to see a moth-eaten pallet against the wall. Other than that, and the table, there was a bucket in the far corner. She was too certain of its purpose. She yelled for Paxton Re, her face to the door, but it was thick, and she didn't hear anything. She didn't know if he could even hear her.

She was exhausted but a bit more selective than the pallet would allow. Once, she wandered close, but the smell, old mold and sour, drove her back.

She paced the close confines for what seemed to be hours and finally took a seat against the wall.

Half asleep and unable to turn her roiling brain off, she stared at the slowly dying flame of the candle. When it finally gave a last sputter and extinguished in a puddle of its own fluid, she continued to stare into the abyss, the image of the flame burned into her gaze.

*****

The next morning, not knowing if she had slept or not, she was jerked from her cell, Paxton Re nowhere to be seen.

"Where's my friend?" she asked of the soldiers, but she might as well have saved her breath for all the interest they showed in her.

Now, stepping out of the castle, she didn't know how to define her part in all of this. The king seemed to think she could locate the talisman he required. But how? And where was Paxton Re? Was he still in his cell being kept a prisoner until she succeeded in their quest?

She squinted as the rising sun shot a brilliant ray into her still-sensitive eyes, then gaped at the procession that greeted her. This couldn't all be for her, she thought right before her gaze happened on the elven king and his magistrate.

"What the hell is this?" she whispered as King Mallevorn stepped to a forward position on his balcony.

"My warriors." His voice reverberated off the walls of the courtyard. "For many lifetimes we've heard tales of a talisman of unimaginable power."

In the hush that filled the area, Naomi heard a hawk scream far in the distance. Each man present seemed to pull in a collective breath.

"Now, I, your king, have evidence of its location."

The sensation of a breath held released with an audible whoosh that had Naomi glancing around.

He certainly has their attention now, she thought.

"You, my brave soldiers"—he passed an outstretched palm across the field of men before him—"will accompany one who will be entrusted to bring this talisman to me. You are the finest of the elven nation—the bravest and the brightest. You will aid when necessary, keeping her safe during this quest."

Gesturing to a company of iron-clad elves—swords on their hips and upright spears in one hand, an end planted on the ground—the king continued, "My elite soldiers. Your strong arms will battle foes who think to stop this journey."

Shifting, he held a palm toward the middle group.

"My magic wielders. You shall stand before all threats to keep the talisman out of the hands of men—for man blood . . ." At this the king's mouth turned down. "Will surely locate what you seek. But the talisman will be delivered into elven hands.

"With you, my magistrate will travel." When King Mallevorn gestured to his side, the darkly cloaked figure stepped forward. In this bright courtyard, light seemed to be absorbed into his frame.

A shiver passed through Naomi. She was not happy to be traveling with the magistrate. He gave her the creeps.

The king turned finally to a small group of elves wearing leathers of varying shades of browns and greens.

"My hunters."

At the king's words, a lone woman stepped from the ranks. She gave a deep nod toward the king.

"My hunters," the king repeated. "With you I send the map and information on the location of the talisman. The location, long secret, will be found only with stealth and a keen insight into this land. Captain Lefaye, you will ensure the talisman is found. That is the first step. Allowing the others to do their parts."

He hesitated and then, with a deep breath, turned to where Naomi stood on the stairs. Alone but for the two guards who brought her here.

"This woman." He sighed again, dropping his arm to his side. "This woman," he repeated, "will accompany you, my finest elven troops. Her role in your adventure will begin when the talisman is revealed. Until then, you must do everything in your power to keep her safe. She has an essential part to play in retrieving our prize."

At his words, Naomi glanced around. Her gaze drifted over the assembly of elves in the courtyard only to see that they all watched her.

"It is reported," the king boomed, "that she—a child of man—has elven blood. I've not seen evidence of this," he lied, "but it gives me confidence that the rumor must be true as this is an elven quest."

Silence descended, and in the final moments before turning away, King Mallevorn stared straight at Naomi. It was all she could do to hold his gaze, a cold shiver running down her spine.

When he left the field without another word, the men milled for a moment before filing out. A man in the leather uniform of the hunters ascended the stairs with a light step.

"You're to come with me."

Naomi nodded. Following the hunter down the stairs and across the field, Naomi became aware of stares directed her way from the departing soldiers. She knew less than they, and figuring there was little she could do about their curiosity, she kept her eyes on the back of the elf she followed.

Down hallways too numerous to count, he led her until he finally proceeded into a small room.

Naomi gazed around, taking in the various gear. Packs, clothing, cold weather provisions, and weapons—swords, knives, shields, and spears.

"Am I to be armed then?" she asked. "I had nothing when I arrived."

The hunter indicated a small table to the side of the room.

"Outfit yourself. No weapons." Then he made his way to the door. "We leave within the hour."

"Wait," she called as he made to leave. Turning, he raised one eyebrow to her. "Do you know anything of my friend? A dwarf named Paxton Re?"

The elven hunter shook his head and planted himself by the door, watching her every move.

Naomi wanted to find Paxton Re, but she didn't even know

where to begin. At this point, she wouldn't even be able to get herself back to her cell. She was hopelessly lost in the castle. Other than the soldiers in the yard, she was without companions or friends. An image of Laina rose in her mind. Where was the girl? She had been sent from the throne room last night, and Naomi hadn't seen or heard of her since.

Naomi took a deep breath, the flat of her palm placed to her heart. She was as much a prisoner as if she were called one. She had no choice but to continue with the hunt for the talisman—whatever that turned out to be. If King Mallevorn could be believed, for her to locate Darklin Vale and a way home, she would need this object. She would need to find it if she hoped to leave this place with Paxton Re.

Resigned to her fate—at least for the time being—Naomi walked among the items in the room, selecting provisions she thought she would need. There was so much, and she could only carry a limited amount. She had just shoved the last of her selection into her pack as another soldier came into the room.

Ignoring the hunter at the door, his loud voice startled her into turning. "You! Come wit' me."

Naomi shouldered her pack and followed him. She gave the other elf a look, but he stared straight ahead.

Back down the hallway they went, reversing the path she had taken to get there. When he led her out a different door, a field spread before them. Seeing it from a different perspective, she gazed over the wide avenue the soldiers, trappers, and magic wielders who marched down. The troops' movement raised a fine dust that quickly coated her throat, and the din of their footfalls blocked out other sounds.

Her escort gestured a small distance away where the line of soldiers broke off and the company of wagons began. He leaned in and shouted, "This way," earning a nod from her.

She hurried and dropped in between a wagon and the next team of horses. They moved, stepping quickly to avoid being trod upon.

Her day quickly became focused on a forced march through a world hemmed in by walls of dirt. Naomi kept her gaze on the spinning rear wheels in front of her, and she concentrated on staying in front of the push behind.

Once, she attempted to speak to the soldier who still paced her, but the dust caught in her throat and almost caused a coughing fit that may well have gotten her trampled.

She was unable to tell the passage of time—the darkening of the day more sensed than seen until suddenly she no longer saw the wagon before them. It wasn't too much longer before the entire train came to a halt.

The scratch of flint and flare of light had her turning to the soldier beside her.

"This way," he said with a jerk of his head.

Like phantoms, the two moved through a quickly assembling camp. Fires burned at regular intervals, the scent of food rising from some of them. Horses were stripped of tack, bringing the pleasant scent of sweaty equine and hastily spread hay.

"Sit here," the soldier barked. Before she had even taken her seat, a young elf stood before her with a tin bowl and a hunk of bread. Naomi rose from a partial crouch and took the bowl. She swallowed hard—spittle filled her mouth at the smells. She would have eaten anything at this point, but the aroma rising from this simple fare had her striving not to devour the meal in one bite. Sitting, slow and silent, her eyes glued to the steaming bowl, she heard those around her shoveling the stew into their mouths.

Naomi gave in to the urge and took a bite. Then another and another. Her bowl was empty too soon, but her belly was full. Just as she set her bowl aside, the soldier again showed up. With a gesture, he indicated for her to follow him.

A city of tents began not far from where they had eaten. Walking among them, the soldier stopped before a small structure.

"Sleep here," he said and then walked away, the dust and

smoke enveloping him.

"Well," Naomi breathed, "I guess it's just me, then."

When she shimmied into the tent, she found two thin blankets. After wrapping up in them, she huddled into a ball and was soon fast asleep.

CHAPTER THIRTY-FIVE

A boot in the hip brought Naomi to her feet. The tent was gone, and all around her were the noise and commotion of the breaking of a large camp. Amid the chaos, she spun in a slow circle, trying to orient herself. Even if she knew this land, which she didn't, she would be lost. She was a prisoner just as surely as if she were bound.

The second and third days passed much the same as the first—hours blended one into another. Thirst and exhaustion were her constant companions. She would barely get her sparce dinner down before stumbling where directed to collapse, sleep claiming her before she hit the ground.

On the fourth day, the contingent made an abrupt shift in trajectory. Suddenly, the dust that had plagued their days lifted to be replaced by a sharp, cold wind.

Naomi gasped as a gust swirled her hair and cut through the light cloak she wore.

"Damn, that's cold," she muttered, stopping to look to the mountains that were now visible with the removal of the layer of dust. She hadn't even had time to take a breath when she was shoved from behind, almost falling to her knees. With a hiss she spun to face the soldier.

"Keep moving." He brandished a long knife. Taking the chance that, for now at least, she had value, she threw a gesture at the guard and turned back to follow the caravan.

*****

They marched until the duo moons had risen in the far sky, but the mountains got no closer. Were they going all the way to them? What in the world was this talisman she was supposed to find? There was no one to ask, so the best she could do was keep up and keep her eyes and ears open.

Like every other night of their forced march, dinner was handed to her by a young lad. As soon as she had eaten, she was taken to a small tent already set up for her use. She was both pleased and bewildered to realize she was becoming accustomed to the ritual of her days. Before drifting to sleep, Naomi pushed up the sleeve of her tunic, and in the scattered firelight filtering through holes in the tent, she studied the vine marking on her arm. If she couldn't see it, she wouldn't know it was there—no raised lines met her fingers. It caused her no pain but did her no good. Paxton Re had said, in his short and concise way, that it was a staff that had disappeared into her hand. She thought she must have misunderstood him, or he was being cryptic. She studied the mark for a while, but exhaustion overwhelmed her confusion and she fell asleep. This night, she slept soundly.

*****

She was up and ready to move before they came for her. Earning a few quizzical looks, she simply stared back at them and waited. The soldier who followed her during the day pushed through the few who surrounded her, and with a growl at being denied his morning kick to her backside, he tossed her an apple and turned away. Naomi ducked her head to hide a grin while she hurried to catch up.

By the end of the second week, Naomi had fallen into the

routine of the army. She was no longer a burden. In the morning, she broke down and repacked her own tent, only requiring aid to place it in the wagon. Once or twice, she had helped in both preparing and dispersing their meals, earning a small smile from the cook and young elf who assisted him.

Day by day, the mountains got closer and closer, and the air around them more and more bitter with the cold. One morning when she awoke, Naomi found a heavier cloak and a pair of gloves lined with something akin to rabbit fur. That morning, after breaking their fast and repacking the kitchen, Naomi watched as a unit of trackers headed out ahead of the caravan. She hadn't seen the map that King Mallevorn spoke of, but she heard whispered conversations about a passage through the mountains. Wandering through the encampment, all of them waiting to hear something from the trackers, she caught sight of a figure she recognized. She ducked behind a pile of wood, watching until the man entered one of the large, central tents.

The sprog. The one she encountered upon entering this land and again in the town where they met Laina. Now, why would he be wandering freely through an elven camp? And what was in the large tent he had entered?

Curiosity filled her, driving her to move forward on light steps. No one saw her, no one stopped her, and she made it to the back of the tent. She heard something inside and leaned forward to pick up on their voices.

CHAPTER THIRTY-SIX

The next day, when the man stopped in front of her, Naomi's gaze shifted from the bowl in her hands to the boots planted on the soil at her feet. She swallowed hard and slowly raised her eyes to the man's. Her first fleeting thought had been that it would be the soldier, but although this one was a military man, too, he was of a higher rank.

"Get up. Come with me."

Naomi rose slowly to her feet. She studied the man. He was older than most men in this complement. His clothes neater, his bearing stiffer. She hesitated as he walked away, secure in the knowledge that she would follow him.

*****

They had walked for some distance, the motion loosening muscles that had begun to tighten during her meal. Unsure what was coming, Naomi rolled her shoulders and stretched her back muscles.

She saw the large tent as they neared it, recognizing it as the one she had listened on the night before. As they drew closer, two guards stepped from within. They drew the curtains back, straightened at attention, and allowed the officer and her to enter.

At first, coming from the dim light of morning into the darkness and silence of the tent, Naomi thought it was empty. As her eyes adjusted, a dark form became visible at the rear. When it moved, stepping toward her, she took an instinctive step back, her body hitting that of the soldier. With a small grunt, he shoved her forward hard enough to drive her to her knees. From her prone position, she looked up into the glowing eyes of the magistrate.

For all the things she had seen in this world—some wonderous and some terrifying—Naomi was ill-prepared to face the magistrate. Was he magic or simply evil? Was his one of the voices she had heard the previous day? And who all had he been speaking to?

Keeping his gaze on her, he moved forward, and she noticed he seemed to float in the air. What kind of being was this?

Her heart beat so hard, she felt it in her throat. Each breath quivered as she pushed it back out. She couldn't meet his eyes. Could only stare at the ground between them. When he was within arm's reach, he extended his hand to her. The last thing in the world she wanted was to feel the touch of his skin on hers. Clasping her hands together, she resisted his silent command.

The quake began deep inside and moved to her extremities. By the time her hands were shaking so bad she couldn't keep them clasped together, she realized she was reaching for his hand.

"No," she breathed just as she felt the touch of his cold, clammy flesh wrap around hers.

"Come, my dear," he intoned, his voice barely audible. When he gave a pull on her hand, she was compelled to follow him, her body doing the opposite of what her mind ordered. When he stopped and placed a finger under her chin, forcing her gaze up to him, she clamped her eyes shut, forbidding her body to follow his pull. She was in charge for a moment. Then her eyelids popped open, her gaze meeting his. She felt it, like a draining of her will. Then she didn't know anything.

"There, my dear," he whispered. "Isn't that better?"

Naomi didn't answer. Her blurry gaze rested on the canvas wall behind the magistrate. Keeping her hand in his, he moved her to sit by the rear wall of the tent. Like a puppet, she obeyed.

Stepping forward, the general asked, "Why do you want her here?"

With a growl, the magistrate turned on the other man. "What I want and when I want it are business only to me. You are not to question my desires and decisions."

The military man had dropped to one knee, his eyes on the ground. Now, he quaked, uncertain if he would survive his venture into this tent. For a long time, the general stayed as he was until finally the magistrate beckoned him forward.

"Now, General. Where are we and how long until we reach the valley in the mountains?"

Glad for his reprieve, the general stepped forward to point to spots on a map that was laid out in the back corner of the magistrate's large tent. The two men discussed the coming days, secure in their knowledge that the woman's mind was locked far away.

* * * * *

Naomi became aware of a dense, gray fog surrounding her. She couldn't make out anything around her, no landmarks to guide her way.

After a while the faint sound of voices made their way to her as if carried in on the wind. She tried to understand what they said. Tried to determine from what direction they came, but everything seemed to swirl around her. She was tired. More exhausted than she had ever felt in her life. What had she been doing to tax herself in this manner? Maybe she had been out for a long jog. Maybe that's why she was here. Had she gotten lost?

When voices came again, this time louder than before, she spun in a circle, sure she should be able to determine from where they came. She took a step, calling out.

"Hello."

When no one answered her, she called out again.

"Hello."

This time when the voice came, she made out some of the words—*Caravans. Troops.*

Naomi blinked slowly and a blurry image of the interior of a tent began to form. She was in one of the darkened corners, a large brazier in the center giving off light and heat. When the voice came again, her eyes shifted toward it. Two men. The magistrate and that general. Though it was clear they discussed something, the deferential tone of the general made it obvious he would agree to anything.

Naomi didn't move her head. Didn't move her body. She didn't even change the cadence of her breaths. She remembered the magistrate approaching her. Remembered his touch. Then there had been nothing until the fog. Had his touch done that?

The men spoke freely with her in the room, so Naomi figured they thought she was still under whatever kind of spell the magistrate had used. What reason would he have for wanting her here? Just to look at her? To know he had bested her? Yes, she could believe that. He was just that kind of man.

When their conversation stopped, Naomi stayed very still, staring at one spot in the room. A shadow approached her, and she knew it was the magistrate.

Kneeling in front of her, his back to the fire, she couldn't see his face, but she could smell him. She allowed herself to slowly blink but kept her eyes unfocused, her mind tight.

"My dear," he whispered, running the tip of one long-nailed finger down her jawline.

Sheer will kept her breathing even and a shiver of revulsion contained.

Straightening, the magistrate turned to the general. "Come, I would see a layout of our plans." With the general in tow, the two men left the tent.

Naomi stayed where she was, afraid it was a trap. She waited five minutes, then ten. When everything in and around the tent remained quiet, she slowly made her way to her feet. Glancing around, her gaze came to rest on the map the men had been studying. Taking tentative steps, she approached the table. She recognized the marking of their location. A symbol indicated the city of Eldenblair behind them. Mountains in front of them. And within the mountains a symbol. This was their destination. She didn't have to be told to know it was so. It looked to be a fortress of some sort. Quickly, she studied the map, looking for directional details and landmarks. A river, it seemed. And a drawing resembling a bird. Chicken perhaps. Time flew, and before she knew it, she heard a commotion of people coming toward the tent.

She ran back to the corner where they had left her. Situating herself back down, she mimicked her position from when she had first regained her wits. She was just in time, as the front of the tent was thrown open and the magistrate, general, and guards marched in.

Walking immediately to where she sat, the magistrate stood over her quiet form. Bending, he held a hand to her.

"Come, my dear."

Naomi hesitated a moment, unsure if this was a trap.

His voice firmer, the magistrate again said, "Come."

Naomi blinked, and without raising her gaze, she placed her hand in his. When he pulled her to her feet, she allowed it but didn't rise on her own. The magistrate ran another fingernail over her jaw and said, "Wake, my dear. It's time for you to return."

Naomi blinked and then blinked again. Looking up into the magistrate's eyes, and with a small squeal, she jumped back, overturning a small table, earning a chuckle from the man.

He spun, his cloak flowing out around him. He ordered the guards to take her back to her tent. Naomi went with them willingly, her mind spinning with the information garnered from the map.

Back at the fire, her stew cold and coagulated, Naomi pondered her situation. She knew where they were heading, but not why. She had to assume that the fortress was their destination as marked on the map. Was this the location of the talisman? What if she could escape? Escape and make her way to that location before the army reached it. If she could get the object, she could make her way to Darklin Vale and meet up with her friends. Then, they could free Paxton Re.

But first, she had to free herself.

*****

The next day, it seemed as if every time she looked up, it was to meet the eyes of the magistrate. Even in the bright light of day they seemed to glow from within. She would dip her head, looking away, which seemed to please him since when she peeked, a small smile quivered around the corners of his mouth.

That night, the same occurrence happened. She had just finished eating and the general appeared. Taking her into the heart of the encampment, he led her into the large tent of the magistrate.

She began to wonder about the magistrate. Who was he? How did he come to be in the position he was in? Did he learn his magic, or did it come naturally to him—and he chose to use it for evil purposes. Would he be necessary for her to claim the talisman?

These thoughts swirled in her mind as she sat in the corner of the tent. After that first night, the influence of the magistrate waned more and more. By the third night, she barely felt the sleeplike effects of his touch. Each night, again and again, he left her on her own within his tent. So often that she began to wonder if he was doing it on purpose. An effort to see what she could or would do. But each night, when he and the general and guard returned, he went through the motions of releasing her from his spell.

This night, she smiled to herself, feeling superior as she acted scared and confused upon waking. When the magistrate dropped in front of her, grasping her chin in his bony hand to peer into her eyes, she gulped and held her breath.

Could he decipher her thoughts? Had she acted and thought rashly?

But then the magistrate released her and rose, then walked to the map. The general still occupied his place by the drawing, looking down, studying the parchment.

"So, General." The magistrate joined him to study their plan. "We're almost to the beginning of the shale slide. From there, large boulders cover the ground to either side of the path into the mountains."

"Yes, Your Eminence. Not many have traveled beyond the boulder fields into the Yon Mountains. Fear holds many of them back."

"Fear," the magistrate spewed the word. "Fear is for small minds. There is nothing within the mountains to fear. And everything to gain. When we locate the talisman, we'll be the most powerful men in the land."

The general tilted his head to look at the man beside him. "Other than King Mallevorn, of course."

"Yes, yes, of course. Of course," the magistrate said with a chuckle. The opening to the tent flew open and two guards entered.

With a wave of his hand, the magistrate indicated Naomi. "Take her back to her tent." He barely glanced at her before returning to the map.

Naomi spent the next night and couple days wondering how to escape. She was always surrounded. Always watched. Sooner or later, there would come an opportunity. She just had to be ready.

CHAPTER THIRTY-SEVEN

The muffled sound of a cell door closing had Paxton Re opening his eyes. A day before, he and Naomi had been separated. He protested, but all he had gotten for his efforts was a lump on the head and several lost hours.

He knew Naomi had been in the cell across from him. He saw enough that first night before they threw him in here. Now, with the sounds outside his quarters, he held his breath and listened. He thought for a moment that he heard her voice, the timber and cadence different from others, but the walls and door were just too thick to know for sure.

From a small hole high on the wall of his cell, light filtered in, and he could just make out the parameters of his room. When the voices continued in the hall, Paxton Re rolled from the questionable comfort of the mat he had crawled to the night before and hurried to the door. At this motion, a splitting pain shot from the back of his head, over the top, to lodge itself above his eye. He clamped a hand to his eye but continued until he could lay an ear against the portal.

Now, the voices were gone.

Had he missed her? Was she still there or taken elsewhere?

This girl, this problem that had come to be his, had also come to mean something to him. It had been a long time since he had any family. He had been thrown out of what he had at a young age—been on his own for almost as long as he could recall. Friends were plentiful, but only for what he could get from them. This girl, this outlander, was different. She had wormed her way under his skin until he couldn't see where he stopped and she began.

And the others in their company. Willing to follow the girl. Willing to lay down their own safety to see her home. What had become of Adalard and Bob? And now he didn't even know where Naomi was.

Paxton Re looked across the span of his cell, the diffused light allowing him little visibility. How would he get out of here? He could do the girl no good if he was trapped in this prison.

When a scratch came on the door, he thought he must be imagining it. Then it came again. Softly, so softly.

"Paxton Re?" His name drifted up from the small opening at the bottom of the door—right where it met the ground.

Paxton Re dropped to his belly, his cheek pressed to the cold stone.

"Paxton Re?"

"Laina," Paxton Re whispered back. He heard shuffling and a scrape at the door. He was on his feet, stepping back from the portal when the key clicked in the lock. For a moment nothing happened and then with a grunt, the small elven girl pushed the door open.

Light from lanterns in the hallway spilled into his cell and over him, blinding him to everything but Laina backlit in the doorway.

"Come," she whispered to him. "We must be quick."

Not questioning her, not even stopping to think, the dwarf slid through the small opening. When Laina stopped to pull the door shut again, he leaned in to aid her. She locked the door and pocketed the key. On the floor lay two packs. Next to them lay a sword and short knife. Picking one pack up, she handed it to him. Paxton Re took it without question. When she picked up the second and then the weapons, he followed her down the hall and out of the prison.

Partway across an open inner field they heard voices, and the elven girl moved them back within the shadows of a building. Two guards passed within touching distance, and for a heart-stopping moment, Paxton Re thought they were caught. But the two moved on through the night, continuing their conversation about what they might eat in the barracks to break their fast.

As soon as the soldiers turned a corner, Laina and Paxton Re were again on the move. Though Paxton Re followed the elven girl without protest, it soon looked to him as though she had led them into a blind alley. He was about to protest, perhaps give her some aid, when she stopped and reached into a bramble. An audible click caught the dwarf's attention, and when the girl stepped through the bushes, he followed her.

Outside the fortress wall, Laina closed the small door they had walked through.

"Come, quickly," she whispered. "It'll be morning soon, and we need to be away."

*****

An hour later, halfway up a hillside, Laina paused and pulled out a container of water. She took a swallow and then handed it to the dwarf. After he drank, she put the flask back in her bundle, shouldered the pack, and again headed out.

"Laina."

She glanced back but kept up her pace. "We have to be on the other side of this hill before the sun breaks," she said. "We're too visible here." Paxton Re gave a nod, readjusted his pack, and hustled to catch her.

Laina and Paxton Re were well away from the city, the sun almost at its apex, when she finally stopped and turned to the dwarf.

"We need to get Naomi back," she stated.

Paxton Re stared for a moment, sure what he was about to say was obvious, but not knowing how else to put it. "Don't you think we should be following her then?"

Laina nodded, but she put up her hands in a consoling gesture. "Yes. I understand what you're saying. But I'm sure I know where they're going—at least the first part of their journey." She paced away from the dwarf and then back again, her agitation evident. "We'll catch them before they get too far, and we'll free Naomi."

"Well, what are we waiting for?"

Laina's brows drew together. "You mean . . . you mean, you trust me?"

A sharp response quivered on the dwarf's tongue, but undermining the girl's confidence wouldn't do either of them any good, so he crushed his first impulse and softened his tone. "Of course I trust you, girl. This is your land after all. You brought us here, and I'm sure you'll be able to get us out of this mess."

Laina took him at his word, and smiling, she patted him on the arm.

"So?" He indicated the way they had been heading.

Laina looked that way and then, with a tip of her head, she looked back at him.

"Should we be going?" he prompted.

"Oh. Yes, yes." The elven girl stumbled forward a step or two. Getting her bearings, she turned to smile at Paxton Re and then hurried in the direction they had been heading.

Paxton Re gave a sigh and shook his head, but he followed the girl into the noon sun hoping he knew what he was doing—and that she did, too.

They hadn't gone too much farther when he called out to her.

"Do you know what this talisman is that the king thinks Naomi can get for him?"

"Yes." She led the dwarf to a shady tree with a log lying

beneath it. "Let's sit for a moment and have some food. We can talk."

Paxton Re slid the bag from his back and sat on the log beside her. When he opened his pack, he was pleased to see provisions. Enough for a few days.

"The talisman," Laina began, "is an old story. It's the kind that is told around campfires or alehouses. No one knows what it looks like or exactly how it works, but it's supposed to be eons old—formed back before there were even elves to covet it. And it's supposed to have immeasurable power, but I've never heard what it could actually do."

"So, it's a fairytale," he said with a shake of his head.

"Maybe," she agreed. "But then, maybe not."

"Why do you say that? It sounds as though no one has even seen the thing."

"Well, that's true enough. But do you think the tales would have survived so long if there wasn't some degree of truth to them? I don't know what my cousin wants with it, but I bet it really exists. I bet whatever it does, it's powerful."

"We'll need to get to it before that magistrate does. No one will be safe if that one has his way. But first, we need to locate and free Naomi. Answer me something." Paxton Re took a bite of jerky from his pack.

"Yes," Laina prompted him when he didn't continue.

After repacking his provisions, Paxton Re secured the tie on his pack. "What is with the staff? Why did it disappear and then the vine appeared on Naomi's skin?"

"The Bloodline."

"What in the world is that?"

"It, too, is an old story. Let's find Naomi and then we can all discuss it."

CHAPTER THIRTY-EIGHT

One day, Naomi's fortune changed, and she wasn't even watching for it.

They were partway through the day, stopping to take a small break and get some fresh water from a nearby stream, when Naomi heard a shout. Raising her head, she looked in the general direction and then went back to sharpening a blade she had been given. When another shout came, she stood, slipping the knife into a scabbard at her waist. A wind blew through the camp from the mountains, bringing with it a harsh smell. And as she watched, a ripple seemed to move through the camp. Curious, not yet concerned, she glanced at the soldier who traveled with her. He, too, was looking into the camp toward the mountains.

A scream traveled to them on the wind, and caravans began shifting and tumbling over as though thrown by a huge hand. Men scattered all around her and Naomi stood spellbound, watching the tumult move toward her. As it neared, she knew in her brain that she should move, but she was frozen, unable to make her body respond. A wagon flew toward her, but a hand grabbed her shoulder and pulled her out of its path.

She landed hard on the ground, the wind knocked from her. Twisting, she rolled to see the soldier behind her, his neck impaled by a joist from one of the wagons. Quickly squatting beside him, she pulled his short sword from its strap. Turning it in her hand with the blade pointed downward, she leaped over his body and fled into the boulder field beyond the caravan.

People ran all around her. Soldiers. Trappers. Seeing no magic wielders, Naomi stopped and looked back. Where were the magic wielders? In the distance, beyond large boulders and sparce trees, the sounds of battle still raged. Booms, crashes, and the occasional scream colored the air.

Now curious more than frightened, Naomi made a large circuit of the area and came at the roadway behind the disturbance. A long, deep gouge disrupted the path, with turned-over wagons on either side. Farther down the road, out of sight beyond a small hill, a grove of trees had toppled. Stretching her neck, Naomi scanned the area, sensitive to changes. She was ready to bolt, could feel her body already turning to flee, as she took a tentative step forward. The shouting of men drew her on, her eyes jumping back and forth, ever watchful for danger.

When she crested the hill and looked down, her mind went blank, and she couldn't move. At the base of the hill, amid the wreckage of overturned wagons and slaughtered livestock and men, lay the carcass of what she first thought was a huge worm. Step by step she advanced down the hill. Step by step she got closer to something she thought she would only see in a horror movie.

When it shifted and rolled, she jumped back brandishing the sword, only to realize it was the magic wielders who moved the thing. And now she saw it wasn't a worm, exactly. On its belly were hundreds, if not thousands, of small, segmented legs. Occasionally, one would flick and the entire complement of men, her included, would jump back.

Someone stood just behind her. She turned to see another magic wielder—obvious by his long cloak.

"What is it?" she asked.

"A borgie."

"Borgie," she repeated.

"Old magic," the man whispered.

Now, Naomi turned fully to the other. "What do you mean by old magic?"

Seeming to realize what he had said and whom he had said it to, the magic wielder turned from her to circle the borgie. Naomi followed close on his heels.

On the downhill side of the borgie, a group of men gathered, mostly magic wielders. There were spears sticking out of the creature's flesh like porcupine quills. A yellow, sour secretion ran down its skin from each of the holes. Naomi pursed her lips, her nose crinkling at the smell.

Two uniformed men stood to one side, discussing how to move the carcass, and barring that, how to get the caravan back up and running and around the creature.

Naomi stared, fascinated and appalled by the destruction. Soldiers hustled past her, their attention solely on getting the carcass of the borgie moved and getting the caravan again on its way.

For a time, Naomi watched them work. When she became aware of a nagging in her mind, she first ignored it, enthralled by the dismantling of the remains. When the tickling became more troublesome, she paused her thoughts of the borgie to listen to her inner voice. Eyes widening imperceptibly, Naomi glanced around. No one paid her any attention.

No one paid her any attention.

Naomi stepped back. This was her chance. She may not get another one. She needed to take this one and act.

When she reached the edge of the boulder field, she slid between two giant rocks. She took deep breaths, calming herself and trying to get her thoughts in order.

Could she risk going back into camp to get her things? Some rations? Even a water flask? She decided quickly that another chance like this wasn't likely to come again. She needed to take advantage of it and get gone before someone came looking for her.

Above the boulder field, a sparce forest of trees began. Glancing up the hill, the long shadows showed how late in the day it had become. Naomi was no outdoorswoman. She had grown up in the suburbs of a large city and then moved into the city as an adult. The most she knew of the wilds was the large park within the sprawl of urban. But, if she could get far enough away by night, she was sure she would lose anyone who tracked her.

Water would be her greatest challenge, but just days ago they had stopped by a large river and filled their water canisters. That water was flowing down out of the mountains. That same water shouldn't be too hard to find.

Keeping low, boulders between her and the complement of men who worked to clear the road, Naomi kept up a steady pace. Once they got the camp packed up and the way clear, the detachment would continue up the path into the mountains. She needed to be away from that area before someone realized she was missing.

When she cleared the boulders, she moved through the sparce undergrowth and the occasional tree. She glanced over her shoulder every so often, certain each time that she would see soldiers rushing up behind her. Each time there was no one, she was relieved and worried that she was missing something. Were they circling around her and would be waiting at the rise of the hill? Perhaps she should have continued farther across the field of stones. Maybe come toward the valley beyond from a different direction.

Looking once more behind her, Naomi took a deep breath. Short of circling around and getting farther to the north, she just needed to continue the track she was traveling. At least the ground was rocky, and she didn't think she would be very easy to track. But really, that was just wishful thinking. She knew next to nothing about tracking. With a mental shrug, she put her concerns in the back of her mind and hurried on.

*****

Night had fallen by the time Naomi stopped to rest. Pushing north, it was a couple of hours before she heard rushing water. By then, she was beyond simple thirst. When she saw the river, she broke into a run. Dropping to her knees on the bank, she scooped handfuls of water down her throat. Freezing, coming straight from the snowpacks, her hands felt numb in no time, and still she continued to drink.

Finally, thirst momentarily quenched, she sat back on her haunches and surveyed her surroundings. More trees and scrub foliage grew around the edges of the river. Too far and too fast to cross, she couldn't put the river between herself and anyone who might be pursuing her. And if she walked along the bank with its cover, she was more likely to leave tracks in the softer soil. But she didn't want to lose sight of the river. It was the only water she had.

Knowing she needed to be up and moving, Naomi took a moment to rest and think back to the map. She needed to get to the object before the magistrate and his men. The object King Mallevorn claimed she needed to complete her quest to locate Darklin Vale and get back to her own world. For the first time, a nagging suspicion arose that perhaps the king was not as well-informed as he insisted. What did he really know about this talisman? Her only hope was that with it in her possession, she could force the king to release Paxton Re. And get them out of the land of elves. Instead of getting home, she seemed to be getting farther and farther away.

Naomi gave herself a mental shake, and with one last drink of the cool water, she was back on her feet and moving upstream toward the top of the mountain.

When she again tripped on loose rock, she finally admitted to herself that she needed to stop soon and get some rest. She was asleep on her feet, and before long, she was going to get hurt. There were no moons tonight, and that was a blessing and a curse. She was harder to track on a black night, but she was also at a disadvantage with no light. Everything appeared to her in shades of black and gray. Twice she had run into trees, the second time knocking her head into a branch.

Continuing to walk but keeping her eyes peeled for somewhere to get some sleep, Naomi almost missed the small opening in the side of the hill. When she stepped close to it, she squinted to see the opening clearly, and a stale scent of old water came to her.

This is as good as any, she thought and headed toward the cave with resolve. She planned to go into the cave just far enough for some cover. Taking her short sword in one hand and her knife in the other, she moved into the cave.

CHAPTER THIRTY-NINE

Bob woke up at the break of morning. The sun was just peeking over the horizon. Even early, he heard the clang of pots and the soft sound of women's voices.

He had been with the Tinkers for many days. They had accepted him readily enough. He was a hard worker, willing to do what was asked of him, and they were happy to have another able-bodied man who knew how to use a sword. Not everyone liked Tinkers. Some peoples and communities were downright hostile to them.

He was invited to share a caravan with one of the single men—Henivar—and they had become fast friends. He liked living with the Tinkers, but always in the back of his mind was the nagging image of Naomi. Where was she? Was she okay? Where were Paxton Re and Adalard? Did they survive the spiders' attack?

Just last night the talk around the fires was about the move to their summer haunts. North, the leader said. North for the summer months. It would be cooler there. They would travel, stopping at the small towns. They had wares to sell, and the communities enjoyed the entertainment they brought. They put on small plays and sung. And the whole while, some of them would steal from the unwary. They said it would be a profitable summer—it always was.

Bob sat silently, warm by a small fire, and listened as the plans were laid. The trip north would take him close to where he had lost his companions. It seemed the Tinkers were circling around on their travels. He thought maybe he would let them pass by that area. Maybe he would just stay with the Tinkers. But in the back of his mind there was always that tug, and Bob knew better. He knew he would watch for his chance. Watch for when he would step away from this life and back into the one he had before.

Now the Tinkers were breaking camp. Everyone had been fed, dishes cleaned, belongings packed. Horses were strapped to the caravans or saddled. A couple dogs ran between people and under animals and wagons, barking in the excitement of the move. Children ran after the dogs, squealing with the barks. Even with the strain of getting everything packed and moving, the adults were excited. Summer in the north was a good time for the Tinkers. A time of easy pickings, good weather, and rest.

Bob did his part in loading the wagons. He liked taking care of the team of horses that pulled their caravan. Tonight, he would give them a good brushing. Now he got them strapped into their braces and hooked to the wagon. Backing easily into the tack, the horses knew what was expected of them. With a final pat to the neck of one of the horses, Bob climbed aboard the seat of the colorful wagon. Henivar gave a crack of the reins, and leaning into their harnesses, the horses pulled the wagon forward.

The procession didn't stop until the sun had been down for hours. The leader, a large man with a booming voice, knew the way well and navigated with the stars and his memories. Bob helped build a firepit while the women fixed a quick, but filling, meal. Music began before dishes were taken away, and when someone broke into song, a couple began to dance.

Bob usually enjoyed the festive way the Tinkers lived. Each day was special and a gift. But tonight, he was unsettled. He rose from his spot by the fire and moved away from the crowd. Between and past two of the wagons, he moved into the grass field that surrounded the camping spot. He couldn't get Naomi out of his head. He never should have quit looking for her and the others. His failure was weighing on him more and more, and he couldn't shake the feeling that his friends were in danger.

He was certain that by the end of tomorrow, or maybe the next day, they would be in land familiar to him. There was no longer any confusion as to what he would do. He couldn't live with himself if he didn't find his lost companions. His only choice was to move on without the Tinkers when the time was right.

CHAPTER FORTY

Naomi splashed through another stagnant puddle of water on the floor of the cave. She had already moved in farther than she had planned, but worry over getting caught kept her hoping for a better hiding spot. The cave was long but narrow, and although she had no light to see, she kept her shoulder to a wall and moved forward. Her exploration was taking her time she didn't have as every step was a tentative feeling with her toe before putting her foot down. The last thing she needed to do was fall into a crater within the heart of the cave.

Time played with her. In the absolute dark, she didn't know if it was a minute or an hour. No sounds from outside the cave came to her, and the farther she went, the more lifeless the air became.

Finally, unable to go any farther—fear beginning to take hold of her—she sat, placing her back to one wall and her feet against the opposite side. The only belongings she had were the knife and short sword, and with one in each hand, she drifted off to sleep.

*****

Naomi jerked, her eyes popping open. She didn't know what woke her, and with no light, she didn't know what time it was or how long she had slept. She was exhausted and sore. The stone hadn't done anything for her muscles, which felt prone to cramping. And she was thirsty and starving. When her stomach rumbled loudly at the thought, she gave a wry grin and a small nod. She needed to find some food.

Naomi made her way back to her feet and began the arduous trek out of the cave. She had gone a few feet when a thought stopped her, giving her heart a jump.

Had she turned the correct way? Was she moving farther into the cave? Could she get lost in a cave that she thought was a straight path? Had she missed a turn off or two? Scaring herself, and beginning to panic, Naomi took a deep breath.

Think. When she walked into the cave, she had turned and put her shoulder to the wall. Getting up, she reversed that. Almost certain she was moving in the correct direction, Naomi continued slowly down the cave path.

When she saw the first faint light in the distance, she gave another sigh. That had to be where she had entered. Now, she just had to find something to eat.

Naomi stopped at the mouth to the cave. She listened. It wouldn't do to rush out and fall into a trap set by the magistrate. When all she heard was a soft whistle of wind, she moved slowly forward. Keeping her eyes open as the area outside the cave came into view, she was relieved to see she was alone. Without having to worry about an immediate capture, Naomi's stomach gave another growl.

"Yes, yes," she said under her breath. "I hear you."

"Who are you speaking to?"

With a gasp, Naomi spun around, her sword and knife raised. But there was no one behind her.

"Hello," she said, looking left and right, then turning in a complete circle. Deciding it must be delirium, she stood for a moment longer. Keeping her eyesight sharp, she moved away from the mouth of the cave. She remembered, from the night before, the general direction of the river. She needed to get some water. She had read once that a human could go weeks without food—though the physical exertion of being on the run would affect that—but she would be toast without water in a matter of days. Not for the first time, she wished for a container of some sort. If she could move away from the river, she would have a better chance of losing anyone who tracked her.

She heard water first and then a glint of morning sunshine off the stream caught her eye. Rushing forward, Naomi dropped to her knees on the riverbank. The cold water was as refreshing as she remembered from the day before. When she had her fill, she splashed water on her face and over her head. She was still feeling the effects from the night spent in the cave, and the crisp water did much to refresh her.

"Okay, Naomi," she said out loud. "What's your plan."

When someone giggled behind her, she spun, landing on her backside partially in the water. She swung her head looking for where the sound had come from, but once again she was alone.

"Hello!" she shouted, unnerved by sounds when she was obviously the only one here. She pushed to her knees and leaned forward to stretch her hands out into the space around her. Nothing. Dropping her hands and head, she gave a sigh.

"God, girl. You're losing your mind."

This time when the giggle came, she lifted her head, her jaw set.

"Who's there?"

Picking up the weapons she had dropped upon reaching the water, she stood, her fisted hands on her hips.

"Who are you?" she asked.

The giggle came from the side, and she spun to face it.

"You!" she shouted. "Come out. This isn't funny."

This time, the laughter came from the other side. She spun, hoping to see who mocked her.

"Damn it! Come out. Show yourself!" Naomi stomped her

foot, ready to begin throwing punches at the air. Just as she thought to make another demand, the air in front of her began to sparkle. When two large blue eyes appeared and then tilted as if studying her, she took a hurried step backward. Her foot met wet rock, and she fell back, flailing her arms. The being became fully visible, grabbing an arm to stop her fall, and it hauled her out of the stream.

Naomi pulled her arm free, jumping to the side. Keeping the apparition in front of her, she moved backward, the sword and knife at the ready.

"Whoa, whoa," she said, shaking her head. "Wha-what are you?" The being tracked her, moving forward every step she took back. Naomi stopped moving, then took a deep breath and a large swallow. The being shimmered in the morning sun. A variety of colors came off it. Yellows, lavenders, pinks. All soft hues and welcoming. The lines of its body were indistinct, as if in flux. It seemed as if the harder she tried to see its edges, the harder they were to capture.

"Hello," she said softly.

"Hello," the word came from the being, but no mouth opened to speak it.

"I'm Naomi." She touched her own chest.

"I'm Naomi," came from the presence.

"No, no." Naomi shook her head.

"No, no."

"No, wait." Naomi held up a hand.

"No, wait."

Naomi stopped taking. Placing her hands on her head, she tried to think of what to do. When the entity shifted, lifting appendages to its head, Naomi sighed. What in the world was this thing? And did it matter? She was sure this entire world was full of magical beings. She needed to get away from this area. Get to the fortress marked on the map in the magistrate's tent. Nothing else mattered. Nothing else could matter. This being was interesting, possibly dangerous, and she needed to stay focused.

Keep moving. Get to the fortress. Get the talisman.

Giving the being a last look, she continued her journey upriver. Once or twice, she looked back, but she appeared to be alone.

Naomi stopped often to take drinks from the river. It helped to keep her belly full and kept her energy level up. She knew that wouldn't last long. By tonight, tomorrow morning at the latest, she would feel weaker. She kept her eyes open for anything edible. When she came across a small growth of plants, she dropped to them and dug around the roots. Unearthing a few, she bit into one.

Spitting it out, she dropped the plant. Bitter. She washed her mouth out in the river. This was a whole new world. She didn't see plants like the ones Paxton Re had shown her. Without his knowledge, how could she make the decision of what was safe to eat?

The sun was past its zenith when Naomi stopped for a rest. She was failing faster than she thought she would. Though keeping her hydrated, the water no longer helped with her hunger. When was the last time she ate? Dinner the day before yesterday? Yes. That was it, and she hadn't had much. The magistrate had called her to him during her mealtime. She had no option but to go to him.

Finding a small shady spot at the base of a growth of scrub trees, she sat, shifting the sword in her belt to lay down her leg. She was just drifting off, not even realizing she was falling asleep, when the air began to sparkle in front of her.

Naomi watched as the apparition took its unstable form. It appeared to be kneeling, leaning forward to stare at her. Still in a partial doze, Naomi raised one hand, fingers extended to touch the aura of the being. When she encountered it, a small shiver shot up her arm and across her chest, making her catch her breath, but she didn't remove her fingers. She moved her gaze from the eyes of the being to where her fingertips met its face. When she couldn't see the first two knuckles of her fingers, she jumped. There was still the tingle, becoming constant now, from where they joined, but no pain. She felt no fear, just a curiosity.

The spirit didn't move, didn't come forward or shake off her touch, and after a time, Naomi dropped her arm to her lap. Her eyes closed, and the last thing she saw before falling asleep was the fading of the spirit.

* * * * *

She came awake with a hand on her arm, and before she even had her eyes open, she was being jerked to her feet. A complement of soldiers and trackers surrounded her. They ripped her weapons from her frame, dragged her forward, and shoved her to her knees. Naomi's gaze swung everywhere. When had they come upon her? How had she not woken? The noise was almost deafening. Men yelled at men, horses nickered and blew, rattling their tack. A large bird flew over, drawing Naomi's attention.

Why not? More the merrier.

An officer approached her, his higher rank obvious by his uniform. When he stopped and looked down at her, one of the soldiers grabbed a handful of her hair and wrenched her head around so she faced him. She couldn't help the grunt of pain that escaped her at his rough handling.

"So, this is the girl that's caused so much commotion." He kneeled to look her face-to-face. Taking her chin tightly between his finger and thumb, he said, "Not so dangerous, are you?"

Naomi's eyes shifted from his to just behind him. The air shimmered, seeming to vibrate. When the entity moved, Naomi barely had time to shut her eyes. At the screams, her hair was released. She tucked into herself, forehead to the ground, and waited for the pain. As abruptly as they began, the shrieks ended. Lifting her head and then straightening her body, Naomi surveyed the carnage. Piles of ash surrounded her. Some still resembled curled bodies, but even now the breeze was blowing them away.

Naomi tried to stand, but at first, she couldn't get her shaking legs to respond.

She was all alone. Just the sound of the wind and her breathing were evident. In the distance came the scream of the raptor as it hunted.

Pushing to her feet, she steadied herself and took a large step over the officer's remains. When she spun in a circle, she heard a soft nicker and moved beyond the trees to find one of the horses. All the rest had either run off or been destroyed.

Naomi walked to the horse, speaking gently. She placed a palm to its nose and had to smile when the animal blew out its breath into her hand. This would make travel quicker. Had the entity meant to leave her a horse or was it just luck? It really didn't matter. The horse was welcome. Walking down the body of the animal, Naomi ran her hand down the beast's neck, over a rudimentary saddle, and to a loaded pack slung across the back of the saddle. For a moment, she kept her hand on the pack, hopes swirling in her mind. With a deep breath, she opened the top and reached inside. She pulled out packages of food—all wrapped for travel in water-resistant fabrics. Dried meats and vegetables, breads—even a package of some unknown substance. When she took a bite of it, she found it was sweet and chewy. After a couple more bites, she rewrapped it and placed it back within the pack.

Keeping her hand on the hind end of the horse, Naomi circled to its other side. The pack on this side was also full, and in front of it was a skin full to the brim. She uncorked it and brought it to her lips, pleased to taste fresh water. Suddenly, the success of getting to the fortress looked a lot more certain.

Naomi strapped the flask back onto the saddle and continued her circle around the equine, this time ducking under its neck. Careful to avoid stepping on any of the quickly disappearing ashes, she made her way back to where she had slept. She retrieved her weapons, sliding first the knife and then the short sword into her belt. She needed to hurry. It was imperative she get to the fortress before the magistrate and his army. She needed to find the talisman to be in a bargaining position to get Paxton Re back.

Mounting the horse, Naomi leaned forward to whisper soft words to the animal. Its ears twitched and turned in her direction before it lifted and dropped its head twice. Directing the mare uphill to follow the river, Naomi gave a soft thank you to the spirit. She scanned behind her but saw no one.

CHAPTER FORTY-ONE

The magistrate raged. Just this evening a trapper had made his way back into camp. He had been with the expedition trailing the woman. He had been out hunting, coming back only in time to see the captive erupt in a swirling, shiny pulse of light and motion, frying everything within a short distance. Scared, uncertain what he should do, the man had hustled back to find the main camp.

What weapon had she gotten ahold of in the short time she had been gone? Mere days and she had wiped out a full complement of men. Something else was at work here. He must find out what it was, and a way of reclaiming the woman. He might even be able to take control of the weapon.

With this thought, the magistrate stopped his furious pacing, his mind turning.

Yes, he thought. With this new deadly weapon, he would be unstoppable. Not even King Mallevorn or—dare he speak it?—Charmot could stop him. He would be the most powerful person in the world.

With a smile on his lips—a smile that had men he passed more worried than his rages—he moved slowly back to his tent.

CHAPTER FORTY-TWO

Adalard looked back the way he had come. Far below him lay the base of the valley, and above that a large stretch of treed area. He had crossed above the tree line and into the snow sometime in the past night. It was cold now, but the cold had never bothered him. His dense coat kept him comfortable even in the bitterest of weather, and just to be certain, he had acquired a heavy cape that covered him from head to foot.

He didn't know where he was going. He had lost Naomi's scent some miles back, but something within kept him going. He was just following a sense, a pull that kept him moving first toward the mountains and then into them. He hadn't stopped long enough to question his decision to let this instinct guide him. He just went with it.

The whipping of snow pulled at his cloak, causing it to billow out behind him until he grabbed it and brought it back around his body. The storm was picking up. He would need to find shelter soon or commit to traveling through the worst of the tempest. And it looked to be severe. Where first the sky filled with black clouds, now they were gray and heavy—swirling with fury. The wind's howl hurt his ears.

Step by slow step, Adalard made his way farther into the storm. The snow was thigh-deep and grew deeper by the minute. When he crested the top of a hill and looked down into the next pass, it was to see mountains rising beyond it, layer upon layer of snow-covered crags. If only he could get to the other side of the pass. Get to higher ground beyond the edge of the next mountain range.

A sudden gust of wind hit him, almost driving him to his knees, and he moved resolutely forward.

Adalard was pushing through snow chest-deep by the time he scaled the next rise. Darkness had almost fallen, and he was preparing himself to continue when he saw the jumble of large rocks. At some time in the distant past, there had been a massive rockslide creating a rock pile like some giant's house of bricks. He moved to them and then between them where the drop in the wind's fury was obvious and welcome.

Adalard pushed forward, able to turn corners and put more space between him and the storm. Coming up against the final rock, unable to go beyond this space, he pulled the cloak around his form. Adalard sat with his back to one of the walls and attempted to find sleep.

*****

The quiet woke him, a soft, insulated sound as if he were removed from the world outside his haven. He didn't know how long he had been in this cocoon of stone, but at least he had found some rest. Even in sleep, the instinct had pulled at him to up and away, and now that the storm had ended, he was anxious to be gone. He shook out the cloak and made his way back through the halls of stone to the entrance. When he got to where he thought the exit should be, he faced a wall of white. He was snowed in.

Adalard arched his hands, claws extended, and began the arduous task of digging himself out of this snow and stone coffin.

By the time he broke through the barrier, the sun was at its apex and streamed through the gap he created. Encouraged, he doubled his efforts and soon had an opening large enough for his big body to pass through. He walked to the path, leaving his tomb behind, only to realize the path along the mountain had been swept away during the night. An avalanche, he thought. For the entire side of the mountain to be gone, it must be an avalanche. He glanced back at the stone he had just come from and knew he had been lucky. The crash of snow, ice, and rock could easily have taken him with it.

He scanned the area, looking for a way ahead, but the passage through the mountains was gone. Adalard knew he could go back. Could forget the girl and the quest. Forget that Maude had charged him with aiding Naomi. When he turned to again look at the chasm where the path was, his eyes were drawn to the mountainside that had been scrubbed clean by the avalanche. It was almost completely vertical. Parts of it had an appearance of curving outward.

Adalard exhaled steaming white vapor. He would continue where he was led or die trying. He stepped to the wall of stone and looked up. Distending claws on all four appendages, he dug in with his hands and feet. Over and over, he pulled one from the rock and ice and then another to plant them higher and higher in the wall.

Only once did he look back and down. The world seemed small and very far away. For a moment, he wallowed in the peace of it.

When the ache and pull at his shoulders intruded, Adalard again began to climb.

He pulled himself over the edge of the wall, panting and straining to get his body over. With the passing of the storm the previous night, the sky was clear, the stars bright. In their light he could see the mountain range before him, the light reflecting off their snowcaps. Rolling to his back, he worked to quiet his breathing and still his heart. His claws retracted and his digits bloody, the werebeast centered his thoughts. Almost immediately he felt a pull, like a silken cord around his chest. He rose to his feet, and step by plodding step, he continued his hunt for the girl.

CHAPTER FORTY-THREE

Paxton Re sat across a fire from Laina. They had been traveling for days, and he was more lost than he had been at the beginning. She assured him she knew exactly where they were and that their travels were taking them where she thought they would bisect the trail the magistrate traveled. At that point, they would be able to rescue Naomi.

Paxton Re had his doubts. Just this morning, Laina had stood at an intersection of rivers. She had studied the different directions, even turning to look back the way they had come. When he questioned her, she had given him a large, toothy grin and, indicating one of the ways, began again to walk. He had followed, having nowhere else to go, but worried just the same.

Would he ever see Naomi again? How could he come to her aid if they couldn't locate her?

Distrustful by nature, Paxton Re kept his suspicions to himself but watched closely.

"How much farther do you think?" he asked across the flames.

Laina leaned to the side to better see him and gave a shrug. "It shouldn't be too much longer." When she stood and made her way to sit beside the dwarf, he watched her. "I had thought we'd see them by now. Something must have slowed them down."

"Naomi?"

"Maybe. Maybe not." She gave another shrug. "It's hard to say. There are plenty of dangers out in these lands that could have gotten in their way."

Paxton Re's brows drew together. "A group that large? Doesn't seem like there'd be much that would slow them down."

"You'd be surprised," she muttered. "If we don't see evidence of them tomorrow, we'll track back the way they should be coming. See if we can locate them."

Paxton Re nodded his agreement, but his mind was spinning. Could this be an elaborate trap? But to what end? He had already been a prisoner.

"Let's get some rest," the girl offered. "We can be up and moving early tomorrow."

Paxton Re gave a grunt of acknowledgment and stood. Gathering his belongings, he wrapped himself in his cloak and lay down, his back to the fire. He heard Laina following his suit, and judging by her breathing, she drifted quickly into slumber. Paxton Re lay as though asleep, but it was late in the night before he found it.

*****

They traveled for some time the next day before they saw the devastation of the attack upon the army. Slowing, Laina and Paxton Re approached the area hidden from the camp by staying behind closer and closer hiding spots.

What had happened here? Paxton Re thought.

Almost as if she'd heard his thoughts, Laina whispered, "A borgie."

"What's a borgie?"

"It's a large scavenger. A type of insect."

Paxton Re studied the single track scooped out of the land. He laid his hand on the torn-up ground. "Must be a pretty big bug."

"Yes," Laina answered. "They can grow to enormous sizes." As the girl spoke, she walked through the destruction. Stopping occasionally, she eyed pieces of wagons and where dried blood made black splotches on the ground. Large areas were covered by a chalky substance.

Touching one of these with her fingertips, she said, "Looks like they cut up the borgie. Maybe to make room for them to get through." When she continued through to an overlook, Paxton Re followed her.

Laina peered down the incline and then stepped back. "Yep. They dumped it down there."

Paxton Re stepped forward and looked. At the bottom of the defile lay pieces and parts of what once was a large insect. If she hadn't told him what it was, he never would have been able to identify it. Large fleshy parts, mostly dried up, flaked off in the breeze. More of that yellowish substance stained the area all around the carcass.

Laina turned away and walked again through the area.

"Must be what slowed them down. That's why we came out ahead of them and didn't see evidence that they'd passed. Why we had to double back to find them. But they must have taken a different route than we were on."

"Can you tell how long it's been since they were here?"

"Days, maybe," she said, shielding her eyes to look around them. "They're leaving a trail, with so many men, so following them won't be a problem."

"Well, enough of this delay. We should have been trailing them in the first place."

Laina spun around to stare at the dwarf, her eyes showing her hurt at his words.

Paxton Re didn't like the feelings her expression brought to his chest. "I told you from the beginning we should be following them."

"I did what I thought was right," she responded.

"Well, now. Here we are. Trailing them anyway."

"Right," she said and turned from him to continue on their way. "And aren't you the smart one."

Paxton Re didn't do more than grunt at her words. At least now he knew they were on the right trail. He could follow it plainly on his own. Now finally, they would get to Naomi and be back on their quest to get her home.

* * * * *

That first day, they didn't come within sight of the large complement of men, but on the second, they heard them. Footfalls and voices, even low voices, of so many carried through the wilds. Laina and Paxton Re caught them by nightfall. The troops were finishing their evening meals and bedding down when the duo snuck closer.

Coming in from the dark toward an area lit by multiple small fires, they were almost invisible to the guards who paced around the camp. Getting closer and closer, the two waited for the watch to pass their area and then moved in. They located an area full of tack and hunkered down.

The camp was a busy place with people coming and going. Animals were led past. Food trays taken into tents and retrieved when empty. Soldiers came and went. Repairing weapons, gathering fuel for the many fires, and keeping watch. Paxton Re and Laina ducked down often when soldiers got too close, and once, they thought they had been seen, but the watch passed them by.

They kept their ears open. As things slowed down, most of the units finding their beds, two soldiers passed the tack area, their conversation catching Paxton Re's interest.

"How much longer do you think we'll chase her?"

"As long as it takes," the second answered, glancing around as if afraid of being caught discussing something that wasn't his business.

"Seems like we've been out here for ages now."

"I wouldn't worry about it. Just keep to your job and you won't be gettin' in any trouble."

The first nodded his agreement but didn't stop the conversation. "I'm wondering how the wife and kids are doing with me being gone. You know my children are young. Everything will fall to my wife now. All the chores I'm not there to do."

At his words, the second soldier grabbed his friend's arm, whipping him about. "You listen to me," he hissed, "and you listen good. All you're doin' is worrying yourself to no end. You're here to do a job, and you'll be here until the job is done. Quit worrying about your family and start thinking about what's gonna happen if someone hears you complainin'. The girl will be found when she's found. That's for the magistrate and officers to worry about." When his friend nodded, his eyes downcast, the second soldier put a hand on his friend's shoulder. "Go and get your stuff. We'll find a nice warm fire to bed down next to. You watch—this'll all be over before you know it."

At his words of encouragement, the first soldier's head came up, and his anxious eyes met the others. "Do you really think so?"

"I know so." The other nodded and sent his friend off. He shook his head. "Silly sot. Gonna get us both dead if he don't watch out." With those words, the soldier headed to the center of the camp.

Paxton Re looked at Laina. Her eyes were wide in amazement.

"Sounds like Naomi got away on her own," he whispered.

"Yes." She nodded. "But where did she go? It sounds like they've been after her."

"We need to locate the magistrate's tent."

"What?" she practically yelled and partially stood. Paxton Re gestured her to sit back down, but she didn't lose any of her intensity as she leaned forward and got in his face.

"What do you mean find his tent?" she hissed. "Are you trying to get us killed?"

"No but listen to me. There must be something in his tent that will give us an indication of which way she went. And why."

"Great," she said, sitting back on her haunches. "How do you propose that we not only locate the tent, but enter and search it?"

"How about this." He sat forward, now invading her space. "We steal cloaks from two of the soldiers. They've been walking by us for hours, and I couldn't tell you what any of them look like, they're so covered up. We will be able to wander about freely within the camp."

"I don't think it will work," she said with a shake of her head. "I'm sure to be recognized. And, well I'm sorry, but you're short." When Paxton Re simply looked at her, she added, "Far shorter than any elf. You'll be noticed."

"Give me another idea, or I'm going to go with this one."

"I don't have another idea." Taking a deep breath Laina said, "But I think you should stay here. I can keep my hood up, especially since it's night and chilly. I'm less likely to be noticed. I'll find something and then come back and get you."

"No." He shook his head. "It was my idea. It's not right for you to take all the risk."

"Well, you're going to have to deal with it. Wandering around this camp isn't something you can do. Even cloaked."

Paxton Re stared at her for a long moment. Finally, he nodded and sat back. "All right. You go. Find the magistrate's tent. Find some information as to where Naomi went. Come and get me and we'll be away."

"All right. You stay here."

Before he could say more, the elven girl was gone.

Laina found a cloak easily enough. They were lying all around the camp, thrown over armaments or laid out for soldiers ready for bed. The camp, though busy, was coming down for the night hours. She wandered about freely. No one noticed her either because they didn't know to look, or because they couldn't imagine anyone would have the guts to be in their camp.

When she saw the large tent in the middle of the camp, by

itself, she knew this must be where the magistrate slept—if he slept.

Laina leaned against the nearest tent. She watched, and when no one was coming, she stepped out. Her plan was to hurry across the open area, stopping only when she reached the main tent. Just as she straightened and made to step away from her concealment, a group of soldiers turned to the large tent.

"Think he's in it?" one of them asked the others.

"Didn't see 'im leave, and I've been guardin' this here tent most of the day."

"That don't mean nothing." He slapped the one soldier on the shoulder. "I've seen you guardin' with your eyes closed and your mouth open."

Offended, his friend slapped his hand away. "What you mean? I'm a good guard."

The entire group agreed with him by nodding their heads, but they looked at each other through the sides of their eyes and smiled behind the soldier's back.

"Well, I am," he insisted.

"Yes, yes. Of course, you are," his friend agreed. "You're the best tent guarder in the whole army."

The men jostled each other, moving past the main tent and into the body of the camp. Laina watched them go, sure that now would be her chance. She again made to step away from the relative comfort of her concealment when a large voice came from within the main tent. With a hustled footstep, she moved backward. Crouching, she watched from her hiding spot.

The doorway of the large tent was thrown open, a drape flung up and over the entrance. Laina peered into the darkness, not sure who was there. She had watched the tent for some time and hadn't seen anyone coming or going. She hadn't seen or heard any motion within and had been certain it was empty. Now, here was the first evidence that someone was there. But where had they come from?

The voice was joined by another, and the two came closer to

the opening. When he spoke, Laina recognized the voice of the magistrate.

"I am doing all I can. Tell your master that."

When another answered, the hair on Laina's neck stood on end and a shiver passed down her back.

"My master knows all." The voice was so low, Laina took a step forward, intent on hearing what was said. "I tell him nothing. He tells me, and he tells you. And what he tells me is to locate the girl. She will be the key to all he desires."

"Yes, yes." And now she saw the magistrate's silhouette. "I know where she's heading. We're on her tail and will have her any time now. Please, tell him that."

Something was off with the magistrate, but Laina couldn't tell what. She moved a step closer.

"My master already knows the words that come from your mouth before you speak them. If you want to live, show your value, and get the girl."

"Of course, of course."

Laina watched incredulously as the magistrate genuflected before the stranger. Her breath caught in her throat. Laina never thought she would see the day that the magistrate humbled himself before anyone.

From behind her Laina heard a noise and she hustled back to her hiding spot. When she again looked toward the opening, both men were gone. She couldn't go into the magistrate's quarters now. Not now that she had seen him there. She would have to stay hidden and, when he left, sneak in and look for clues to Naomi's location.

The girl huddled down against the neighboring shelter behind some tack and other belongings that lay there. She watched the large tent through the night, and when her eyes grew tired and grainy, she ignored it. When she fell asleep, it was as if the Land of Nod had crept up and sprinkled sleeping dust.

*****

When a foot landed on her backside, Laina jumped and came quickly to her feet only to be confronted by a young elf.

"What are you doing sleeping here? Ya trying to get out of your work?"

Laina quickly realized he had mistaken her for one of the troops in their camp and not as an outsider. She straightened her tunic and weapons, slicked down her hair, and tried to look contrite.

"I'm sorry, I am."

"As you should be." The elf looked around them. "No harm done. Get back to your unit and get packed up. Word is we're leavin' right soon."

"Thank you." She tipped her head to him. "Thank you, I'll do that." She hustled off into the camp, pulling her hood over her head to cover her face.

Laina berated herself for falling asleep as she walked across the camp and then took a wide turn to make her way back to the center tent. As she neared it, she slowed, keeping an eye open for the young elf. Wouldn't do to get caught back here. She was sure he would make more of it if he found her by the magistrate's shelter again.

Hanging out on the far side of the tent, Laina helped a trio of soldiers load up their wagon all the while keeping an eye on the entrance. When the magistrate, cloak flowing from him with the speed of his walk, left trailed by three attendants, Laina decided this was her chance.

She slipped away while the soldiers were lifting a heavy crate, making sure they were focused on what they were doing and not on her. She slipped behind the large tent. After wiggling a stake for a moment, she pulled it out of the ground. She lay in the dirt, worming herself under the edge of the canvas.

Inside it was almost completely dark. A filtered light made its way in by a crack in the canvas to the side of the exit. Laina crouched at the edge of the room and waited for her eyesight to adjust.

The first thing she saw was a large table occupying a place of importance in the middle of the space. Beyond the table was a sleeping pallet—so he did sleep after all—and a large chest she assumed held personal articles.

Making her way to the table, she studied the design. She knew this land and easily recognized the Yon Mountains. She had been to their base many times on hunting trips but never had a reason to venture into them. Her gaze locked on an image set in the middle of the mountains. It appeared to be a depiction of a castle, or fortress of some sort.

Was this where Naomi was heading? Was this where the talisman was located? She wished Paxton Re were here with her. His different perspective may offer answers to some of the questions rolling around in her head.

She walked around the map, looking at it from different angles. She noted a couple areas of interest. Perhaps geological formations that would lead them to their goal. She would talk to Paxton Re about it, but none of it changed her mind. The area marked in the center of the map. The area with the structure upon it. That was where they needed to go.

CHAPTER FORTY-FOUR

Naomi stopped after a couple hours, not only to allow the horse a drink and the chance to forage for some grasses, but to walk for a bit so the blood could return to her backside.

She had ridden before. Had a best friend who kept horses stabled and occasionally they'd ride together, but she had forgotten the toll it took on your body if you weren't used to it. Stretching, she arched her back and then stepped forward to do a few lunges across a particularly grassy area where the horse grazed.

She had been looking for a distinctive outcropping of rocks in the distance. A marker from the map. If distances were true on the chart, she should be able to locate it anytime now.

Leaving the horse to graze, Naomi walked away a short distance. She was just short of a crest in the land and she jogged to the apex. What she saw caught her breath. On the other side of a small gully was a stone edifice with a cluster of trees growing out of the top. There didn't appear to be room for all the foliage. It seemed that each tree would tumble off in a strong breeze, but there they were. Had she come to the gully from a different angle, she might have missed it entirely. She propped one hand on her hip and the other shaded her gaze.

"Looks like a damn rooster," she muttered. When she had

seen the image of a chicken on the map, an image drawn as if by a child's hand, she had almost discounted it. But there it was. It relieved a lot of the tension in her shoulders to realize she was on the right track. Turning away from the gully, she looked down the hill and watched the horse calmly clipping at the grasses.

The horse had been a godsend. The more she thought about it, the more she was certain the shimmering entity had left it for her.

"Hello," she called, not really expecting an answer, but curious if it was still with her. When the day remained still, she gave a shrug and headed back to the horse. She remounted and, with a little kick, had the horse trotting up the incline.

When she and the horse crested the hill, she was amazed anew at how the rock and trees resembled a rooster. Now, as she neared the stone marker, she lost sight of the image of a rooster and was reminded how luck had played a part in her noticing this point on the map.

The closer she got, the more obvious the deterioration of the stone was. It appeared that what once was an entrance into the mountains was now just a jumble of rocks. The tree roots were breaking it down until soon there wouldn't be anything here.

Seeing the map within the tent now in her mind, Naomi turned the mare so that the setting sun was on her left. They continued down the gully until its gradual turn had them going the wrong way. Dismounting the horse, Naomi kept a rein in her hand as she made her way up the rocky bank. Once near the top, the mare broke into a trot, pulling the rein loose.

"Hey, wait!" she yelled, but the mare crested the top and disappeared. Making her way over the rise, Naomi was relieved to see the mare not too far away, once again grazing on a clump of green grasses.

Naomi squinted into the setting sun. This was as good a place as any to spend the night. She removed the mare's saddle and, with a rope she found within the saddlebags, did a quick hobble on the animal. She didn't seem prone to wander, but Naomi would rather not lose her.

*****

The mare's nicker brought Naomi awake when the sun had yet to rise. She lay still, listening for more, unsure why she had woken.

When the horse grew agitated, stomping and giving a higher, shriller call, Naomi rose and went to her. Obviously, something was disturbing her. Petting down the mare's neck, Naomi laid her forehead to hers.

"That's a girl," she crooned to her companion. "That's a good girl. What's bothering you?"

As if understanding, the horse threw her head and gave a high-pitched call. Seeming almost in answer, a howl sounded in the night. A second and third called from different areas of the mountain.

"Oh, hell," Naomi said as the horse stomped her foot and again threw her head. This was not a good situation. A fire would be helpful, but Naomi knew she didn't have the time to find fuel and start a fire big enough to dissuade wolves from attacking. If she was smart, she would grab what she could and leave the horse to her fate, making her escape while the canines were occupied. Just the thought of that turned her stomach. She wasn't overly fanciful or thinking there was a good way she and the mare would survive this, but she just couldn't sacrifice the animal that had been true to her, aiding her in her quest. One thing they could do, at least try, was to take flight. It was possible that they could escape the net the wolves were setting.

Leaving the saddle, Naomi grabbed the sacks, not only for their foodstuffs, but for anything else that may be useful, so she didn't feel she was leaving everything behind. Quickly, she unhobbled the horse and threw the bags over her shoulder. With a leap and the aid of her mane, Naomi pulled herself aboard the mare. Grabbing the reins, she gripped with her knees, pulled the mare's head about, and gave her a kick.

Needing no additional encouragement, the mare leaped forward, her goal to gain freedom in the night. Naomi held on, leaning over the mare's neck with one hand twisted in the mane, and the other guiding where she could. The night was dark, the moons not yet risen, and their flight was mostly on instinct.

When the first wolf surged from the dark, Naomi and the mare screamed in unison, the horse planting her hooves and performing a maneuver sure to throw her rider. Like a tick, Naomi clung to her back, allowing the animal to go where it may. The horse plunged on, taking leaps and declines in equal daring. For a time, Naomi wasn't in control, only going where carried.

When a clearing appeared before them, Naomi again took the reins in a firm hand. If they could outrun the pack, they may find safety on the other side of this valley. Understanding that the mare, if allowed to run with abandon, would most likely lead them into a trap, she scanned the distance and quickly made a plan. Controlling the mare was paramount. She would run herself out, depleting energies if not controlled.

Taking small hills in a leap and bound, Naomi peered over her shoulder for their pursuers. When she couldn't see anything, and hadn't heard anything, she pulled on the reins and caused the mare to drop from her frenzied dash to a canter. Maybe, she thought, looking left and right, the wolves had decided to pursue easier prey.

Just then, a massive gray beast jumped at them from in front. The mare planted her feet, skidding to a stop. Unprepared, Naomi was sent over the horse's head, airborne until she hit on the ground, knocking the air from her lungs. Unaware for a moment, the only thing that kept her alive was the pack's desire for the horse. Catching her breath, she shook her head and looked over her shoulder. In the limited starlight, Naomi saw the mare fighting off four huge wolves. A yelp sounded as a hoof struck one in the side, rolling it away. The mare reared, averting a killing bite on her throat, but the wolf caught enough to draw blood. The smell drove the hunters into a frenzy.

Incensed by the slaughter she was sure to see, Naomi

advanced on the wolves with a scream of rage. When two of them turned on her, she roared her anger, gesturing to them to come to her. Just as the largest of the two, fangs slathering, got within reach, a light blazed from Naomi, and she dropped to her knees. Wolves forgotten, she cradled her arm to her chest, a pain filling her being that originated in the vine on her arm. Horror filled her as the pain intensified, and a burning sensation shot from her fingertips. Before her eyes, a leafed wood grew from her palm. Elongating and filling out, Naomi soon cradled a wooden staff. On the staff, glyphs glowed in the darkness: shapes and symbols that she didn't recognize. She advanced on the wolves, guided by a wisdom and battle knowledge she could only glimpse. A small piece of her perception knew the mare still fought for her life—could hear the cries of the animal as the wolves caught her again and again with fang and claw. But the larger part of her consciousness was centered on the staff.

Hungry for blood. Wanting to feel the soft give of flesh to timber. She relished the battle in a way she never could have imagined.

As though sensing the difference, scenting the threat, the wolves began to back away from her. One, still occupied with the mare, thinking an easy meal was eminent, didn't feel her coming. It had just turned, just looked her way, when its head cracked from the force of her blow. The body of the beast dropped where it stood. The blood that stained the staff disappeared, absorbed into the glowing timber.

With the spilling of slayer blood, the remaining wolves turned and fled into the night.

Naomi, flaming staff in one hand, eyes wild and untamed, spun in a circle, seeking out another foe, the wood spinning in a protective arc. When none presented themselves to her killing rage, she dropped to her knees, threw back her head, and shrieked into the night. The mare, agitated and terrified, screamed with her.

*****

When Naomi opened her eyes, she didn't know how much time had passed. Lifting her head, she sought out the horse, seeing her standing just where she had been. Muscles still twitching on the mare's flank, Naomi could only presume she hadn't been out for long.

When she tried to stand, it was to find she couldn't. Not only was the mare twitching, but Naomi was, too. Taking a deep breath, Naomi tried again. This time she got to her feet. The glowing staff was gone. All that was left was the mark of vine still aflame with some inner light, a debilitating exhaustion, and an elation she couldn't understand.

Naomi stumbled to the mare. Running her hands over her, she surveyed the damage done by the hunters. Nothing that wouldn't heal.

CHAPTER FORTY-FIVE

The sun was rising when Naomi and the mare crested the next hill. After the wolf attack, neither she nor the horse wanted to be there, so bemoaning the loss of the saddle, she mounted up and they headed out. Her adrenaline having passed hours ago, Naomi couldn't get her thoughts off the glowing staff. It was an amazing weapon, but more than that, something had filled her when the mark reacted to the threat of the wolves. With all the amazing, crazy—okay, Naomi, she thought. She had to admit it . . . Magic—of all the magical things she had seen in this world, this one took the cake.

Continuing to think about the battle, fear again lifted its head. From the point of the staff erupting from her flesh, to its absorption into her, she hadn't been herself. Or at least not just herself. The killing rage. The thirst for blood. She would never be that. Where had that come from? What if she lost herself within the heat? Her heart thumping, she knew she could never let it overtake her again.

Now, with the sunlight throwing a large shadow off her and the horse, Naomi turned her thoughts to the map. She didn't believe, as she once did, that finding the rooster outcropping was luck, so what came next?

The rhythm of the horse's motion a soft lullaby, Naomi's hands loosened on the reins and her thoughts flew back to the map. Mountains. She was in the mountains, and they stretched for miles. Her destination, the fortress, lay almost smack dab in the middle of the mountain range. To get there, she would keep her back to the rising sun, but there may be clues along the way.

Think, she told herself. Allowing the horse to pick her own trail, Naomi closed her eyes and went back to that central tent.

* * * * *

When her eyes popped open, for a moment she didn't see what lay before her, still in her mind and in that tent. Then the greens, blues, and startling whites of the mountain leaked into her vision, and she was again aboard a horse, crossing mountains, fleeing an army, and trying to get her friend back safely.

A river. There had been a river on the map. It flowed between two of the mountains, and the more she thought about it, the more certain she became that it was a means to getting through the pass.

"Okay," she said and gave the mare a pat on her neck. Gathering the reins, she directed the horse down a small incline and headed up another, changing their route to intersect with the river.

"You're a good girl, old horse."

Naomi didn't expect to find any civilization this far into the mountains, so it was with a startled look that she and the horse crested a hill to come upon a small settlement nestled in a valley between two hillsides.

"What in the world." At her voice, the horse's ears twitched. Naomi studied the buildings for a few moments. They looked to be abandoned, but when she urged the mare closer, she saw small tufts of smoke rising from several of the chimneys and knew there must be people here. She walked her horse down the snow-packed main street, only to have people step out on their stoops to stare at her. She found herself staring back at them, for they reminded her of Paxton Re, and she wondered if they were a community of dwarfs.

Hairy, the men had long, dark beards that reached the middle of their chests. Both the men's and women's hair were long and coarse, standing in halos around their heads and down their backs. They were dressed in dark clothing, the women wearing dirty white aprons over theirs. And as of yet, she didn't see any children or animals.

When she was partway down the main street, she came upon a building that seemed to be a place for commerce. Several people stood at its open door, and from within she could see shelves of foodstuffs and other goods. She turned the horse toward these people and, when stopped, swung her leg over the horse's neck and dropped to the ground. Unable to halt a small moan that escaped her lips as she straightened, Naomi faced the townsfolk.

"Good day," she began, not even knowing if they understood her or not. One of the men stepped forward and bowed his head at her. He said something she couldn't understand, then moved the people on the walkway aside. Then he indicated for her to enter the store. It was her turn to bow her head to him, and with slow, measured steps, she preceded the man and the others into the building, keeping her hand close to her knife at her belt.

Naomi strolled down one of the aisles, with an entourage right behind her. When she reached for a small sack of what might be flour, her sleeve shifted up. At the sight of the mark on her arm, a communal gasp went up behind her. They jabbered to each other and to her, reaching for her arm, caressing the skin. Trained from birth to be polite, Naomi waited a moment and then gave some resistance to their touch. She tried to extract her arm from their grip, smiling and keeping her voice light. They were backing her into a hall, touching, jabbering. She thought she could get out of there, away from their touch. Maybe with some food to take on her way.

It wasn't until the mare screamed that her sense of danger

went into overdrive. She swung her head, stood tall on her toes, and searched outside the windows for the horse. The animal was surrounded. The mare was throwing her head to release her reins from a male who held them. Naomi pushed at the townspeople, but there was always another to fill the space.

When the horse cried out again, the mark on Naomi's arm flared with a blinding light. The people fell back, crying out and covering their eyes. Taking her chance, Naomi leaped over one after another. Her way to the door was clear, and she broke into a run. She pulled her sword from her hip, pushing back the urge to let the staff extend. Fear and anticipation warred with each other, and fear won. She didn't know what the staff's magic did to her the one time she had used it, but until she knew more, she didn't want to be overcome with the lust to draw blood.

Swinging her steel sword, Naomi cut a path through the dwarfish people until she was at the horse's side. With a grasp of mane, she leaped to throw her leg over the mare's back. One hand still gripping the sword, Naomi grasped the reins, wrenched the mare's head around and, with a kick, sent her at full speed out of the town and into the forest surrounding the hamlet. For a time, she could hear pursuit—perhaps it was the promise of fresh meat—but as they climbed out of the valley, she left the townspeople behind.

CHAPTER FORTY-SIX

Naomi kept up their pace through that day and the next night. By the time they stopped, exhaustion was sitting hard on them both. Looking to the far sky, Naomi watched a storm move their way. Wind blew her hair from her face and whipped the mare's mane.

Snow, she thought. They needed to find shelter to ride out the storm.

Naomi dismounted. She led the horse and watched the forest around them as the day darkened. Snow had begun to fall, blowing in a tempest, before Naomi passed within a bramble of trees and bushes. In the center, perhaps from the use of other animals, was a beaten-down area. The trees canopied at the top, and the bushes all around provided welcome shelter. She stripped the horse of her remaining tack and the bags she had strapped across her back. From the underside of some of the bushes, Naomi pulled grasses and some dried summer flowers to rub the horse down. Her wounds were healing well, though she would probably always have marks from the wolves' teeth.

When Naomi finished rubbing her down, she offered the grasses plus any others she could pull, and the mare was eager to add them to her scant meal. They would soon head back into snow within the pass, and feeding her and the horse would become even more difficult.

Naomi decided to let tomorrow's worries take care of themselves. She lay within the shelter of the trees and, with the sound of the horse's breaths, fell asleep dreaming of the rush of excitement that came with the eruption of the glowing staff.

* * * * *

It took three more long days for Naomi to reach the river. They heard it long before they saw it, and just before Naomi smelled the water, the mare picked up her head and increased her pace. When the river came into view, Naomi slid from the horse's back. She tied the reins to a tree and quietly made her way to the water's edge.

CHAPTER FORTY-SEVEN

Bob watched the passage of the grasslands. The Tinkers and their wagons made good time knowing where they were going, keeping to the trails utilized by Tinkers for eons.

Bob didn't know where they were. And he had come to the realization that he may not ever recognize the land and which way he should go. One thing he did know, however, was where Naomi had been going.

He had been to the troll's stronghold once before. He was quite young but had done a service for the tracker. Now Zulrajas could repay that service. Bob was certain he would have to refresh the troll's memory, but once that was done, he would likely be happy to help. Well, at least Bob hoped so. Trolls were notorious for their bad tempers, but Zulrajas had been all over these lands. He was sure he would be the one to direct them to Darklin Vale. Maybe he could even talk him into taking them there.

Bob had become friends with the Tinkers. Family really. Surely, they would allow him to take some provisions to see him on his way. His problem was that he wasn't certain of this. Should he talk to Mazition, the head of the Tinkers, or just take some foodstuffs and go?

When the Tinkers stopped their caravan for the evening, pulling them in a circle for better security, Bob was still undecided. He was afraid to confront the leader, but to just take and disappear felt like stealing. He didn't want to reward their charity with an act of thievery.

The Tinkers had eaten, drank, and danced by the time Bob made up his mind. He would speak with Mazition. Nerves eating at his belly, Bob made his way to the chief's wagon.

At his knock, Mazition called for him to come in. Bob took a big breath and pulled open the rear door to enter the wagon. Mazition wasn't alone. Two of the other top men sat with him, a map open before them.

"Bob," the leader said. "Come." He gestured for Bob to join them. Mazition smoked a large pipe of tobacco, and he offered it to Bob.

"Thank you, no," Bob declined with a shake of his head.

Mazition set the smoking device aside and faced Bob squarely. "What can I do for you, Bob?"

It's now or never, Bob thought before he plunged into the tale of what had brought him to this place, this night.

The three men listened without interrupting, letting Bob tell his story in his way. When he wound down, Mazition looked from his visitor to the two men who sat with him.

"Interesting." He nodded at Bob. "What would you like from us?"

"I've enjoyed my time with the Tinkers. I appreciate all you've done for me, but I must get back to what I should be doing. I must find Naomi and help her in her quest. I promised her I would help her to get home, and I must do what I promised."

Mazition moved around the other two men and approached Bob. Laying his arm about the boy's shoulders, he pulled him into a quick sideways hug.

"Bob, you are one of the Tinkers. We would no more think of letting you go on without us as we would kick one of the family out. Why, we'd be happy, not only to transport you to where you wish to go, but assist you in any way getting your friends safe."

Bob was flabbergasted. He never expected the chief of the Tinkers to be so understanding and helpful. He stumbled a bit in his thanks and then got it out.

"Thank-thank you Mazition. I really appreciate your help."

"Of course, my boy." With a slap on Bob's shoulder, Mazition returned to his seat between the two men who watched their interaction closely. "Now, go and get some sleep. We'll head out to find your friends at first light."

Smiling, Bob stumbled from the wagon and returned to the one he shared with Henivar. A great weight had been lifted from his shoulders.

As the door shut behind the young man, one of the men turned to Mazition.

"What was that all about?"

"Remember a few weeks before we found the boy? When word came out that there were stirrings of Charmot? Talk of battalions of sprogs moving through the land."

The man looked at his companion and then back at Mazition. He gave a small nod. "Yes. They were on the hunt."

Mazition leaned back in his chair, again taking a large draw on his pipe. "What do you think the odds are that what they're looking for is a woman from another world, come into this one without permission?"

The two lieutenants again looked at each other.

"And what do you think the reward would be if that woman was found and given to Charmot?"

"It would be risky," one of the men said.

"We'd have to be careful," the other chimed in.

"Yes, yes," Mazition agreed. "All of that and more. But when have the Tinkers not been willing to do a daring task for great reward?"

Mazition rolled up the map they had been studying. His plan for their future changed with Bob's visit. His mind filled with the dream of the riches that would overflow their wagons when they turned the girl over to Charmot, and he dismissed his two lieutenants. Pacing within the wagon, he puffed on his pipe, mind flowing with plans.

Tomorrow he would again talk with Bob. He would get a destination from him. A heading to this Zulrajas in the mountains. The troll might be a problem, but he was certain they would come to an understanding. Trolls were as mercenary as Tinkers.

Finally able to calm his spinning mind, Mazition stripped and climbed into his bed. One never knew where good fortune would smile on you. Tomorrow, he thought. Tomorrow they would begin the hunt for the greatest treasure in the land.

CHAPTER FORTY-EIGHT

Unaware of how many different groups searched for her, Naomi awoke to the sounds of morning birds calling to each other. Rolling to her back, her hood falling from around her face, she looked into the mare's face as she chewed on a mouthful of grasses and breathed on Naomi. She gave a chuckle and ran her hand over the mare's soft, warm muzzle, then leaned up and gave her a quick kiss.

Rolling away from the horse, Naomi dropped her cloak with the saddlebags and walked the few feet to the riverbank. They had come upon the river late in the evening the night before, and since it was too dark to investigate, she had wrapped herself in her cloak and fallen asleep.

Naomi squatted at the river's edge, rubbing her hands together in the cold mountain water. Glancing over her shoulder, she monitored the mare. She hadn't even thought about hobbling her the night before, yet here she was. Naomi was lucky and thankful for that. But surprised, too.

The mare nickered and tossed her head, then wandered down the bank to drink. Naomi watched her the whole way, wondering about this world she had arrived in and what she didn't know about the creatures that resided here. A horse was a horse in her world . . . but here? Might she be more?

"Hello."

Naomi wrenched her eyes from the mare and gazed out to where the call had come from. There on the water, floating against the swift current, was a raft. Standing on the raft was a man? Her first thought was that it was a man, but the more she studied him, the more unsure she became. A long cloak covered his form. All except for his head and his arms.

Long, skinny arms, she thought.

"Hello," he called again, waving those arms.

Naomi lifted a hand, leery of this stranger. And what was he doing way out here? And on a raft moving against the flow of water?

The man bent and retrieved a long pole. With it he navigated the raft toward her side of the river. This seemed to be a lot simpler than it should have been. As though the water were working with him. As he pushed down on the riverbed, his long arms bent, bony elbows pointing up. He was kinda freaking her out.

As the man approached the bank, Naomi moved backward. When he beached his raft and jumped off it to the ground, Naomi put even more space between them.

He gave her a toothy grin and turned to pull his raft higher on the bank. He shook out his cloak and then, wrapping it around his frame, again turned to face her.

"Hello," he said.

"Hello," Naomi returned, uncertain what was happening and what she should do.

"Are you going upstream?"

An image of the map popped into Naomi's mind. She did think she was going upstream. Hesitantly, she said, "Yes. Yes, we're going upstream."

"Well, great. Great. No need for you two to have to walk the whole way. A lot of it's hard going. Boggy at times, blocked with fallen trees some others. If you're wantin', and have coin to pay, I can get you upstream in half the time."

The decision was made for her with his words. Coin. She

didn't have any coin.

"Thank you," she said, "but we'll keep going the way we are."

When she turned to go to her packs and the man took a step in her direction, Naomi spun to face him again. Unconsciously, her hand went to the hilt of her sword. At her quick movement, the raftsman moved back a step.

"No pressure, you know." He put his hands up. "Just . . . well, it's just the going upstream is mighty rough. I think you might be regretting your decision in the next couple of days. By then, I could have had you where you're wantin' to go."

"Look, mister . . ." And Naomi gave an internal sigh. "I don't have any coin to pay you. I don't have anything of value at all." When he just looked at her, she added, "So see, there's no reason for you to wait around for me to change my mind."

"Well, now, I'm thinkin'." He paced in front of her, his cloak billowing in a peculiar way. "You look to be a woman on a mission. Maybe something important?" He raised an eyebrow at her. When she just stared at him, he gave a small cough and again paced. "Anyway, maybe, at the end of your journey, you'd be givin' Ol' Humphrey a taste of what you find."

Naomi gave it some thought. It would be speedier to be ferried upstream—assuming Ol' Humphrey could be trusted, that is. Her core of honesty insisted she be true with him.

"Humphrey." When he faced her, she told him, "I can't guarantee there will be any payment at the end of my travels."

"Yep, yep," he said, rubbing his hands together. "I have a nose for these things. You let me worry about that, little lady."

Should she tell him she was being hunted? Maybe the best pay to be had from her would be to turn her in to the magistrate. With that thought, she decided to keep her situation to herself.

"Okay," she said, turning to grab her packs. "You're sure you can get us upstream?" At his nod she added, "I'm interested in going to the headwaters."

"Yes, yes. We can go to the beginning of the Breakling. That's the name of this here river. Breakling. It's been around for as long as there's been mountains. And that's been a long, long time, I'll tell ya. But I can get you to the very beginning. Very beginning. High in the mountains."

"And the horse isn't going to be a problem?"

"No, no. Many times have I trafficked animals. Come." He gestured toward the raft. "Get your things and your horse."

Naomi approached the horse. Putting the reins around the mare's neck, she slipped the bridle over her face and tightened the straps.

"Come on, girl." She gave a small tug on the rein. Docilely, seemingly with no concern in the world, the horse followed the woman aboard the raft. Naomi stood with her in the middle of the craft, legs spread, keeping her balance. With the first pull, there was a gentle sway, but nothing like Naomi had expected.

"Hang on, my ladies," Humphrey called. "It might get a bit choppy farther up, but I'll keep us to the middle of the river."

In awe, Naomi watched the miles fall away. Had she traveled by land, what looked to be taking them hours would have taken weeks, if not months. She had certainly lucked out finding the raft man. No sooner had that thought entered her mind than Naomi was turning slowly to study their deliverer.

It had been awful lucky, hadn't it. And he had agreed to take them with no pay, and no real promise of pay.

I have a nose for these things. You let me worry about that.

Hadn't that been what he said? Let him worry about it. How many people, in her world or this one, would do something without some form of payment? Not many, she decided.

Naomi got a firm grip on the mare's halter and called to the stranger.

"Humphrey!"

He looked from his study of the river to her, a wide smile on his thin face.

"We need to go to shore."

When he shook his head at her, she took a steadying breath.

"Just for a moment. I need to do something." Let him think she needed to pee. Let him think whatever he wanted. She just needed him to land this raft. The more she thought about it, the more her nerves pinged around under her skin.

"Humphrey, really. I need you to let me off the raft."

All he did was shake his head at her and go back to his survey of the water.

Naomi released the horse and, with wide ambling steps, approached the man.

"Humphrey." She didn't shout. Didn't need to since she was quite close to him. When he ignored her, she grabbed at the arm of his cloak.

"No!" he yelled, shoving her away.

Falling, Naomi grabbed even harder on the cloth, pinwheeling her arms. As she fell, tumbling off the raft and into the rapid current, the cloak came with her. When her head broke the surface, she gulped a lungful of air and spun to face the raft that continued to travel up the river—as she was swept down it.

Squinting, she stared at the spectacle. On the raft, next to a franticly stepping mare, was something from a nightmare. Multiple arms, all hunched and hanging below his knees, reached for the horse. When he moved on horribly bowed legs, the raft rocked, terrifying an already frightened horse. Just as she was about to be swept around a bend in the river, Naomi saw the mare leap from the raft to swim toward the far shore.

Naomi turned and began to swim toward the bank. Her routine sport was running, but she could swim, and it didn't take her long to make it to shallow water. The current had swept her far downstream. She had no idea where she was.

She clamored up the bank, sopping wet, hair and clothes dragging at her. She had just gotten to the cover of trees when she heard Humphrey call.

"Hey lady. Lady what happened? Where are you?"

Naomi peeked around a tree to see the raftsman on his craft moving against the flow of the water. He had donned another cloak that he had gotten from somewhere. He scanned the edge of the river, searching for her. Naomi's gaze dropped to where she had come out of the water. Did she leave tracks?

When Humphrey didn't stop, didn't even slow, her breath returned to normal. She needed to get out of here.

Moving quickly, almost running, Naomi headed upstream. As she moved, her hair and clothes began to dry, but she didn't even notice. Where was she going? She had nothing. The mare, and all her provisions, had gone into the river.

Kicking herself, she couldn't believe she had been so stupid as to get on the raft. Just when things were going well, she had to put her foot in it.

CHAPTER FORTY-NINE

The magistrate watched the sprog who paced his tent. He had never liked this man thing. Never trusted him. If he didn't desire the power that Charmot could give him, he would have him killed. The magistrate's dark thoughts stopped, and another entered.

Could the sprog be killed?

Perhaps, he was dead already. The magistrate had heard tales of how a sprog was created. According to legend, it all started with a man—but he didn't remain a man for long. Painful it was. Dark magic. And in the end, Charmot had his army of lackeys.

But he was not a lackey. Charmot had come to him. In a dream. A dark, seductive dream. There were many things the magistrate wanted. And Charmot had promised him all of them.

Power.

Wealth.

A kingdom.

But Charmot wanted something, too. He—it?—wanted the woman, Naomi. The magistrate knew she came from another world, though he didn't know how. He knew she was coming before she made it to Eldenblair. Before the king saw her. It was he who told King Mallevorn to send Laina to intercept the girl. The dwarf had been a surprise, but no matter. He quickly separated them and had the woman under his control.

But then she got away. He had wanted to execute the guilty party who hadn't been watching her but then the sprog turned up. Out of the blue with an army of lackeys behind him. He had already known the girl had fled. He told the magistrate to fall back. Charmot wanted her on her own.

Wanted her to fulfill some destiny. He didn't understand it, but with the instructions, the sprog had brought a large bag of gold coins. They were for him, the sprog told him. For him as thanks from Charmot. And he was to listen to the orders this sprog gave him.

Oh well, he thought, running a coin between his thumb and forefinger. He would put up with this thing for a bit longer. But when this business was finished, he would ensure that the sprog saw his last day.

CHAPTER FIFTY

When Laina got back to where Paxton Re hid, she was certain she knew where they needed to go. She knew these mountains. Had grown up in their shadows. And she knew the Breakling River that was shown on the map. She had crossed it before where it spilled into the valley. They could circumvent this army. Make haste to the headwaters and work their way down to the fortress. That way, they would bypass those hunting Naomi.

Now she just had to convince Paxton Re that this was the right decision.

Moving through the near pitch of night, even with her elf sight, Laina almost stepped on Paxton Re before she saw him.

"Hey," he whispered in her ear, causing her to nearly jump out of her skin. She didn't know dwarfs could be so stealthy.

"Jeez, Paxton Re. Make yourself known." She placed a hand to her heart.

"What's got you so jumpy?"

"Oh nothing." She rolled her eyes at him. "Just sneaking into an enemy camp. One with a being far more powerful than me and battalions of soldiers at his beck and call. Nothing, nothing at all."

"You're grumpy."

"Grumpy? I'm not grumpy. I'm never grumpy. I'm not the

kind of elf who gets grumpy."

Paxton Re looked at Laina from the corner of his eye, not sure what he should say. The silence between them stretched, and finally the girl took his arm, moving him farther from the encampment.

"I'm sure I know where Naomi is . . . or at least where she's going."

"Great," he said, looking off into the distance as if he could see a line from them to her.

"Yep." Her energetic response had his internal nonsense meter jumping into hyperdrive.

"What's wrong?" he growled at her.

"Nothing's wrong." They continued into the forest.

"You're acting funny."

Laina gave a little twitter of a laugh. "I'm not acting funny."

"Okay." Paxton Re set down his pack and swore not to move another foot until he knew exactly what was going on. "You're a crazy little elf, but you've always been honest. Out with it."

At his first words, Laina's temper bristled, but as he talked, she accepted what he had to say.

"You are right. About me being honest . . . But I'm not crazy. And I'm not little."

Paxton Re regarded her with a patience he was surprised he even had. He knew something was up. Something she didn't want to tell him. He had always thought of situations like this as something of a bandage to rip off quickly. Say it and get it done. When he didn't say anything, Laina took a couple steps and then spun to face him.

"I do know where Naomi is going. I'm almost one hundred percent sure. The thing is, I think we'll have a better chance, not only finding her, but not getting caught trying, if we head where she's headed by a different route."

"Okay."

When the dwarf didn't say anything else, Laina stalled. It couldn't be this easy. He had questioned every decision she had made all along the way. How could he now have nothing to say? No opinion to give?

"You agree with me?"

"Well, in theory, yeah. I need to know more—know where we're going and how we'll get there, but this is your land, after all." When she didn't answer, he gave her a bump with his elbow. "Right?"

Laina gave a small start. "Right. Yes, of course, right. I'm just wondering where Paxton Re is and who you are."

With a scowl the dwarf regarded her.

"Okay, anyway." Laina led him into the night. She knew how to get to the delta. From there it shouldn't be too hard to get to where the fortress was located on the map.

*****

Paxton Re and Laina walked throughout the rest of the night and most of the next day. Laina explained her plan to him as they walked, and in true dwarfish fashion, he tore her plan to pieces. She came to understand this was all right because having it in pieces allowed them to put it back together. Stronger. Better.

Now they had a course of action that they both approved of.

It didn't take long for the plan to fall apart. Their personalities, in general, were that Laina was cheery and optimistic and Paxton Re was grumpy. In the mix, these two were oil and water, especially when they first awoke.

Laina came to look at this as her daily challenge. Getting him up and going. And with a civil comment to the day.

About a week into their joint travel, Paxton Re and Laina came upon the Breakling River where it spilled into the valley. The plan was to cross it and reach the headwaters from the opposite side. Here it was wide, and it was deep, but Laina knew of a crossing farther upstream, so they headed that way.

Groups of travelers passed. Some traveling up the river and

some coming down. Varied types and shapes of boats moved about on the water. When they rounded a broad curve of the river, the crossing was ahead of them. It had been some time since Laina had been here, and in that time, a small community had sprung up: What looked to be a store, a livery, and a larger nondescript building that might be used for a gathering spot. The crossing, which was a rope strung across the narrowest part of the river, was attached to a pole on a raft. Two strong men worked the rope all day, taking turns, to pull the raft back and forth across the river. Near the actual crossing a small structure stood. Laina led Paxton Re to this spot.

Pushing open the door, the duo entered to the din of an argument.

"Why that's highway robbery!"

"Sorry, sir. That's the cost of passage." The man behind a makeshift counter didn't even look up to acknowledge the shouting man. He continued to make marks in a ledger open on the desk in front of him. When Laina walked up to him, he looked up and gestured for the other man to step aside.

"Yes, ma'am. How can I be of service?"

Laina opened her mouth to tell him, and the man pushed back in front of her, shoving her into Paxton Re.

"Now, just wait a minute—"

The man stopped, the blade of a knife now drawing a small bead of blood from his throat. His eyes rolled toward the dwarf who stood beside him, knife in hand.

"Now, maybe you should just be waiting a minute," Paxton Re growled. "All I see here is an elf with bad manners. I thought all you fairy folk were extremely proud of how highborn you all are."

It was quiet as the interior of a coffin. When the elf in question gulped, it was heard by all. Holding it for a moment more, Paxton Re pulled his knife away from the elf's throat but kept his eye on him. The elf, finally showing some self-preservation, stepped back, hand to the small wound. Laina watched him move and then turned back to the proprietor.

"We're looking for passage across the river," she said in answer to his previously asked question.

"Yes, ma'am. Of course." The elf kept a wary eye on Paxton Re, who kept an ear attuned to the group behind him. Just because the man had been cowed, there was no reason to assume he would stay that way. Give him a moment for anger and humiliation to set in. Have his group start egging him on, and Paxton Re might need to kill someone.

"It will be about two hours before the conveyance is turned around and back onto this side of the Breakling."

Laina gave a sigh; there was no help for the wait. "How much for passage?"

"Two coppers," the man said, and his eyes shifted to the party behind them. "Apiece."

Now Paxton Re turned his full attention to the conversation. He didn't have any money, elven or otherwise.

Laina reached within her jerkin and pulled out a small bag cinched at the top with a leather band. "He's right, you know. It is highway robbery." And she dropped four coins into the man's outstretched hand. They clinked together and, in a wisp of a movement, the man had them out of sight. With his other hand, he indicated the room and the area without.

"You're welcome to wait inside, or we have some lovely sitting spots outside."

Laina glanced about the room, and outside to the muddy, trodden area. With a lifted eyebrow, she turned back to the man.

"We'll be back." She headed toward the door, Paxton Re on her heels.

As the door closed behind them, she spoke over her shoulder to the dwarf.

"Figured we might as well check out the town, as it is. Might find some useful provisions." Paxton Re just grunted in response, so Laina led them down the stairs and toward the town. Behind them, peering out the windows, the traveler elf and his group watched them go.

* * * * *

Paxton Re and Laina stepped out of the mercantile, their packs once again full of provisions. They didn't know how many days it would take them to make it to the headwaters of the Breakling River. Or what would take place after that. How far would it be to the fortress? Would they find Naomi there? And what would they do if they didn't?

They stood on the stoop and watched the group from the crossing office make their way down the opposite side of the street. The group kept glancing their way and whispering among themselves.

"I think we may have made some enemies," Laina said.

"Let them come," the dwarf rumbled. "My sword is thirsty."

Laina turned to look at him, a smile breaking across her face. "Your sword is *thirsty*?" She had the pleasure of seeing a blush shade his cheeks. With a small laugh, Laina slapped him on the shoulder and walked down the stairs to the crossing.

More travelers had gathered there in the time they had been in the store, and it looked like the raft would be full for the next crossing. Standing on the shoreline, just down from the dock, Laina and Paxton Re watched the raft near this side of the river. With each heave on the towline, the vessel neared the dock. Full of fares and stacks of cargo, the raft gave a mighty thud as it met the landing. People and animals streamed from it. When the riders had been depleted, two men from within the office came out and began off-loading the cargo. Sooner than she would have thought possible, the raft was clear, and people began to board. Laina and Paxton Re took their places in line, inching forward until they stepped aboard. Laina led them through the pack until they were toward the front open side of the raft. A rail had been built around the vessel, and turning to face the passengers, Laina leaned against the barrier.

They watched with interest as the elves from before made their way aboard. The group took surreptitious glances at them but kept their distance. Along with them, there were other groups of men and women, dirty from their travels. A family—a father, mother, and three children—pushed their way on, pulling a nanny goat with them. A merchant with a handcart covered in bells made his slow, noisy boarding, and just as they were getting ready to cast off, two soldiers galloped up demanding to be allowed on. The raft was delayed as the transaction was completed and the men walked their horses aboard.

Laina and Paxton Re exchanged a look. As a unit, they turned to face the water. As far as they knew, no one knew they were even out here in the wilds of the Yon Mountains. But he had been seen entering the city, and Laina had lived her life in and around this area. What if it were reported to King Mallevorn or even the magistrate? All and all, it would be better to have a covert trip through the mountains.

When the rope to the other side was pulled, everything on the raft moved with it. Laina grabbed the post she stood near and put one foot backward to maintain her balance. Paxton Re gave a grumble, and when Laina raised an eyebrow at him, he muttered, "Don't like the water. Dwarfs prefer the earth."

"Do you really have any preferences?" She raised her eyebrows at him.

"For an elf, you're funny." With that last parting quip, Paxton Re moved down the rail, past the goat, to a corner. He put his back to the pole, crossed his arms over his chest, and scowled at the crowd.

It would take almost an hour to make the crossing, and from there they would follow a road into the mountains. Laina had been that way before and knew farther up, the road turned into a trail. She had it on good authority that the trail petered out some miles after that. She had never heard anyone tell of being all the way to the headwaters, but the river came from somewhere. They would just need to follow it to its source. According to the map in the magistrate's tent, the fortress was located on the other side of the river. Laina had told Paxton Re that she planned on leading them to it from the opposite direction as the army that hunted Naomi.

When they neared the other bank without any interactions with the other passengers, Laina strolled over to Paxton Re in the corner of the raft. She followed his gaze out to the water.

"The soldiers could be a problem," she muttered.

"Yep. Been keeping an eye on them."

"We should probably be one of the first off. We could blend into the crowds on this side. Let them leave before we go anywhere."

At this, the dwarf gave a jerk of his head. Along with the soldiers, he had been keeping an eye on the band of elves. He was sure he had the leader cowed, but with all his pals with him, he might again find his courage. Paxton Re planned on being prepared for that eventuality.

The raft bumped into the dock, and everyone crowded the front. One of the rope men pushed his way through, yelling at them to step back and give him room. When a couple didn't comply fast enough, he gave them a shove and unlatched the gate of the raft. It crashed down onto the pier, making the raft shift. As soon as the gate came down, there was a commotion in the back and the two soldiers, now mounted on their horses, pushed through the passengers. No one stood a chance against the large animals, and everyone stepped aside. Paxton Re and Laina watched from within the group as the two raced their animals off the raft, down the dock, and into the forest.

"Wonder what has them in such a hurry?" one of the travelers said.

"Long as it ain't us, I don't care," his companion answered.

Paxton Re agreed silently with them. Now he and Laina only had to worry about the troop of elves.

With the soldiers gone, the two waited for the rest to unload before making their way to shore. Paxton Re watched the troublemakers until they were out of sight. He gave a sigh and hoped they would decide to take their troublemaking somewhere else.

"Sun's gonna be setting before too long," Paxton Re muttered as they walked into town.

"I was thinking that," she answered. "Seems to me, it would be best if we kept walking this evening. Get out of the town and away from the crowds."

Paxton Re didn't answer, just nodded, and hiked his pack more firmly on his back.

CHAPTER FIFTY-ONE

Naomi walked the better part of two days before exhaustion stopped her. She knew she was going to crash—could feel it coming over her like a gray fog—so she began to search for somewhere to hide and sleep. She had stayed close to the river, navigating based on its twists and turns. Every so often, she would get as close as she thought safe and study the river and the other side. She didn't just miss the ease and speed of travel with the horse; she missed the companionship. Being alone was scary. And lonely.

Now, hiding and resting was on her mind. She had nothing with her and was dressed in shades of brown, so when she saw the large pine, she knew it would have to do. The tree was at least forty feet tall, its lower boughs so heavy, the ends drooped to the ground. Naomi ducked her head, closed her eyes, and, careful to leave no evidence of her passing, forced herself between and beyond the boughs. Sharp with age, the pine needles scraped her arms and parts of her face they could reach. When she passed beyond them, the area under the pine was dry and lined with ages of dead needles.

Naomi dropped to her knees, pulling herself to lay with her back to the trunk of the great tree. She blinked twice, the haze deepening until she dropped into a deep sleep.

Almost immediately, the bed of pines began to shift and

move. Small eruptions occurred all around the sleeping woman, and small twittering noises flowed through the area. When a pile of needles burst upward, a small pointed green hat squeezed out followed by an arm and then the rest of a small body.

Large eyes peered at the girl. Soon, the first creature was joined by many more. Each wore a hat, of varied colors and shapes, but their small bodies were covered only with a thick pelt of wiry hair. Feet, large for their size and devoid of hair, kept them balanced on the soft bedding. Other than the large eyes, the only feature visible was a bulbous nose that twitched as they picked up the scent of the girl's blood now drying on each scrape.

A conversation seemed to be taking place between the creatures. Finally one, braver than the rest, moved within an arm's reach of her. Lifting a lock of hair, he sniffed. Looking over his shoulder, the fellow chirped in its language to its companions. He took another look at her and then, one by one, they disappeared back down their holes. A moment of stillness filled the small clearing and then the ground again moved. A single gnome climbed from his hole. He turned and leaned in only to pull forth a small daisy-like flower. Stepping easily through the bedding of pine needles, he tucked the flower behind one of the girl's ears. He looked on for a moment and then, like a shot, was back down his hole and gone.

Naomi slept through the day and into the following night. When she woke up, she didn't at first know where she was. There was only darkness and the scent of pine. Sitting, she remembered what had brought her to this place and time, and for a moment she allowed herself to worry for her comrades. Where were they now? Had Bob and Adalard survived the spider attack? Was Paxton Re still imprisoned in the cells at Eldenblair? How long would it be before he gave up? Decided she wasn't coming for him.

Naomi wiped her eyes, which had filled with tears. She couldn't despair. Couldn't become so lost in desperation that she stopped. She needed to set her sights and finish this task so she could rescue Paxton Re. When that was done, they would locate Adalard and Bob. And she needed to hurry. Again, wiping her eyes, Naomi felt something in her hair. She pulled it from the strands and let it fall into her palm. A flower? Glancing around her, she looked for where the flower could have come from.

Finally, with a shrug for this world and its mysteries, she secreted the flower within her tunic.

Naomi listened for a moment before parting the boughs of the great pine and pushing out from its cover. In a crouch, she listened again, scanning all around the tree. There was nothing but the far-off call of a forest bird. Standing, she stretched a body gone to cramp from her long sleep. She was thirsty and hungry. The thirst she could quench with water from the river, but the hunger she would have to ignore. It wasn't the first time she had been hungry, and it probably wouldn't be the last.

After making her way to the river, Naomi hid near the forest's edge for a long time. She needed to know that Ol' Humphrey wasn't going to appear suddenly running up the river on his magical raft. After a time, she made her way to the bank, staying low and concealed by long grasses. Drinking her fill, she then snuck back to the tree line. She studied the water, sure she would see the raft coming down it. When she didn't, Naomi turned from the river and slowly made her way upstream.

As she walked, she counted backward over the days she had been traveling. She must be nearing the fortress. The river was becoming narrower and narrower. Soon she must arrive at the headwaters.

It was later that day when Naomi saw what appeared to be a small wild orchard in the bowl of two hills. There were maybe a dozen trees, all the same shape and size. Craggy boughs sprouted from trunks with thick, gnarled bark. The leaves were small and a dark green color. The veins a bright purple. What caught her eye was that the branches appeared to be laden with some type of fruit. As she neared, she studied the growth.

The fruit ran from bluish when small, to light yellow on the largest. Naomi studied the bounty, her stomach cramping and her mouth watering. She looked from the orchard to the surrounding hillsides. This had to be a trick. A trap. Why would these trees have grown here? There was no evidence of a past town or even a farm.

Slowly, keeping her eyes open, Naomi moved toward the trees.

Birds called and bees buzzed—at least she thought it was birds and bees. When one of the buzzing creatures flew by her, she tracked it with her gaze.

Yep, she thought. Pretty close to a bee.

At the first tree she laid her hand upon it, not sure what to expect. Nothing happened, though the bark was particularly rough. The trees had a sweet scent that the breeze blew to her, stirring her hair. Naomi grasped a low-hanging fruit and, with a tug and twist, snapped it from the branch. She froze, waiting, images of the apple trees in the *Wizard of Oz* filling her thoughts. When the day remained serene, Naomi lifted the fruit to her mouth and took a small bite. Sweet and juicy, it exploded through her senses. Past the point of hungry, her body opened to welcome the nourishment. Naomi finished off the first fruit and began on another as she plucked more. Arms full, still consuming the second one, Naomi climbed the back hill. Partway up, she stopped, turned, and sat down. She couldn't move anymore. Tired, drained of energy, all she could think to do was eat.

The fruit went down easily. Finishing the fourth one, she thought enough to hesitate before taking a bite of the next one. Currently, her stomach was growling, wanting more and more, but soon all that fruit would be apt to make her sick. Sitting now, letting her system settle, Naomi heard the wind whistle through the tops of the trees in the orchard. The tall grasses that covered the hill she sat on and the one across from it moved in its gentle touch.

When she heard the clang, coming as if from a distance,

Naomi stopped thinking about the next fruit and listened. There it was again. Standing with a twist to face uphill, Naomi let the remaining fruit drop. Hearing the sound again, she made her way slowly up the rise of the knoll. At the top, she looked down on what could only be a road. Long unused, it was weed grown. The ruts mostly filled with dirt blown over the years. Almost in a trance, she stepped down the hill, having to catch her descent when she almost fell end over end. Coming to the road, she turned to follow it as it moved away from the orchard. As she passed through a cut in a hill, the small valley opened up before her. She stood still, mouth agape. Across the valley she saw the grayish, rough-cut buildings.

She had found the fortress.

This ends part one of

The Quest for Darklin Vale, Book I: Coming of the Storm

Continue the story with

The Quest for Darklin Vale, Book II: When Silence Falls

Other Titles by Vicki B. Williamson

*****

Ellen Thompson Thrillers

Finding Poppies

Key of the Prophecy

Faith of the Curé

The Pedagogue Chronicles

Maya's Song

Sylvan's Guise

Tessa's Flight

To learn more, please visit:

Vickibwilliamson.com

Facebook.com/FindingPoppies

Made in the USA
Coppell, TX
08 March 2026

73332981R00156